A FAR
BETTER THING

Visit us at www.boldstrokesbooks.com

A FAR
BETTER THING

by

JD Wilburn

2021

ISBN 13: 978-1-63555-834-0

THIS TRADE PAPERBACK ORIGINAL IS PUBLISHED BY
BOLD STROKES BOOKS, INC.
P.O. BOX 249
VALLEY FALLS, NY 12185

FIRST EDITION: FEBRUARY 2021

CREDITS
EDITORS: VICTORIA VILLASENOR AND CINDY CRESAP
PRODUCTION DESIGN: SUSAN RAMUNDO
COVER DESIGN BY TAMMY SEIDICK

Acknowledgments

First and foremost, I want to thank Rad and everyone at BSB for taking a chance on me. I genuinely hope I don't disappoint y'all. That having been said, there were a lot of people who helped this book come to fruition. I want to thank my buddy Jax Meyer (A Marine's Heart series, *Rising From Ash*) for always having my back, even at one in the morning when I'm freaking the hell out. I want to thank Lucy Bexley (*Must Love Silence, Just my Type*) for always checking on me and allowing me to unload on her whenever things got too rough. I want to thank Lily Seabrooke (too many to fucking name) for simply being an amazing and beautiful dazzling star, and reminding me that I am one, too. Lastly, I want to thank my family, especially my mom. You always knew I was a writer and you always told me to follow my dreams and get it done. I love you, Mama.

Dedication

This book goes out to Buck and Lorelai.
Without you two babies, this book wouldn't have happened.

PROLOGUE

Detective Bo Alexander looked around at every officer in the room and wondered when everything she had ever known had come crashing down around her. Was it a specific moment that could have been avoided, or had it been inevitable? From the moment she first placed the Galveston Police Department badge on her chest, had she been destined to completely forego everything she'd ever known in favor of a moral compass that no longer pointed North?

She turned around at a raised voice behind her. Detective Gerald Guthrie was lying to a woman on the phone because he didn't have the heart to tell her that her son was most likely one of the victims of a shootout.

"If you have information, it belongs to me!"

The woman was shouting loud enough for her to hear it from the phone he held away from his ear, after he'd told her they had a promising lead but didn't clarify what it was.

He sighed and pinched the bridge of his nose. "I just think you should prepare for the worst. Mrs. Smith?" Apparently, she had decided to end their conversation.

The longer they strung the mother along, the worse it would be when the truth came out. Of course, the body they found was too mangled to be positively identified, but wouldn't it be better to just break her heart now? Or was it better to lie?

To his immediate right, Detective Sergeant Paige Gill was telling their lieutenant a story that obviously involved quite a bit of emotion, if her wild hand gestures were any indication. Bo caught the last bit of the story.

"—and I swear to you, to this day he doesn't know. Obviously, we're better now, but back then? He's lucky all I did was cheat."

Again, she wondered if it was better that way. Better to lie. Everyone did it, right? What was a lie to save someone's feelings? No matter where she turned in the squad room, it was all the same. Lie after lie after lie. All to save face. But lies got people killed.

She thought about her own lie. The little secret no one knew. She thought about Cass Halliburton.

Hers was a lie that could get her completely discredited as an officer if it was ever found out. But then, if it didn't affect the way she did her job, what should it matter? If smoking marijuana made Sampson less likely to get a use of force complaint, and taking Adderall helped Heath get through multiple doubles a week, then why should it matter? Cops chose every day to walk away from crime scenes without making arrests or writing reports. Settled at the scene, they called it. Why shouldn't those officers be given the same consideration if it was all for the better in the end?

Six months ago, that line of thought never would have crossed her mind. Right was right and wrong was wrong. Period. Cass Halliburton didn't see it that way. Maybe she used to or maybe she never did, but she certainly didn't now. Bo thought back to when the two of them had first encountered each other. She thought about hindsight and if she'd have agreed to take the case if she'd known then what she knew now.

CHAPTER ONE

Six months earlier

Newly minted Detective Guthrie asked Bo, as his former field training officer, to accompany him on a surveillance run on the top floor of an abandoned donut store that overlooked a mechanic shop owned by a man named Dusky Nelson. While nothing was off about the mechanics themselves, Mr. Nelson was one of the top members of the Galveston chapter of the Voleurs, and there had been rumors floating that he was using the shop as a front for something more nefarious than overpriced oil changes and the brass had decided it was a good case for him to get his feet wet on.

He'd asked Bo to come along because he trusted her input and knowledge and he didn't want to be alone in the cold and dark. She agreed because most of her cases were in the tail end stages, and the Voleurs tended to be involved in quite a few of the cases she ended up investigating. When she was a narcotics officer, they owned the dealers she busted. As a detective, their club came up more often in her work than she was comfortable with. She followed the stories, did the research, and generally knew who was who in the ranks, and that was the information Guthrie needed to make good notes for his case tonight.

It didn't hurt that she understood how miserable it could be on a cold night by yourself, having to force yourself to stay awake, trying not to miss anything on your comms because you were sniffing too loud, and trying to make sure your inside man didn't get killed. Assuming you had one.

While it didn't usually get anywhere near freezing in southeast Texas, this December was a cold one. The temperature, according to Bo's phone, was twenty-seven. Cold by any standards, but to someone whose usual outfit of choice was shorts, it was almost unbearable. She sipped her coffee slowly and shrugged her shoulders up slightly to push her thick leather coat farther up her neck. A glance at Gerald told her he had just done the same.

"It's fucking cold."

He laughed quietly and looked over at her. "I wish I could say I was used to it, but I haven't been used to it since a year after I left Montana. I acclimated to the heat and forgot what the cold felt like."

She squeezed her eyes shut in an attempt to stave off a sneeze. "Is there any particular reason you chose the coldest night of the year to do a stakeout in a building with no power?"

He grinned at her. "You mean besides the obvious fact that nothing was happening during the day? Sergeant Gill told me to come out here tonight when she handed me the case. There's no real intel, and she wants to know if this is worth putting man hours into."

Bo made a mental note to kill Paige Gill when she next saw her. "You're so lucky I like you, Gerald."

"Aww, that's sweet, but I think my wife would have something to say about it if you and I hooked up."

She glared at him and started to respond, but he held up his finger and pointed. Bo looked down at the street to see Frank Newman—a scrawny, ginger, twenty-something-year-old who had been in just enough trouble to be a good CI—walking toward the closed mechanic shop with his hands buried deep in the pockets of his sweatshirt. She had suggested Frank as a good source of information, so it made sense that he ended up being the insider.

"He's the one you have wired?"

Gerald nodded. "I originally suggested using one of our undercovers in the gang tonight, but that kind of fell under the same umbrella as why we're here. No real intel means no proof of wrongdoing, which means—"

"No way to spin the need for an undercover. I got it. So, he's the wire and we're here to see who, if anyone, shows up?"

He nodded again. "That's the plan. Frank already had connections who could get him in contact with Nelson for some 'extra work' so I had him ask around and this is where we're at."

"So, Gill didn't actually say come out *tonight*. She just said to check out the building and tonight is when it ended up being?"

A third nod.

"I hate Frank. Be sure to tell him that. I hate him. It is a smart setup, though. I'm proud of you."

Gerald blushed and then once again pointed toward the shop. "Someone just let Frank in the side door."

"Let's see what happens, then." They stopped talking and Bo checked her computer to make sure everything coming in over the wire was being recorded.

"You're late, Frank."

Bo assumed that was Frank's contact in the gang. She didn't recognize his voice, so she couldn't bring a name to mind. Low level, most likely.

"My bad, Hernandez. I was getting some ass. You really think 'sorry, I have to go do some work with the Voleurs' is going to fly when my girl wants to get laid?"

Brad Hernandez. Bo had seen his name come up in a few of the reports she had fielded from street officers running stings on the Voleurs. He was a low-level dealer and newly minted member of the motorcycle club. Brad growled deeply and said, "If she was worth being property, it would have."

Property of the Voleurs was the label given to any woman screwing a member of the gang. Obviously, Frank's girl wasn't so lucky. Bo barely resisted rolling her eyes.

"Guess it's a good thing I'm not a Voleur, huh?" Frank said.

There was a moment of silence as the two men entered the main garage, judging by the sound of echoing footsteps and the added voices Bo could now hear. The footsteps stopped and Brad spoke again. "Now that we're all here, everyone, listen up. My name is Brad. This gorgeous man beside me is Marcus Sindel, aka Jersey Boy. He's going to tell you all what's going on."

"Make a note of that, Gerald. Jersey Boy is one of the Voleurs' regional VPs." The distant rumble of a motorcycle registered in Bo's ear, but she was too busy notating the important points of the current meeting to take much notice.

"The boss will be here in a minute." Sindel's thick New Jersey accent made Bo's ear itch and she fought the urge to scratch it. "Every single one of you is here to make money for the Voleurs. If you have a problem being involved with such an illustrious organization as my Voleurs, you leave now."

Judging by the lack of sound, no one moved, and Marcus continued. "There are parts all around this shop that will be sold to various dealers whose names will be provided for you. These dealers are already standing by waiting for you tonight, so you will not screw around in any way. You are to get your dealer name from Mr. Hernandez here, and then collect your respective parts and get the hell out of my shop. You will be gone by the time the boss gets here, or you will be fired. The boss is not to see your face at any point. If you get in her way, I will get in yours."

Frank cleared his throat and asked quietly, "Who is the boss? I thought we were working for you guys. That's what Brad said."

"Cassidy fucking Halliburton is the boss, you dumb sack of—" A scuffling sound stopped Brad short of completing his sentence.

Bo looked up from the notes she was writing to stare at Gerald, who looked just as surprised as she was. "What the fuck, G?"

Gerald shook his head. "I don't know. Nothing in the little bit Frank told me suggested Halliburton's daughter would have any part in this."

Daniel Halliburton was the worldwide president of the Voleurs, and his daughter, Cass, was second in command. She would have absolutely nothing to do with something as small-time as a chop shop.

Frank spoke up and echoed their sentiments. "W-what's she coming here for? I thought this was just parts and shit?"

"You ask too many questions. The boss does what she wants. Your job," the deep voice got even closer to Frank, "is to do what *we* want. Got it?"

Frank's voice seemed to jump an octave. "Got it."

Bo didn't have to ask who Frank was whimpering to. She had been investigating the Voleurs long enough to recognize the voice of Dusky Nelson aka the Judge. "That would be the owner of the building," she murmured. Gerald nodded to indicate he heard her and marked it in his notes.

The motorcycle's rumble was now a loud roar and Gerald tapped Bo on the shoulder. "I think our new target just showed up."

Bo stood and stretched her legs, then cussed out loud as she looked out the window and locked eyes with Cass Halliburton, who smirked as she pulled off her helmet to let her blond hair loose.

"Fuck!" Bo sidestepped quickly, but it was too late. "She saw me."

Gerald chuckled and shook his head. "And I thought I was the rookie."

"Shut the fuck up, Gerald."

A thick East Texas accent cut through to their earpieces, and though Bo hadn't heard it before, she could only assume it belonged to Halliburton.

"Who the fuck are all these people in my building?" Cass asked.

The New Jersey accent answered. "Boss! I, uh, wasn't expecting you yet."

"No shit. What part of 'only the two of y'all' did you not understand, Marcus?"

"See, I just thought that you wouldn't mind if maybe we made some extra money before you showed up."

Cass must have whispered something because the only response was mumbled. Bo felt her heart beating against her chest. The surveillance was blown, but if Frank could keep his head about him, maybe there was a chance he would still be okay. The poor kid was probably terrified, though. She was trying to figure out a way they might be able to let Frank know they had been made without alerting Cass, when she thought instead of the reputation the woman had. Many an undercover cop had been killed without a second thought when this woman was involved. She felt her stomach roil.

She frowned and glanced at the computer that was transcribing word for word what was coming through to them. "Gerald, why is Cass Halliburton still talking?"

He looked perplexed but slowly answered, "Well, I would assume it's because she's the boss?"

She shook her head and began to gather her weapon as a sense of dread grew. "No, Gerald, why is she talking if she knows I'm here? Why hasn't she just thrown everyone out? She saw me, Gerald."

"Because…she's going to…make an example. Shit!"

Cass spoke again. "You thought going against my orders was a good idea with GPD watching us from the building across the street?"

Bo slammed the laptop down as she bolted across the room and into the stairwell. She yelled for Gerald to follow her as she heard the words, "Take care of this, Sindel."

They didn't make it two steps out the door before the first gunshot rang out, quickly followed by six more. As they ran across the street, Bo keyed up her mic and yelled, "Shots fired at Nelson Auto Shop! Officer requesting immediate backup!" When they burst into the shop, Bo was knocked backward by a bullet to her chest. The armored plate she wore took the brunt of the force, but she swore when a second bullet ripped through her arm. It was only through years and years of repetitive training that her muscle memory took over and she switched her gun into her non-dominant hand, focusing the weapon at her attacker. Gerald shot twice at the man standing over Frank's dead body, who Bo could only assume was Marcus Sindel. He was dead when he hit the floor. As his partner Dusky turned to fire at them, Bo fired one shot to the right of Dusky's heart and he dropped like a stone, blood slowly seeping through the navy blue shirt he wore.

The shooting stopped and all Bo could hear over the ringing in her ears was the phantom echo of gunshots in the air. She scanned the room to make sure no one else would pop out, then holstered her gun. She checked Nelson's pulse. It was weak and getting weaker, but she didn't bother applying pressure to his wound. The paramedics were on their way and there wasn't really anything she could do to stop a chest wound from bleeding. Besides, he'd signed his death warrant when he fucking shot her.

Gerald turned and emptied his stomach in the corner.

Cass Halliburton, it seemed, had escaped through a back door and left a pile of bodies in her wake, Frank's included. Bo's stomach rolled at the carnage, but she had seen enough dead bodies as a detective for it to not get the better of her in public. She didn't fault Gerald his weakness, though, because she knew as well as any cop that you never really got used to it, and seeing a dead body that you were the cause of was much, much more than just seeing a corpse at a crime scene.

She got to her feet, moving cautiously until she decided she probably didn't have any broken ribs and the vest had done its job. Thank God she'd decided to splurge and get a rifle plate to go with her vest. Had she not, the Kevlar might have kept her alive but the shot to the chest most likely would have incapacitated her, at the very least. As it was, it barely knocked her backward. She led Gerald out of the garage, away from the bloodbath. "It's okay. Call your union rep, and then call your wife. Get everything squared away with them and I'll take point on all this until you catch up, okay?" She looked up as the night shift supervisor careened into the parking lot, gravel flying behind him. "Fucking took them long enough."

Gerald walked away, phone to his ear as the sergeant ran up to Bo. Before he could begin his rant, she held up her hands to stop him. "We're both fine. I got hit in the chest, but my vest took the bullet. I took a second round to my arm and it hurts like a bitch, but other than that I'm fine. Gerald is shaken up, but he's not hit. We have quite a few bodies so we're going to need the ME."

"All right." He sighed deeply and ran his hands through his hair before shaking his head and looking behind her. "I'm sorry it took so long to get here. We had another issue on the other end of town I was tied up at. Everyone should be arriving soon. Your sergeant is also on her way. She'll take over with you two once she gets here." She waited until he walked away before removing her vest and gingerly probing at the small bruise forming in the center of her chest. She nearly hadn't worn the vest since they were just supposed to be watching, but given the nature of who they were watching and what they were known for, she'd changed her mind at the last second. Thank fuck for that.

When the cavalry arrived, the scene was chaotic, to say the very least. The radio call sent out had gathered every available officer, and the night sky was lit with red and blue so bright it could have been day. A total of eight bodies were removed from the scene. The black-and-whites searched the area, but there was no sign of anyone who'd been in the building. A team of paramedics secured Dusky Nelson, who was miraculously still alive. Bo hoped that maybe, if she were lucky, he would survive long enough to be a key witness in whatever shenanigans were going on.

"Ouch! That fucking hurts!" Bo jerked her arm away from the medic cleaning the wound in her arm.

"It's just a flesh wound. Stop being a baby." She kissed Bo's cheek and shoved her off the back of the truck. "Call me later. Maybe I'll be able to make everything else feel good to make up for it."

Bo couldn't help but laugh as she shook her head. "You're crazy, Stef, but maybe. First, though, I need to check on my officer. Thanks for the cleanup." She walked toward the squad car where Gerald was standing, but she waited until he was off the phone before she approached him. "Is everything okay?"

He nodded. "I'm okay. I think I just wasn't expecting this, of all places, to be where I shot at someone for the first time. SWAT, maybe, but not here on what should have been just a shitty cold surveillance run."

She raised her eyebrows. "You work for GPD and you've never shot at someone until now?"

He shook his head. "I've been extremely lucky. I'm a white cloud."

"White cloud my ass. This turned into a shit storm tonight. I'm glad you'll be all right, though. Is your wife going to be good? Your rep contacted your lawyer?"

"Yeah, I took care of everything. How long before I'm back on the case?"

She shrugged as their commanding officer walked up. "I'm sure she can answer that, though. Sarge?"

Sergeant Paige Gill clapped them both on the shoulder. "A few days. You'll both be put on three days mandatory R and R leave, and then since this is obviously a good shoot, we'll let you come back to desk duty. Until then, we've got it from here. You two go write your reports and turn in your duty weapons for evidence. Give IA a couple of weeks, max, to run the investigation and you'll be back on full duty. As of right now, you're on paid leave. Stay with friends, don't do anything too stupid. Oh, and I'll also want reports from you detailing everything that *doesn't* go to IA." She winked and walked back into the fray.

Gerald looked at Bo's shoulder. "Are *you* going to be okay?"

She nodded and grinned but held her arm just a little closer to her body. "It's just a scratch. Now, if you'll excuse me, I'm going to go write my report and then see if I can't get someone to make a pillow princess out of me to work off this excess energy." His laughter followed her as she got into a cruiser and drove back to the station.

She sat at her desk and ran her hands through her hair as she pulled up the proper format to write her report, the smell of floor cleaner and rocket fuel masquerading as coffee to keep her company. She breathed deeply, pulling in the familiar smells as she started typing. While her report flowed smoothly, the thoughts in her head were anything but. Why was Cass Halliburton on the island? There was no way she would be here for a chop shop unless something went horribly wrong and she'd been demoted or something, but Bo hadn't heard anything along those lines. Was she setting something up? More likely, she wasn't overseeing the setup, but the initial production of whatever was being set up. Of course, that only added more questions. What was being set up? More importantly than *what* they missed, though, was *how* they missed it. In her heart, she knew this would only be the beginning.

Chapter Two

B o watched as her best friend, Nikki Sanders, shook her ass to the music as she wiped spilled beer off the bar.

"Fucking party foul, man," the other waitress beside her yelled.

Nikki grinned and threw the towel in a water bucket as she jumped up on the bar to dance some more, much to the obviously immense pleasure of the bar crowd.

"It's Saturday, Francis! Have some damn fun!"

As she danced, Bo came up to her bar and threw a dollar at her feet. "How much for the night?"

Nikki laughed and jumped down, yelling to Francis that she was going on break as she fell into Bo's arms. The other waitress just laughed and waved her off.

"Still keeping your patrons entertained, I see."

Nikki kissed Bo fully on the mouth—lingering just long enough for Bo to tighten her grip—before she answered, "Always, my love. My bar has been on top since the beginning for a reason. I make sure they have fun; they make sure I stay in business." She flipped her long hair back behind her shoulder. "My wife called. She said you might be coming over tonight. You want to talk about it?"

Bo rolled her eyes but nodded. "Can I have a beer?"

Nikki handed her one from behind the bar before leading her to one of the booth seats in the back corner of the bar.

"Now. What the hell happened? If I recall correctly, you said you were going on a…" She paused and looked up as if searching for the correct phrase, her face lighting when she remembered. "'A too damn cold, going nowhere, good-for-nothing stakeout.'"

"That's what it should have been." Bo rolled the bottle between her hands. "But it turned out to be something else. I have one witness who's in the hospital probably going through surgery and another in the wind somewhere. If I could find her—the second witness—I could easily bring her in for questioning, but she's literally the second highest ranking Voleur in the world. She's not going to just walk up to my door and say hello. Not to mention the fact that she should theoretically have absolutely no business on my island. Yet, here she is." She took a swig of her beer and frowned. "I'm behind, and I don't like being behind."

Nikki tapped on the table as she thought it through. "I guess your only choice now is to do what you do best."

"Which is what?"

She smiled. "Be a detective." She slapped the table. "And you don't need me to tell you that, so what else is up?"

Bo grinned and finished her beer. "I just wanted to see you. Your lovely wife must not have mentioned that she offered to make me feel better as she was cleaning out the gruesome wound on my shoulder." Bo made sure to emphasize *just* how bad it was.

"Oh, gruesome is it?"

"Truly it is. I could have lost my arm. And I took a bullet to the chest. My heart is wounded."

Nikki slid over and gently kissed the bandage on Bo's arm, then she kissed her neck before finally kissing her lips again. "Then go ahead and head to my house, and Stef and I will take good care of you when we get home tonight. How's that sound?"

Bo nipped her bottom lip and kissed it gently. "Sounds good to me. I've got to go home and feed Chubby first, though. I'll see you when you get home."

Nikki smiled seductively as she got up to walk away. "See you then, baby."

❖

The first thing Bo noticed when she approached her apartment door was the wet mark under her door mat signifying it had been moved. Thankfully, she was never one to leave spare keys in such obvious places. She glanced over the railing around the side of the apartment and saw that the living room light was on as well, something she hadn't noticed when she pulled up. She looked out over the parking lot but didn't see any suspicious vehicles. Slowly, she drew her backup weapon and approached the door, but there was no sound coming from inside. She edged it open, and immediately noticed the leather jacket hanging on her coat rack, the bold emblem of the Voleurs on the back. The second thing she saw was her massive brown and white pit bull, Chubby, lying on the couch wagging her tail at a woman with long blond hair sitting in Bo's recliner, wearing a black T-shirt with that same logo opposite "Vice Presidente" on the chest, and a pair of chaps covering blue jeans that looked painted on.

She carelessly threw the tattered copy of *A Tale of Two Cities* to the side and quoted, "'It is a far, far better thing that I do, than I have ever done.' Sounds like complete bullshit to me, don't you think? What kind of stupid fuck gives his life up for a made-up notion like love?"

Bo glanced at her dog to make sure she was genuinely fine, and then turned back to face Cass Halliburton, who was stretching like a cat as she stood. "How did you get in my house?"

Cass grabbed her jacket from the coat hook. "One of my many skills, Detective Alexander."

Bo didn't lower her gun and moved into a better position. "And my address? Are you so invested in whatever you're doing in Galveston that you already knew who I was?"

An eye roll preceded a sound of disgust from Cass. "Your address is anything but unlisted, Detective, and seeing as how your name seems to pop up quite a bit whenever one of my boys gets arrested, I'm well aware that you've had an interest in us for quite some time. Some of my boys told me you were the one I needed to watch out for, but if finding me in your apartment is truly all you're worried about at this point then perhaps I was wasting my time looking into GPD. If you're the best they have then I have nothing to worry about."

"So, you're here because you're worried? About me, or about what I could do to your business?" Bo took in the leather chaps framing the perfect ass, the tight T-shirt, the way her hair moved. She was fucking hot, and she fucking knew it. Bo ignored the familiar pull she felt in the depths of her stomach.

Cass's laugh was patronizing. "No, I'm not worried. You're not a threat to me, but I am here to warn *you*."

They'd been circling each other like alpha lions preparing for battle, but the answer was so abrupt and without pretense that it stopped Bo in her tracks. "Excuse me?"

Gone was the smiling woman Bo had walked in on and in her place was a woman who had obviously earned her spot as second in command of the largest criminal biker gang in the southern United States, if not the world. "I'm here to warn you, Detective. Galveston Police Department isn't prepared to handle what you'll walk in on if you continue to pursue my boys and me in our endeavors on the island."

"So, you're worried about me." Taunting probably wasn't her best idea, but it was the only defense Bo had to being caught unawares in her own apartment. She was lucky she hadn't walked into a bullet. Again.

"I enjoy my business, Detective, and I don't want to ruin what I have going here. Hypothetically speaking, killing you would certainly do that. So no, not worried. Warning. Stay away from me and my boys. Leave us alone, and we'll leave you alone."

"With all due respect, Miss Halliburton, this is my island and I'll do as I please. Unless you want to confess to whatever the hell it was that happened tonight and tell me all about the chop shop you're apparently in charge of, kindly see your way out of my apartment."

Cass moved into Bo's space, forcing her to turn the gun away or jab it into her stomach. "Or what?"

More out of instinct than anything, Bo grabbed her by her arm and twisted it around, slamming her face-first into the wall behind them. "Or else. I'm a cop, you've broken into my house, and you were at a mass shooting tonight. There's no reason on earth why I shouldn't arrest you right fucking now."

Surprisingly, Cass laughed, and it threw Bo off just enough for her to whip around and slam her fist across Bo's nose. She felt it crack and automatically went to cover it. As quickly as it started, though, it was over, and Cass held her hands up in surrender. "Assault on a peace officer is a class B misdemeanor. Take me in, Detective." When Bo hesitated, a slow smile spread across Cass's face. "Except there's no evidence that I broke in, is there?" She glanced behind Bo in the direction of the bedroom. "I could always wait for you to go get your handcuffs and we can fight it out? Since you want so bad to bring me in for questioning about the mass shooting I was at. Then again, you didn't see my motorcycle when you drove up, right?" The threat in her eyes was clear. She wasn't walking out of this apartment in cuffs.

Bo snarled and yanked Cass up by her shirt, leaning in close to her. "I don't fucking think so. When I bring you in, it's not going to be on some bullshit charge that you'll be able to talk your way out of. When I bring you in everyone is going to see it. And you'll know for a fact that it was me who brought you down."

"Did I do something to piss you off?" The cocky smile was back. "You seem overly aggressive."

Bo opened the door and threw her out before slamming it in her face. For a split second, she contemplated doing exactly what Cass had suggested and running to get her cuffs, but she knew as soon as she thought it that it was a bad idea. Even if she had been so inclined to chase her down and bring her in, it would be just as easy for Cass to say she'd been invited inside and Bo had assaulted her as it would be for Bo to tell the truth of the matter. Cass's version wouldn't hold up in court, obviously, but it would be enough to get Bo taken off the investigation. And any questioning about the shooting would be ruled inadmissible. In the end, her original statement stood; when she brought Cass Halliburton in, she was going to make sure every piece of evidence she gathered had Cass's name written on it in permanent marker.

A wet nudge on her hand reminded her of her pit, sole witness to the whole debacle. "You could have easily stopped that, you understand? What use are you as a guard dog?" Chubby simply wagged her tail and then sat down, lifting her paw to say hello. "Useless. I'm fucking bleeding and you're asking for a handshake. Are you hungry?"

She spent the next hour feeding Chubby and cleaning her face and clothes. When she was satisfied that her nose wouldn't start gushing blood as soon as she released pressure on it, she kissed Chubby's massive head and left, ensuring that she locked the door behind her. The spare key was left hanging by the door where it belonged.

She got to the house five minutes before Stef and Nikki. While she had originally planned to be lying mostly naked in their bed when they got home, Cass's fist changed her plans. As it was, she barely made it to the couch where Stef and Nikki found her with a bag of frozen peas on her face.

"Jesus Christ, Bo. What happened?"

While Bo gave Nikki the short version of events, Stef immediately bent down to give her face a cursory examination.

"It could be broken. If it is, it could cause a lot of complications in the long run. Do you want me to take you to the hospital?"

Bo shook her head, then groaned at the sudden pain. "It's not broken. Just fucking hurts. Honestly, the only reason I'm even here is because it looks better after a shooting if the officers involved stay with family. Otherwise I wouldn't have left my house at all. All I need right now is some Tylenol and a nap and I'll be fine. Think we can manage that?"

Stef looked like she wanted to argue, but instead she and Nikki gently helped Bo off the couch and they made their way slowly to the bedroom. This definitely wasn't the night she'd envisaged having with them. Just another thing to thank Cass Halliburton for.

The party scene was where Cass belonged. It was where she thrived, and it was where she returned after her interesting conversation with Bo Alexander. If she were being honest with herself, it was where she could blend in. No one asked questions in the middle of the club if you were in the right place, and luckily for her, this bar was the right place. Nikki's Place had garnered a reputation around the state as a place where pretty much anything was accepted, and everyone was welcome. Everyone including, much to her surprise, Detective Alexander.

She certainly hadn't been expecting the kiss the bar's owner had laid on the detective. A kiss that promised much, much more by the looks of it. When the detective had walked in, Cass had waited a few minutes and then walked out. Already knowing the address made it easy to find the right apartment and make her way inside, courtesy of a pick lock kit.

Before she had even made her way to Galveston Island, she had done her homework on every officer she was likely to have a run-in with. Bo Alexander was at the top of that list, and Cass was certainly pleased the detective hadn't disappointed. When confronted, she hadn't been expecting Bo to get violent, from what she'd heard about her from the boys on the street, but damn, was she thankful she had. Cass lived for the thrill of the fight, and no one put up a fight like cops. Unfortunately, it had left her high and dry with a massive case of blue balls. "God, she would be so much fun."

"Talking to yourself, honey?"

Cass glanced up from her glass of bourbon to set eyes on a busty redhead who could have given Jessica Rabbit a run for her money. Cass purposely kept her eyes at chest level. "I'd much rather be talking to you." She knew she wasn't imagining that the woman pressed her chest out more.

"I just got off. What would you like to talk about?"

"Well, if you're talking about getting off, let's talk about getting off."

"Oh, I would love to."

Cass grinned and leaned over the table. "Isn't sex such a great distraction from a bad day? What's your name?"

"Sav. And yours?"

"Cass. And I've had a terrible day. My best employee just got fired, I have a new business to run that seems to be doomed from the get-go, and there's a very good chance the CEO of my company is about to come down and put his hands where they don't belong."

Sav made no effort to mask her surprise. "That…sounds like a lot." She glanced down at the patches on Cass's leather, familiar to anyone who grew up on the East Coast, and then slowly dared to make eye contact. "I don't suppose any of that is a metaphor?"

"Of course not! Why would it be?" She grinned. "I could use a distraction. Tell me about yourself, Sav." Sav was flustered, that much was obvious, but Cass could tell she was intrigued. "How about you tell me what you think about good sex?"

A bright red blush was Cass's reward for the question. "I think it's something I haven't had in a very long time." She spoke quietly, almost sadly, but there was an edge that Cass grabbed on to.

She leaned closer, her eyes locked on Sav's. "Would you like to have it with me?"

"Yes." Sav seemed to barely be able to get the word out, but her eyes said it all.

"I'm going home. Come with me. Again, and again." Cass led the way outside to her Harley Roadster. "I really hope you like motorcycles."

Sav couldn't keep her hands to herself. They wandered everywhere they could reach, and eventually, Cass gave up on making it home and pulled into a motel off the seawall. Cass spent the rest of the night working out her frustrations about Bo Alexander on the body underneath her.

The cell phone on the nightstand rang at precisely 0800 the next morning, and Cass answered it without opening her eyes. "Yes, sir?"

"You didn't call me with an update yesterday, Cassidy."

The scratchy, mildly irritated, baritone voice of Daniel Halliburton was anything but surprising, and it was all Cass could do not to groan out loud. "My apologies, sir. Things didn't go as expected and I was playing catch-up."

"And you don't think that warranted a phone call?"

Respectful, Cass. Be respectful. "You're absolutely right, sir." *You're a complete and utter dick, sir.* "I should have called immediately. Would you like the update now?" Amazingly, the woman sleeping soundly beside Cass hadn't stirred while Cass dressed, and as her stepfather requested the update, she walked out of the room, leaving the woman behind.

"Marcus Sindel is dead. He—"

"And how in God's name did you manage to *not* call me after that?" His voice was considerably louder now, and Cass had to fight not to yell back.

"Because I was busy dealing with the detective whose partner killed him." A growl on the other end of the line brought out the forced, "Sir."

"And how exactly did you deal with him?"

"Her, sir, and I dealt with her by—"

"Whatever. I'll be in Galveston in three hours. I expect you'll have an office set up for me by then. From this point on you will be personally in charge of this operation. There will be no more delegating to your lesser officers, and I will expect your future reports to be on time."

You goddamned son of a... "Yes, sir." She started her motorcycle and couldn't help the smile that came when he said he couldn't hear her anymore and hung up. *Find him a damn office? Seriously?* It had been hard enough finding her own space in the small bar the Voleurs used as a meeting area. "Like I don't fucking have enough to worry about?"

CHAPTER THREE

Bo stretched as she woke, opening her eyes when she felt someone lift off the bed. "Good morning," she said around a yawn.

"Hey there." Stef's shaggy black hair was in a mess over her sleep filled eyes, but it did nothing to belittle her thousand-watt smile. "Feel better?"

Bo stood and nodded, not even a little self-conscious about being naked in front of Stef, who headed for the shower. They'd had this arrangement for years, and it suited all three of them, something Bo was always grateful for. She didn't have the time or desire for a monogamous relationship, and Stef and Nikki were polyamorous and enjoyed sharing their bed with her. It was perfect. "Certainly a lot better than I did yesterday."

A low chuckle came from the shower. "So, you said she came to warn you?"

"Yeah, she said that if we continued looking into what she's doing on the island that we'll regret it. Maybe not in so many words, but that's what she meant. Of course, I wasn't looking into *her* specifically, but I guess she didn't know that. Obviously, I'll have to start now. If she's here it means something big is happening."

"Why do you sound so disappointed about that?" Nikki shuffled up behind Bo, obviously not awake as she leaned down to lay her head on Bo's shoulder.

Bo reached back and ran her hand through Nikki's long, dirty blond locks. "Because this is happening right when I'm being put on leave for the shootout. It's going to take at least a couple of weeks for me to be back on full duty and who knows what I'll miss in that time."

"Didn't you say you were going to be on desk duty in just a few days?"

"Yes." Bo groaned softly as Nikki started rubbing out tight knots that had formed in her shoulder. "I'm going to use that time to look through some of my old case files dealing with the Voleurs and see if I can't get a handle on what might be going on, but it's not going to be anything compared to what I'll get when I'm allowed to go back on the streets."

"Why not let someone else take over while you're grounded?"

Bo shook her head vehemently. "Like hell I'll let someone else take over this case. That bitch broke into my house and threatened me. Not to mention she schmoozed my damn dog."

"Sounds like you're more upset about that than anything else." Stef laughed, stepping out of the shower with her hair wrapped in a towel.

"Your wife would be too, if you were anywhere near as cute as my dog." Bo couldn't help the sarcastic response.

"Just because you can't pull off the towel look, harlot."

They laughed, and any bit of tension was broken. "Stef, you work today?" Bo asked.

She nodded while she stepped into a pair of black BDUs. "Yes, ma'am, I do."

Bo turned to Nikki. "Think maybe I could convince you to have a beach day with me?"

She smiled mischievously. "Why, do you just want some alone time with me? Sex on the beach is more than just my most popular cocktail, you know."

Bo grinned. "No, not at all. I was going to invite both of you if Stef didn't have to work, but since she does, it'll just be me and you."

Nikki shrugged and shook her head. "I don't mind at all. I've still got the set of balls in my Jeep."

Bo feigned horror. "I hope you didn't hurt the poor boy you took them from."

"Only a little. I used a sedative."

"Oh good, good."

The jokes continued while they all got dressed and ate breakfast. Bo tried not to be distracted by the prospect of a major investigation coming up, but she couldn't help the feelings of excitement and anticipation. The mandated leave couldn't be over soon enough.

Once Stef left for work, Nik drove them to take care of Chubby and then they headed to the 13 Mile beach access. When they pulled up, Bo commented on how pretty the water looked, even though there was a front about to blow through. She let Nikki take a swim while she got everything set up—minus the towel that was promptly pooped on by a seagull—and once she was done, she set up two goals and they began a game of beach soccer. Five minutes into that, however, their good time ended when someone Bo genuinely wished she didn't know walked up.

Detective Topher Dusek was a greasy slimeball and rat of a man, and that was honestly an insult to rats. He had the type of face that, no matter how much he worked out, was always chubby and slightly too big for his body. He always squinted like he was looking into the sun, and no matter how friendly he sounded, he always gave off a bad vibe. His sandy blond hair was cut into a high and tight and he said things like, "Lock it up, soldier," and, "Dad just got back from the sandbox," even though he'd never been in the military. Bo's innate distrust of him was one of the main reasons she had left the narcotics division. She had no desire to work with people she didn't trust to have her back when shit hit the fan.

"Hello, ladies. Having a good day, I hope."

"We were. Now we're leaving to go eat. Isn't that right, Bo?" Nikki barely glanced at him.

After Topher basically stalked Nikki for two months because she refused to go out with him after meeting her at her bar, her nice bone was broken. Apparently, "I'm a lesbian and I have a wife," didn't translate well into his language. Whatever that was.

"Oh, where at? I could eat." He gave them what looked to be a genuine smile.

Bo tilted her head. "Really more of a girls' day, Topher. Sorry." Bo smiled back at him.

"What the hell is wrong with you, Alexander?"

Well, she had tried to smile. "Got to go now. Bye, Topher."

Bo hoped he would accept their words at face value and continue his jog away from them, but he insisted on helping them pack their gear up and load it into the Jeep. By the time he finally left them alone, they both agreed it would be too awkward and redundant to unpack and stay, lest Topher decide to turn around and jog back the way he came, back toward their setup. With any other person, Bo would have simply told them exactly where they could shove it, in no uncertain terms. The problem was that GPD had a strict policy against altercations between officers, and in certain crowds Topher was just as well liked as she was. Not to mention that, as much of an asshole as he was, sometimes she got the feeling that he really was just genuinely fucking clueless about regular social cues.

"Tortugas it is, then," Nikki muttered unenthusiastically.

"Margaritas at noon doesn't sound like *that* bad of an idea."

"Well yeah, not to you! You don't even like the beach!"

Bo tried to stifle the smile that threatened but, judging by Nikki's glare, she was unsuccessful. "If I didn't like the beach, I wouldn't have suggested a beach day. It's the water I don't like. Now. Margaritas? I'll pay."

"Sold!"

The nachos at Tortugas weren't the best, but damn it if the margaritas didn't make them worth it. They were three down by the time the waitress brought their plate, interrupting an argument about the proper order to dip a chip into queso and salsa.

"You'll ruin the damn queso if you dip it into the salsa first! You're literally the only person in the world who likes it like that, and no one wants salsa in their queso."

Nikki stared at her, half red chip poised to enter the melted cheese, before slowly lifting the chip and crunching down on it. Before Bo could stop her, she dunked the half-eaten chip into the cheese.

"You're fucking hopeless." Bo laughed and started in on the feast.

"So, is everything going to be okay for you at work?"

Bo scoffed and nodded, mouth half full of nachos. "Oh, yeah. I didn't do anything wrong so all we have to wait on is the mandatory investigation. I've got my shirt hung up in the evidence locker so that if it comes to it, anyone who needs to can see the bullet holes."

"Wait, 'holes'? As in plural?"

"Yeah." Bo frowned and cocked her head. "I'm almost positive I told you I got hit twice."

"Did you? I must not have paid much attention."

"I took the first round to the chest, but my vest caught it. I had an armored plate in the front of it so it wasn't a big deal. Would have really fucking sucked without that, though." She touched her nose, which was still damn sore. It really had been a shitty day.

Nikki set an uneaten nacho back down on the plate in front of her. "And what would have happened if you weren't wearing a vest, Bo? You're a detective. You're not a street cop anymore. You know just as well as I do that it's pure luck you were wearing your vest last night."

Bo leaned in just enough to make a point. "That won't happen. I promise you, if I die, it won't be because of a bullet."

"You can't promise that, Bo." Her eyes filled with unshed tears.

Bo took her hand. God, how she hated making people cry. "Look, I can't promise you bullets won't start flying again, but I can promise you that the Voleurs *will* be laying low after last night. Whatever it is that Cass Halliburton is here dealing with won't be something she wants to draw any more attention to. Besides, it's probably just a setup of some kind and she'll be gone within the month. The local boys won't want to stir up any trouble once she's gone, either. You're my best friend. You can't get rid of me that easily, honey."

Nikki rolled her eyes but finally smiled. "Whatever. Just don't get shot again."

"I will try my very best." She held up three fingers. "Scout's honor."

"That would mean so much more to me if you were actually a scout."

❖

Cass rapped her fingers impatiently on the table in front of her as she waited for the meeting to begin. Not only had her father insisted she give up her temporary office in the Voleurs' headquarters so that he would have a throne to rule from, but his habit of being "fashionably" late drove her batshit crazy. He liked to think it made him the center of attention, but being as he was the gang's president and therefore already *had* everyone's attention, it just made him seem like a pompous ass. At least to her.

When he finally walked in ten minutes after the meeting was scheduled to begin, he cleared his throat and threw the tail of his jacket back behind him before sitting down. *Ever the damn drama queen.* She kept her expression neutral.

"I'm sure you've all been made aware that the Galveston Police Department has been tipped that we're running an operation on the island." He turned to the man to his left and asked, "What are we doing to stay ahead of that?"

The man Daniel spoke to was nicknamed Pigsty. He had been in the club almost as long as Cass had and had been scheduled to be Daniel's second in command before Cass usurped him. He didn't outwardly have a problem with her, but every time he spoke she got the feeling of thinly veiled anger, and his words reeked of sexism. He was not happy that the only female Voleur had taken his seat. Pigsty shifted, cracking his back subtly. "The detective that will most likely take over the case will have taken a mandatory leave of absence due to her involvement in the shooting. That will, at the very least, give us a few days to get ahead of her and cover as much of our tracks as possible."

"Who is the detective?"

"Her name is Bo Alexander. She's a by the book cop, but I think if we worked it the right way, we might be able to use that to our advantage." Pigsty shrugged slightly.

Daniel furrowed his brows. "Explain."

"When a cop is strung tight like she is, it only takes the right kind of prodding to get them to break. In this case, to follow a wild goose in the wrong direction." He sat up straighter and seemed to purposely turn away from Cass as he added, "She's also a lesbian."

Cass only *thought* she couldn't hate Pigsty more than she already did. Turns out, she was wrong. "I swear to fucking God—"

Her father held up his hand to stop her. "Could be a good idea. How are we going to move the product and get it assimilated?"

Another man spoke, but Cass wasn't hearing a word of it. She tried to steady her breathing, but she was quickly losing control of it and was beginning to get dizzy with the effort of holding back her retort. *How fucking dare he.* She had thought, once she made her way high enough in ranks, that her father would cease to use her that way. Obviously, she was wrong.

"And there's already drugs being exported, so it shouldn't raise too many eyebrows if that supply suddenly increases."

Daniel slammed his fist on the table, a sign of the meeting wrapping up. "Excellent. Cassidy, our contact at Classic Auto has gotten you hired as the new sales director. See that you keep everything in order over there to make sure our money goes where it needs to go. As for this detective, once she's back on duty, you know what to do."

"I don't want—"

"You want what is best for this organization, do you not?" His gaze was hard and unforgiving.

Cass sighed deeply and bit off each word as she said it. "Yes. Sir."

"And you couldn't even keep Marcus Sindel alive to run this wing of our business so—"

"That wasn't my fault! Sindel is the one who—"

Daniel slammed his fist down again, this time hard enough to make even a few of his most seasoned captains jump. "So, it stands to reason, Cassidy, that you will be more than willing to help this operation succeed. Now more than ever. Whatever it takes, correct?"

Cass shook but made damn sure no one could see it. "Yes, sir." He stood to leave and she waited until everyone had followed him out before standing up and kicking her chair as hard as she could. It had been years, but she could still feel every hand that had ever touched her body because it was what was "best for the organization" and so it was what she should want.

Years of being used to gain intel or to get a foot in the door to a rival gang to facilitate a takeover had taken a toll on her soul. She really thought she was done. She picked her chair back up and sat down, her face in her hands.

Chapter Four

It had been a very long time since Bo had dressed up this way. She ran her fingers through her short-cropped hair, but she couldn't for the life of her get it to behave. This was exactly why she stopped cutting it short the first time. It had gotten almost down to her shoulders last time before it got in her way and irritated her again, causing her to drive immediately to the barber. She finally shook her head slightly and it fell into place. Short hair was a pain in the ass, but damned if it didn't look good. *Not to be conceited or anything.* She buttoned all but the top two buttons of her shirt and looked herself over in the mirror.

After talking to Nikki, she had decided that it would be a good idea for her to try to get in touch with some of her old street contacts to see if any of them had heard what the Voleurs were up to. Sure, she could have asked one of the narco dicks to do it since she was off duty and they were getting paid for it, but after the break-in, this felt personal. Not to mention the fact that Topher was the narcotics supervisor and any request she made would have to go through him. *Not going to happen.*

She hadn't worked the streets in years, but she still had a few people on the dark side of town that would talk to her. She took herself in. The rolled-up sleeve of her button-down showed off a muscular arm covered in a massive tattoo. The tight shirt stretched across her stomach, and she could just make out the ridges of her muscles. The two buttons showed off just enough cleavage to be inappropriate for work. On her face, the two silver rings above her right eye glinted in the fluorescent light, and below her navel, just under the button of her jeans, the fly bulged out just enough that anyone looking closely would see it. Sure, packing wasn't something she would usually do just to go meet contacts, but for the women she was going to talk to, she had to look like she was there to play.

She almost laughed at the reflection of an older version of her teenage self. For a moment, she wondered if it was worth getting back into that mindset, but the thought left as quickly as it had come. If anyone had their finger on the pulse of the underworld, it was the woman she was hoping to find tonight, and that woman would not appreciate Bo's youthful indiscretions rearing their ugly heads. A word from anyone could be valuable, but a word from her old friend was worth its metaphorical weight in gold. She gave Chubby a pat on the head and grabbed her keys before heading outside.

As she always did when leaving her home, she wondered why in the hell she agreed to a third-floor apartment. A cold, brisk wind was all she needed to remind herself that, should she require it, her apartment had a fireplace that was exclusive to the third-floor apartments. She had a feeling she would need it before the winter was over. As she looked up after locking her door, checking instinctively to make sure no one suspicious was hanging around or paying too much attention to her, she couldn't help but smile at the reflection of the moon on the water. A full moon meant tonight was going to be interesting.

Twenty minutes later, she pulled into the parking lot of the Denny's on the seawall and climbed out of her truck. The diner was a few blocks away from where she was going, but it gave her an opportunity to distance her truck from the girls who worked the streets she was headed to. Five blocks toward East End and she started slipping into her role. The girls might know she was a cop now, but they also knew she was one of the few cops who wouldn't get them in trouble. So long as she played the part.

Bo could feel the weight of the dark side of Galveston Island weigh on her shoulders the deeper into the shadows she went. This wasn't a place for the well intentioned even in the daylight. At nighttime, the right person could be murdered just for blinking the wrong way.

She saw the woman she was looking for. Tiffany, thankfully, was one of the few women who hadn't let the weight of darkness bring her down, regardless of what she chose to do for a living. The shadows hadn't blocked out Tiffany's fire, and it was that fire that made her a damn good informant. Bo stood in the shadows, watching, waiting as Tiffany slowly straightened and turned, her eyes falling unerringly on Bo's.

A smile lit her face, and for an instant, Bo was reminded just how beautiful Tiffany was. It was no wonder she made as much money as she did on the streets. In another life, she could have been an African goddess. Hell, maybe she had been. The streetlights above them were out—whether shot out or burned out was anyone's guess—and it afforded Tiffany a path to make her way to Bo without being too visible.

Her body immediately molded to Bo's as she wrapped her long, almost too thin arms around Bo's neck. "Where have you been? You haven't even stopped by to rile us up lately. I missed you."

Bo smiled and leaned almost within kissing distance. "I'm not undercover anymore, babe. You know the department will kill me if they find me here." It was a game they both knew how to play. A game they were both very good at.

Tiffany moved to nuzzle her neck, moaning at the dark, spicy cologne she had on before running her tongue up Bo's neck to her ear. When she whispered, she was all business. "Is everything okay, Bo? The other girls might not know you don't work the streets anymore, but I do. What are you doing here? And what's with the bruising on your face?"

Bo pressed Tiffany up against the wall just hard enough to warrant a glare. It might be uncomfortable, but Tiffany knew as well as she did that it would make this believable for anyone who might be passing them by. Their hands roamed in the pantomime of the act they were supposed to be performing as Bo answered Tiffany's question.

"Cass Halliburton drove into town this week. I need to know if you've heard anything about what the Voleurs might be doing that we haven't heard about." She winced inwardly at how rough her voice sounded. Just because her mind knew she was here for work didn't mean her body agreed.

"Bo, you know those guys don't talk to us, or in front of us. They might deal with the pimps, but the only thing a pimp is going to tell us is 'This guy is going to give you money. Take it.' Nothing we hear would be enough to get you anywhere if it was something big enough for the boss lady to show up. These guys know their game."

She'd had a feeling it was a long shot, but it was still disappointing. "Have they told you anyone is going to be giving you money, then?"

She shook her head. "Nope, sorry."

Bo growled, more out of frustration than anything, and pressed harder into Tiffany's body. She felt bad at the small gasp she heard but didn't think Tiffany would mind. A hard bite on her ear told her otherwise. "Play nice, Detective, or I'll remind you exactly what else my mouth can do to you."

She backed off. "Sorry," she said gruffly as the headlights from a passing car illuminated them briefly.

Tiffany bit her lip in obvious thought momentarily and then said, "You said it was *Cass* Halliburton that showed up at your operation?"

Bo nodded slowly. "Yes, why?"

"Because one of my girlfriends said she went home with a Voleur the other night and one of his buddies in the house was freaking out about a *Daniel* Halliburton coming into town. The name sounds familiar, but I didn't think anything of it at the time. Who is he?"

Bo stared at Tiffany in silence for a long moment before she finally said, "Daniel Halliburton is El Presidente. The worldwide leader."

Tiffany gasped. "Oh my God. What the hell are you getting yourself into, Bo?"

Bo could see Tiffany studying her face in the light. It was only a split second, but anyone worth their salt on the streets could read a person in a lot less time than that. You'd be asking for death if you couldn't.

Bo was confused, angry. She knew Tiffany could see everything and because she trusted her, she let her. Tiffany was immediately on alert. "Tell me everything."

Bo sighed. She hated having to bring someone else in on what she knew, but she didn't really have a choice. The girls had the right to know how dangerous things were going to get, and if they knew, they could pick up on information they might otherwise ignore. "We thought it was a chop shop. Cass showed up and gave orders, which meant bullets started flying. One of her lieutenants is dead and the other is in a coma. I get the feeling that there's nothing going on right now, but they're definitely setting something up. Setting something up that's big enough she didn't mind giving the order even though she knew we were watching."

Tiffany chewed her lip, her eyes searching Bo's. "That's not everything, Bo. I can't help you if I don't know everything."

"They…" Fuck. Giving the next of kin notifications always sucked, but the fact that she knew Tiffany personally made this even worse.

"They killed Frank, didn't they?" Tiffany's voice was flat.

"How did you know?"

She let out a soft breath and shook her head. "I knew something was wrong when he didn't come home the last couple of nights. Even to pay his half of the rent. I just had a feeling."

Bo squeezed her hand. "I'm the one that gave the rookie his name. It's my fault he was there in the first place. If I had known his family wouldn't tell you—"

Tiffany held up her hand to stop an apology she didn't need. "His family hated me. They thought my lesbian ways would drive him away from God. They had no idea he was gay. And Frank knew what he was getting into when he agreed to be your CI, just like I do. It's not your fault. That having been said," she kissed Bo hard enough to make her grunt, "you're hurting my business. I'll mourn Frank later. Thanks for coming by to tell me."

Bo reached into her pocket, still feeling a little ill at ease.

Tiffany ran her hand over Bo's arm. "One more thing. There was a Voleur that came around asking about our pimps the other day. Before Daniel came. Wanted the names of every single one of them, even the ones not on the payroll. I don't know if it's connected to your case, but it could be. He had a buzz cut so I couldn't give you a hair color, but he looked like he probably worked out."

Bo held up three hundred-dollar bills and winked. "Always a pleasure, Tiffany."

As she turned to leave, she looked over her shoulder. "You know I'll always make you scream, baby!" Tiffany called out loud enough for anyone listening to hear. And then she added just for Bo, "Lord knows, I've done it before."

Bo chuckled quietly as she left. What the hell were the Voleurs interested in the pimps for? They already had enough on their payroll, didn't they? She didn't think something like expanding their prostitution business would be enough to get the Halliburtons in town, but maybe she was wrong. But what did that have to do with a chop shop? Was the chop shop even important?

Cass watched, fascinated and surprised at what she was seeing.

She had driven all the way across the island to check on the prostitutes who were going to be used as part of their product moving scheme. At first, she hadn't seen anything out of the ordinary, only a few females and one extremely flamboyant man, whom she could only assume wasn't a prostitute because she didn't think they employed men and he was in their territory, just a few blocks from a local gay bar. She had parked in a lot in the middle of their territory to make her rounds when she noticed a couple back in the shadows—their hands moving frantically and their legs intertwined—but she hadn't thought anything of it. Until she got close enough to hear a name whispered.

Bo.

Intrigued, she moved on from checking out the women and slid into the shadows the couple was using to hide in. She was close enough to be seen if the detective looked hard enough, but she had the feeling she was hidden. The first thing she noticed were the eyebrow rings. Without a doubt, Bo hadn't had those when she'd been staking out the chop shop Marcus ran, and they certainly weren't there in Bo's apartment. Were they new? Or some kind of affectation?

The other thing she noticed were the tattoos covering Bo's left arm. If she wasn't mistaken, they went all the way up and even covered part of Bo's neck. Paired with how Bo was acting with Tiffany—the way her hands were roaming, moving confidently over what few curves the woman had—Cass would have thought Bo and herself no different from each other in that moment. Two people who simply operated more naturally in the dark than in the harsh light of day.

When the detective had left, Cass nearly laughed out loud when Tiffany said she could make Bo scream because she had done it before. Maybe this was the leverage she needed to get the detective out of the picture.

Bo had slept with a prostitute. Maybe not recently, but she certainly had in the past, and that information alone was enough to make her decision-making skills come under question. She tried to ignore the nagging voice in the back of her head reminding her that unless she could prove that Bo paid for the sex, it was mostly a moot point. She understood and honestly respected that Bo had worked hard for her reputation, and she was going to have to work just as hard to take Bo down.

Chapter Five

On a normal day it would have taken Bo and Chubby roughly twenty minutes to jog to the beach access point on the west end of the island, but five minutes down the road, Bo quickly realized that it was once again much too chilly to be in only a T-shirt and board shorts on the waterfront. They headed back to her apartment so that she could change into a set of jogging pants and a loose-fitting long sleeve T-shirt.

While she never needed to be one hundred percent warm to function, she also didn't do well with being just a little too cold. Chubby, on the other hand, didn't seem to notice that it was about five hundred degrees colder than her usual summer runs. She was just happy to be outside, so Bo didn't bother with her pretty pink sweater. Probably for the best, as Chubby really did hate that sweater. *Even if she does look absolutely adorable.*

Bo looked around to make sure that there was no one who would complain before she unclipped Chubby's leash to let her run wild. It only took thirty minutes of playing fetch and accidentally splashing the water one too many times for Chubby to forgo the stick Bo had thrown in favor of her leash. Bo was in the process of re-clipping the leash on the master of the house when a massive black Lab came up and began sniffing Chubby's rear.

"Whoa! Hey there, big fella, where did you come from?" Bo was wary of stepping back from the two dogs, but the big boy seemed friendly enough, and Chubby's tail was wagging, so she relaxed a little. The Lab didn't have a collar on, so she was about to start looking around for his owner when she heard a familiar voice calling out to him.

"Max, get back here, you asshole!"

Chubby turned toward the voice and began to wag her tail, making Bo feel the sting of betrayal all over again. Cass didn't seem to notice who she was running up on until she was so close Bo could smell the sharp scent of her sunscreen. How in God's name this woman managed to wear Daisy Dukes and a tight-fitting T-shirt in the weather they were having was beyond even Bo's reasoning skills.

When she finally noticed who was standing in front of her, her eyes narrowed. "It's not bad enough you had to shoot my lieutenant, now you're trying to steal my dog, too?"

"I assure you, Miss Halliburton, your dog initiated contact."

"Pity." Cass glared at her. "He usually has much better taste in women."

"Your dog could find no better than Chubby. Now, if you'll excuse me."

Bo tugged on her pit's leash and was beginning the trek back home when she heard Cass call out, "Your dog might have good taste, but Tiffany seems a bit below your standards, doesn't she?"

Bo stopped and slowly turned around, every muscle in her body tensed. Chubby seemed to notice the change in her demeanor as she leaned against her leg and growled in Cass's general direction. "You have no idea what you're talking about."

Cass stood with her hands on her hips. "I know that the two of you looked pretty chummy against the wall the other night. I also know that it doesn't take much for a cop to lose credibility in the eyes of a district attorney when they're about to start investigating what could be a high-profile case. In fact," she paused and smiled darkly, "I'm sure a few well-timed pictures presented to the ADA's desk could make even the most innocent of actions seem like something else entirely."

Bo took a step forward and was inwardly pleased when Cass seemed to move back, her eyes widening just slightly. "Be careful who you try to blackmail, Miss Halliburton. Some people don't take it lying down the way your lackeys do."

"I guess it's a good thing I like the idea of you on your knees, then." Cass's faux smile didn't reach her eyes, which were altogether menacing. "I warned you to stay away, Detective."

"And I warned you to get off my island, Miss Halliburton. If I were you, I'd cut your losses and ride away right now."

"And if I don't?"

"Then I guess you'll see what happens when you wake the sleeping giant, won't you?"

As Bo turned away, Cass called out, "Right back at you, Detective."

❖

In the week that she was confined to her desk, Bo went through every case file she had on the Voleurs with a fine-toothed comb. Nothing she found could point her to anything that would suggest Cass Halliburton was needed. Certainly nothing big enough that El Presidente himself would come down because it got fucked up. One thing that did jump out at her was how many of the recent files seemed to suggest that some of the Voleurs were found with rival gang members. She made a mental note to bring that up with her sergeant. Once she was found innocent of any wrongdoing— no-billed—and she was allowed to return to work, she couldn't get there fast enough, much to the chagrin of her dog who sat whining pitifully as she dressed for her first day back.

Bo leaned down to gently scratch behind Chubby's soft white and brown ears. "I promise I'm coming straight home after work; you have my word."

The dog made a noise that quite clearly said, "I don't believe you," but Bo reassured her and gave her a piece of doggy jerky to placate her. Chubby accepted the offering and carried the large piece of dried meat out to the kitchen to set it beside her food bowl for later. The food that was in her bowl she decided was good to eat now.

Bo laughed and finished getting dressed. When she was finished and deemed herself professional looking enough to suffice for GPD dress code, she gave Chubby one final pat on her big blocky head and then grabbed the keys to her truck and walked out, once again making sure to lock the door behind her. She didn't know if it was a lack of sleep or just her cop senses working overtime, but her conversation with Cass on the beach continued to ring all kinds of bells. Every time she lay down, she thought about Cass's statement about getting Bo on her knees, and since their impromptu meeting, she felt like she was being watched every time she took Chubby for walks. She never saw anyone out of the norm, though, and it was only serving to piss her off.

Within twenty minutes, she was pulling into the gated parking lot of the Galveston Police Department and she backed into her usual spot. Five minutes later, she was at her desk with Gerald Guthrie—and his freshly delivered detective badge—sitting beside her with the miniscule file they had on the new operation in front of them.

"So, Sergeant Gill put us together on this one, then?"

"Yeah." She grimaced slightly. "You understand, right? The only reason I've been made lead is because I've got more experience, otherwise this would be your case completely."

He laughed and shook his head. "Trust me, I'm not upset about it. If this shit blows up, I'm more than happy to let you take the brunt of the force."

"Well, as long as you're happy, sweetheart." She winked. "We need to work on getting something out of Cass Halliburton, but I'm not sure how productive that's going to be. I haven't had the opportunity to question her, but from what little interaction we've had I don't think she's going to be the type to let information flow freely. Unfortunately, since we lost Nelson and Sindel, she's the only one we know of for sure that's involved. Since we don't know exactly what they're doing yet, we don't know how many of the members are involved. We can start by trying to bring some of them in, though."

"What about the one they called Brad?"

Bo shook her head. "I honestly think he was just there to gather runners for the chop shop. On the very off chance that they did bring in a complete rookie on the major operation, I can almost guarantee that he doesn't know enough to be useful. If he did know enough, they most likely hid him away anyway. A kid like that who's not used to standing up under a police interrogation would only be a liability."

She absently flipped through a file on her desk. "I was able to hit up an old street source of mine while we were on leave, but they don't know anything either. They did say a Voleur had come around asking for all the pimps' names, though. It isn't much, but I'd like to know why. We lost the element of surprise in the shootout so they're going to be covering their tracks a hell of a lot better now."

Gerald was quiet for a moment. "Maybe we can use that to our advantage."

Bo cocked her head. "How do you figure we do that?"

"Well," he said, "if you think about it, Cass showing up most likely meant she was checking in on the final stages of something? I mean, she doesn't get involved in the low-level stuff, right?"

"That would make sense, yes. So what?"

"*So*, doesn't it stand to reason that if they already had everything set up and ready to go by the time Cass showed up, and then we decided to go in spraying bullets everywhere..." Bo raised an eyebrow at his over-exaggeration and he held up a hand in apology. "We decided to go in and let a few bullets loose, that they would most likely have to move their entire operation, at least temporarily?"

Bo nodded, beginning to see where he was headed but encouraging him to continue just the same.

"So, what are the odds that they've planned to be at that location the whole setup but have a backup ready to go right off the bat? It's not likely, right? If anything they're doing requires more than just basic hand tools, they'll have to do at least some equipment moving if not some outright new rentals, and we can catch them that way. Use the fact that now they're just as behind as we are. See if any of the rental companies around here, car or equipment or whatever, have had any of our boys use their services recently."

Bo laughed out loud and clapped Gerald on his shoulder. "Boy, you're going to make a damn fine detective."

He blushed but seemed otherwise pleased at the compliment. "So, we check out the rental companies, and then what? Where do we go from there?"

Bo pursed her lips in thought and then shrugged. "It's too soon to tell. It depends on what we come up with at the rental companies. If we're lucky, they'll have rented something that requires an address or something else that will tell us exactly where the bastards are. Assuming our job isn't that easy though, do we have any word on what Cass Halliburton is doing to keep busy when she's not organizing whatever the hell this is?" *Other than breaking into my apartment and ruining my day at the beach?*

"No. I've tried to talk to some people, but to most everyone around here on the streets I'm still 'Officer Guthrie' so they don't want to talk to a uniform."

"Okay, so let's focus on what she *might* be doing. She's going to need to be somewhere in charge, a base of operations she can work from, and I doubt she'd use her home, wherever that is."

Gerald tipped back in his chair. "Do you think Daniel Halliburton would allow her to continue to be in charge after the fiasco at the chop shop?"

Bo shook her head. "I think he would want to punish her, but then ultimately he would loosen the reins because he doesn't like to get his hands dirty. One of my street sources thinks he came into town over the weekend, most likely to check on their clubhouse, but I doubt he stayed. Of course, I couldn't legally go busting down doors so I can't say for sure, but the fact that Cass is still here suggests she's still handling things."

They mulled the idea over together—Guthrie working on a court report from an arrest he had made a couple of years back and Bo simply tapping her pencil on her desk as she considered possibilities—but neither of them seemed to be able to come up with a solid idea of what Cass was doing or where she was based given the intel they had. Once Bo started piecing together everything she *didn't* know, however, an idea began to form. Where could Cass go that she would be in charge, would be in a position to further her business, and could watch people coming and going without raising suspicion? When it came to fruition, she couldn't help but laugh out loud.

"Oh my God, I think I've got it. A friend of mine just rented a car from Classic Auto over there by Teichman Road, right? He said, and I quote, 'The new sales director is a hot ass blonde, but she's a real ball buster.'"

Gerald just blinked and Bo sighed and laid it out for him. "Cass Halliburton would want a job that put her in charge. Daniel would have wanted her punished for letting shit get out of hand at the chop shop. What better way to punish a woman like Cass than to sit her behind a desk from sunup to sundown, right there where she can *almost* see the water? Add to that the fact that as a director, she would have the ability to mock up the paperwork for any of the incoming Voleurs to rent a car or a truck to help move shit without ever actually leaving a paper trail." Okay, so maybe the not leaving a paper trail thing was stretching, but Bo could feel it; she was right.

"Not to mention," Gerald said and grew noticeably more excited as he caught on, "it would give them an excellent front to move money. And we know that if someone as high up as Cass is involved, they've definitely got to be making massive amounts of money. But wait, why would he put her at a place where she had a real job? Why wouldn't they just, say, set up their own fake business if they needed to move money and not have a paper trail?"

"Because the Halliburton family already owns Classic Auto, and it's already established as a legitimate business."

"Which means that we would have no legal reason to look into their paperwork or money trail unless they do something overtly wrong. Whereas if they set up a new business, we'd already be looking into their permits and bank statements to make sure everything was on the up-and-up because the Voleurs set it up."

"Exactly!" Bo shut her computer off, grabbed her keys, and stood. "Start looking into the local members. I went through my old case files last week but haven't had time to look at the brand new ones. I need to know if we can bring anyone in for questioning, especially if they're wearing out of town rockers."

"Rockers?"

Bo looked back at him. "Yeah, rockers. You know, the patches on the back of their colors that say where they're from?"

He nodded but still looked mildly confused.

"Colors. Red and gold. If they're members, they'll be wearing the Voleur patches and the patches aka rockers on the bottom will tell us where they're from. Jesus, do you not know anything about bikers?"

Gerald frowned. "I know everything you just told me. I guess I just never heard the proper terminology used before."

"Look, if anything important happens, call me and I'll walk you through any issues you have."

"You don't want me to go with you?"

Bo shook her head. "We don't have enough resources or time for you to go with me everywhere. Like I said, Classic is a legitimate business. Cass isn't going to do something stupid around that many potential witnesses."

❖

Cass groaned as she stood and stretched her back, letting loose a series of satisfying pops down her spine. The desk she had been saddled with was honestly beautiful, but the chair that came with it was so old it made Yoda look like a padawan. In fact, it had probably been called "old" two centuries before, and now her back and ass were on fire. No, actually, fire would have been an improvement from how she felt.

She made a mental note to tell her assistant that she needed a new one. She would do it herself, but it was five o'clock on a Friday afternoon and she was gearing up to leave when her office phone rang. She debated for a second not answering it but gave in and picked it up. "Yeah."

"Hey there, Mrs. Halliburton, there's a woman here who is demanding to speak with you personally. She says she had an issue with something or other and won't speak to anyone but the boss."

Not for the first time, she wished that everyone in this godforsaken business knew who she was, but unfortunately, minus a select few high-ranking managers, to everyone in the office she was simply the new director of sales. It would have been so much easier to simply be Vice Presidente, but she knew their new endeavor was going to require as few red flags as possible, and a brand new Voleurs only business would have been bright fucking crimson. The people who worked here had no idea who actually pulled the strings at the top. That meant they didn't have any information to sell to cops or rivals. It also meant they thought she actually worked there.

She put on her best happy voice and replied, "Go ahead and send her on in, Alice." While deciding not to remind the woman for the umpteenth time that she was not a *Mrs.*, she also decided to forego the chair in favor of standing in the corner behind it.

She couldn't help showing her surprise when Detective Alexander sauntered into the office, grin blazing.

"Hey there, Director! I seem to have a problem and I was thinking that maybe you could help me."

Cass took note of all the changes she could. Bo was wearing polished patent leather shoes, black slacks with a sharp crease down the middle, and a forest green button-up the exact color of her eyes with the sleeves rolled exactly once. *Just enough to cover your tattoos, isn't that right, Detective?* The eyebrow rings were missing, but now that Cass knew to look for them, she could see the small indentions that marked holes just above and below Bo's eyebrow.

The woman standing in front of Cass was a far cry from the woman she had seen with Tiffany in the alley. This woman was all business and even though she was smiling, there wasn't a trace of the playfulness that bad girl would have had. Cass couldn't help but wonder which detective she wanted to get to know more. *Not* that she wanted to get to know her, regardless of her father's mandate.

She moved behind Bo to shut the door and then pulled out a run-of-the-mill office chair, motioning for Bo to have a seat. "What's the problem, Detective? Am I not allowed to have a day job?"

Bo sat, but still seemed to take up much more than her warranted space. "Well, you see, Miss Halliburton, it appears that I am about to have a very big issue with gang members flooding my city, and I'm not sure how to go about stopping them other than to question the infuriating woman leading them to my goddamn island."

As she spoke, Bo's voice grew louder and angrier, and her expression went from smiling to furious.

Cass grinned. "I'm afraid I can't help you there, Detective. Might I suggest, though, that instead of shooting these gang members you so obviously despise, you ask questions first? It seems maybe that could be a good plan of action."

Bo crossed her legs, clearly getting ahold of herself. "It's funny you should suggest that. I was thinking of doing that exact thing. See," Bo's smile was predatory, "I've noticed that there's been an influx of Voleurs to this area lately. A lot of them have been wearing patches suggesting that they're not from around here, and I can only assume that if they're flying their colors, they rode their bikes." When Cass didn't respond, Bo continued. "What's going to happen when it rains?"

"If they're flying colors it means they ain't just a bunch of pussies who throw a cover over their bike when it rains."

Bo seemed unperturbed by Cass's outburst as she went on. "I figure that some of them probably have wives and such that would *not* be as happy to ride in the rain as they would be to take a long, *dry* road trip with their man. Seems to me maybe they'd need a car rental. Maybe even a car rental from Classic Auto on Galveston Island, newly directed by none other than one Miss Cass Halliburton."

Cass stared at her, waiting for the punchline. She knew better than to offer up any information.

"What do you think would happen," Bo continued quietly, "if a Galveston police officer started hanging out inside the lobby and asking questions to everyone who came in here wearing red and gold? Surely you wouldn't have a problem with it, right? If you're not doing anything illegal?"

Cass opened the office door back up. "I think, Detective, if you're not going to buy a car, you and your boys in blue need to stay the hell out of my dealership. Unless, of course, you feel like fighting a harassment charge in the middle of your *investigation*."

As Bo got up to leave, she leaned down and whispered in Cass's ear, "What are you going to do? Call the cops?"

Cass managed to wait just long enough to see Bo exit her dealership before she threw the only thing she could reach in the moment—a glass Dealership of the Year 2012 award—against the closed door. Bo thought just because she wore a badge that she could march in and make threats? *Yeah, fuck that.* Cass had dealt with being controlled by her father long enough to last a lifetime, and she'd be damned if she was going to let this bitch try to do the same thing. The idea of using the detective's obvious sexual proclivities against her was becoming better and better.

Chapter Six

Sergeant Paige Gill was arguably one of Galveston's best detectives. She was next in line for the lieutenant position, and rumor had it she was being groomed to one day take over the chief's spot once he finally decided to retire. Bo was lucky enough to call her friend, and she was especially glad of that relationship as she knocked on the sergeant's door after her impromptu meeting with Cass at the dealership.

"Detective Alexander. What can I do for you?"

Bo handed her a cup of coffee and waited for the inevitable.

"This shit tastes like ass. We have got to hire someone to make our coffee for us. Can we fit that in the budget?"

"I have absolutely no doubt you could manage it if you put your mind to it." Bo slid into the seat opposite her desk.

She grunted in agreement. "What's going on, Bo?"

Bo waited for her to take another sip, grimacing as she did so. "I wanted to run a few things by you about the Voleurs case that Guthrie and I found. Have you got a minute?"

The sergeant pushed the coffee aside. "Yeah, sure. Meet me in the conference room in five minutes."

Four minutes and forty-eight seconds later, she was rounding the corner to enter into the conference room when Topher Dusek's voice made her stop. More so, Paige's subtly irritated scowl made her want to hear what was going on. She leaned against the doorframe.

"So, that was your new Mustang I saw driving like a bat out of hell the other day, was it?"

"Yes. It was," she said. Topher didn't seem to pick up on Sergeant Gill's annoyance.

He rocked on his heels and folded his arms across his chest. "I thought about getting a Mustang. I'd have to get a GT, though. I'd just have to. You know, pure American Muscle."

Bo thought he was going to stop when the sergeant's nostrils flared, but he continued to address her just as callously.

"I just don't think I could be okay with a V6, even if it was a premium edition. A man's got to have a man's car, you know?"

"I'm still the one with a Mustang, Sergeant Dusek." The way she spat out his name made it sound like it was a poison.

"Yeah, but *your* Mustang—"

"You drive a Taurus, Topher." Bo stepped in to stop the inevitable explosion that was about to melt the entire department.

Topher looked over, obviously irritated with the interruption.

"You literally drive a Taurus. Not because you inherited it, not because it was the only thing you could afford, but because you chose it." He opened his mouth as if to interrupt her, but she wouldn't let him ruin this tirade. "You literally walked onto the Ford lot, walked right past the selection of Mustangs—GT, Premium, and otherwise—and chose a Taurus. Not even a souped-up version of the Taurus, just a base model Taurus. So please, take your 'man's man' car talk and kindly shove it up your ass while you're talking to my sergeant."

If his beet red face wasn't enough to make her day, the look on Sergeant Gill's face as she tried her hardest not to laugh absolutely was. Of course, that didn't mean he probably wouldn't try to retaliate later, but at least for now she had shut him up. Bo hated one-uppers and Topher was the worst.

"What are you even doing here? We're trying to have a meeting," Bo asked.

"Actually." Gill tilted her head slightly in apology. "I invited him. Topher has some men undercover with the Voleurs and he can give us an idea of whether or not you're going to be barking up the wrong tree with your investigation. If you run something by me, you should run it by him, too."

Bo was stopped from making a scathing remark on Topher's lineage by a swift warning look.

"Now. What do you have, Bo?"

Topher's smirk made her want to throw something at him, but she didn't.

"The problem is that we don't really have anything. Marcus Sindel is dead, and Nelson is in a coma. We have a foiled chop shop that happened to involve a very high ranking member of the Voleurs. The only other person involved that night was Cass and she's going to be harder to break than fucking tungsten. I noticed, though, that we seem to have an influx of Demons being arrested with local Voleurs. And not because they're fighting, either." She looked over at Topher. "Have you heard anything about that?"

He shook his head but didn't really seem all that interested in what she was saying.

Paige tapped on her desk, pulling Bo's attention back to her. "You mentioned that Guthrie had an idea?"

"Yeah. We believe that the Voleurs will have to move their operation to a new facility due to the shootout, assuming they haven't moved already. His thought was to check in with all the local rental shops and see whether or not any known members have rented any heavy moving equipment. I agree with his idea. Also, Cass Halliburton recently took over a directorial position at Classic Auto. I think we need to see if any of that equipment they might hypothetically move is going there. I also think they'll be using that location as a front to move money. If we can get a warrant to keep track of the money trail coming and going out of there, maybe we can stop their operation before it ever takes off."

Paige gave her a smile that made her chest swell with pride, but she was interrupted by Topher before she could speak. "No, that won't play. She's not doing anything illegal, just working at an office. No judge in their right mind would sign a warrant for that, even if it wasn't a federal level accusation. Besides, the Voleurs deal in drug trafficking and prostitution, not money laundering. If Cass is working an angle at Classic Auto, it's that she needs a legitimate reason to be on the island."

Paige frowned and shook her head at him. "Why would she need a cover to move? It's still a free country."

"Well, technically, yes." He spoke as if addressing a small child and Bo ground her teeth to stop herself from jumping down his throat. "Cass Halliburton is the second in command of a federally known criminal enterprise. Every move she makes is watched and analyzed, and not just by us. Having a big money job offer at a big name car dealership in a world renowned tourist trap is an offer anyone would take, her included. Suddenly, she has a legitimate reason for moving to Galveston that no one can question."

"I guess that makes sense." Paige didn't seem convinced, but didn't seem inclined to continue the argument, either.

"Speaking of prostitution." Bo spoke to the two sergeants glaring at each other and waited for them to both face her. "I spoke to one of my sources on the street and she mentioned that one of the Voleurs has been asking around trying to gather all the pimps. Since you haven't heard anything about the biggest rival gang in the US being allowed to roam freely, have you heard about new pimps? Maybe new women being brought in?"

Topher looked almost furious and Bo thought for a moment that maybe this wasn't the time for blatant pettiness. "Well, *Detective*, don't you think maybe that's where they'll be moving the money of this new operation you're so sure is going on? It isn't fucking rocket science. What did this supposed inquirer look like?"

"No description. Just a buzzcut and he might work out."

Topher rolled his eyes. "Oh, that fucking narrows it down. Let's just go gather everyone on the island that has a bald head and muscles. Oh, wait."

Paige cleared her throat loudly. "What do you propose, Sergeant Dusek? If Classic Auto is simply a cover to give Cass a legitimate reason to move to Galveston and they're not using it to move anything, what are they doing? Why is Cass here? And do not presume to address me the way you just did my officer."

He shrugged nonchalantly, his attitude obviously now in check. "They deal in drugs. That's what their main gig is. Maybe it happened that they decided not to outsource their product anymore.

Maybe they're making it on their own now. You know, cutting out the middleman."

"Are you suggesting that they're starting a drug manufacturing ring right here in the middle of the island?"

"Well, I mean, it's not the *middle*. The only other buildings they own are in the medical district on East End."

Bo stared at him silently, refusing to acknowledge that remark with a comment. She did, however, voice her agreement that it would make sense they might be expanding their already lucrative operation. "It would explain why the Demons have been showing up lately, and why I saw Johnny Garcia at the dealership today. It didn't click until just now that it was him because he wasn't flying his colors, but it was. He was in one of the back offices talking to one of the other managers while I was talking to Cass Halliburton."

Topher frowned, looking serious again. "Johnny Garcia is a high-ranking member of the Demons. What the hell is he doing down this far? In Cass Halliburton's shop, no less."

"It would make sense if the Voleurs really were expanding their drug operation. If they agreed to a temporary truce with the Demons in order to secure a worldwide drug distribution corridor and used the premise of being able to cut out the cartel completely, it could fly." Bo considered the implications of the two biggest biker gangs in the US joining forces.

"Does that sound like something they would do, from what you've heard?" Paige had been taking notes on her computer and was typing rapidly as she responded to Topher's statement.

"I haven't heard anything about the Demons, but it could be, yeah. Especially if they give the Demons control of the docks. It would be great leverage and the Demons would be able to distribute to all their stash houses straight from one of the biggest ports in the US. I haven't heard anything from our brothers in the Port Police, but I can certainly check it out."

Page nodded once. "Do it. Bo, what else do you have?"

Bo cleared her throat before speaking. "Cass Halliburton is going to be hard to break, but I'm almost positive I can get her to at least crack if we lay the pressure on hard. I told her we would put a uniform at her front door to hassle some of her less…legitimate customers. She didn't seem keen on that idea. I say we make good on my promise; you know, make an honest woman out of me."

Paige snorted. "Nothing in this world could do that, Zander, but let me get with the lieutenant about it and we'll get back with you by the end of the day. Anything else?"

"Isn't Cass Halliburton a lesbian? If you can't get the heat on at her dealership, maybe you could get the heat on…elsewhere, Bo." He raised his eyebrows.

"You goddamned son of a bitch." She moved to deck Topher, but Paige held up her hand. "That won't be necessary. If the detective feels that enacting a personal relationship with the target is a viable option, we will revisit the idea. Until then—"

"I'm just saying it's something you should think about. Rumor has it she's a real…hound. Use what you have to your advantage, right?"

"Is there anything else either of you have to add of *value* to this discussion?" Paige's tone left absolutely no room for either of them to continue speaking to each other.

Topher shook his head, looking smug.

"All right. Topher, if you'd like to *actively* help on this investigation, you can contact Port Police and see what you can find out about any possible activity down there. Bo, sit tight and wait for me and LT to get back to you." The meeting was over, but Bo sat there for a second, trying to breathe through the anger still bubbling under the surface. Who did Topher think he was to bring up either of them as being gay? Cass was undeniably beautiful, but she wasn't someone Bo would ever consider pursuing, case or otherwise. Even if she wasn't a criminal, Bo cared too much about her badge to risk it for someone as flippant about right and wrong as Cass Halliburton. She knew better than most that sometimes when you went down that path you didn't get the chance to come back.

When Bo checked the time on her ringing phone, it was everything she could do not to throw it across the room. Her alarm clock was blinking twelve, and she could only assume her power had gone out at some point due to the storm raging outside. Her phone rang again. She might have been grateful for the impromptu alarm, but three o'clock was still too early, and it most likely meant nothing good was happening. "This call had better mean you've got a gorgeous, leggy blonde waiting to suck me off in one of your back cells."

Her friend, Alyssa, laughed on the other end of the line. "No such luck, sorry. But I do have someone else you might want to talk to, though."

"Talking can wait until the sun is up." Bo grunted and scrubbed at the grit in her eyes.

"Not if he lawyers up, it can't. One of the Texas City boys arrested a Voleur probi on a minor charge and he was just transferred here on an outstanding warrant for County. I thought maybe you should know."

Bo continued to rub her eyes, trying to get at least one of them to focus properly. "I can come question him I guess. No one without rank is going to know anything solid, but even a grunt might know something. Maybe he's been muling and can tell me where he's moving boxes."

"He might know something if he's Marcus Sindel's son, Nathan."

Bo could hear the excitement in Alyssa's voice, but knew that to a high ranking member like Jersey Boy even the relationship between father and son didn't come before the relationship between him and his Voleur brothers. Just the same... "Marcus was a hell of a loudmouth. I guess it's better than anything else we have right now. Nelson's comatose ass sure as shit ain't saying anything. Is he screaming for his rights, yet?"

"No, not yet. I think he actually might be too drunk to think about it. He was originally brought in for PI."

Public intoxication among the Voleurs wasn't unusual. Bo rolled out of bed to get dressed. "All right. I'll be there in twenty minutes."

"Bring me some coffee."

"I'll be there in thirty minutes."

Twenty-nine minutes and forty seconds later, Bo was handing Alyssa a piping hot cup of coffee while they waited together for one of the jailers to fetch Nathan for them. Once he was seated in one of the interrogation rooms, they walked in and shut the door behind them. While Bo took one of the chairs directly across the table from the young man, Alyssa opted to stand in front of the door, her arms crossed over her chest.

"Nathan, do you know who I am?"

"You look like a pig to me." The boy sneered, his tough guy facade firmly in place.

Bo wanted to laugh but settled for a smile. "You're pretty damn close. My name is Bobbi Alexander. I'm a detective with the Galveston Police Department. First and foremost, I would like to offer my condolences on the death of you father."

Nathan scoffed at her. "Oink, oink, bitch. That's the only thing I hear coming out of your mouth."

Bo barely resisted the urge to roll her eyes. Barely. It was obvious that Nathan's bravado was hiding the fact that he was terrified. It was too practiced, too over-the-top. Eventually, he would learn what it really meant to stand up to a cop—right or wrong—but that day was not today. "Look, kid. I'm not the enemy here. I'm trying to give you a chance to do the right thing and turn your life around before you go too far down the wrong path. What do you say?"

"You don't know anything about me, lady. Fuck off, and take your psychobabble bullshit with you."

"Have it your way." Bo stood and turned to Alyssa. "Deputy, please have this piece of crap booked on charges of obstruction of justice. Please note in the file that he was known to have information regarding the shooting of an officer of the law and also information regarding the illegal activities of the Voleurs Galveston Island Chapter and that he steadfastly refused to cooperate with law enforcement, thereby allowing multiple criminals to go free. That should be enough to book him on felony level charges and put him away for a good few years."

"Wait, *what?*" The bravado seemed to slip a little.

Bo barely glanced at him. "Make sure you put him in a cell with Little John while he's waiting on sentencing. Lord knows he won't be able to afford a $250,000 bond, and Little John has been awful lonely lately. As I recall, he likes Voleurs."

Alyssa gave a tiny smile. She knew just as well as Bo that the six-foot-eight lumberjack looking man aptly named Little John was as harmless as they came. If he wasn't the type of man to habitually get in trouble and end up in jail, he and Bo might have been friends. Hell, he probably would have been a cop. As it was, he hated seeing "young'uns" in jail, and he made it his life's mission to make sure that their first time was their only time. Nathan, however, did not know that.

"*Little John?* Who the hell is Little John?" His voice was getting higher.

Bo went for the kill. "Also, be sure to send a deputy to pick up Madison Sindel from her house at 5302 Blackbeard Drive. I'm fairly certain she'll be willing to help us, even if her brother won't."

The young man's act shattered. "No!"

Bo tilted her head toward him and then turned to face him, one eyebrow raised.

"Leave Madison out of this. She has nothing to do with the Voleurs!"

Bo slammed her hands on the table. "Are you sure about that, Nathan? I mean, her daddy was killed flying the red and gold rockers and everyone knows Nathan Sindel is little sister's big hero. Are you absolutely fucking sure that she has nothing to do with the jacket on your back, Nathan?" She stood up straight. "Maybe I should just make sure."

"Stop, stop, stop." He sighed deeply as he held up his hands in surrender. "I'll tell you whatever you want to know. Just leave my sister out of this."

Bo could almost feel Alyssa trying not to laugh behind her. She sat down and steepled her hands in front of her. "I want to know what the hell the Voleurs are doing on my island that's so important that Cass Halliburton is personally overseeing it."

Nathan shook his head, his expression one of defeat. "I don't know." He shook his head when Bo huffed. "I really don't know. My father never said anything in front of me that I could have used against him or the rest of the Voleurs."

"Did he have reason to believe that you would have betrayed him?"

Again, Nathan sighed. "No, but everyone knew he wasn't the nicest person, especially to me. That's why I joined up in the first place. I was hoping that maybe if I flew his colors that he would see me as more than just the disappointing son. It didn't work."

"So, can you tell me anything at all that I can use? Did you move equipment or boxes? Did they have you do anything or talk to anyone?"

"Yeah, I moved a bunch of boxes to the shop that you just took down. I have no fucking clue what was in them, though. None of the probis were allowed to open the boxes. I thought that was kind of weird, but I knew better than to ask questions."

"Were there any labels that you could read? Shipping origins or contents? What about equipment rental? Is there anywhere I could get a new address from?"

He shrugged and shook his head. "I know one of them was acetone, but nothing we ever moved required heavy equipment. I guess whatever they were doing didn't require heavy lifting."

"That's all?"

He nodded. "Questions aren't really allowed if you're not a full-fledged member. I know that my father was in contact with a guy he called Diablo. I don't know of anyone in the Voleurs with that nickname, and I know most of the guys in this area. I never saw the guy, and I'm not sure that my father did either, but they had a lot of heated conversations on the phone. They were talking about bringing in equipment and needing the proper chemicals, and apparently Diablo wasn't very good at holding up the timetables he promised. When my father couldn't deliver on the timetables *he* promised, Daniel decided he needed to send Cass. I only know that because my father wasn't very happy with Cass coming to town and he was very vocal about the fact that he blamed it on Diablo.

They were just starting to be ready when the shootout happened. I know they had to move locations, but I don't know where they moved."

Bo perked up. "Just starting to be ready for what? What did they need the acetone for?"

"I don't know."

"You're a probi, Nathan. Why didn't they have you doing grunt work? You can't tell me you didn't go anywhere in the last few days."

Nathan's eyes flashed and he sat up a little straighter. "They allowed me to plan my father's funeral. So no, I didn't do anything or go anywhere except a funeral home the last few days."

Bo sighed and stood up, then moved to Nathan's side of the table, clapping him on the shoulder. "I'm sorry, Nathan. I really am. But listen to me, okay? You're a good kid. Why don't you consider losing the jacket? You haven't screwed up your life so bad that you can't make a comeback, but if you keep wearing those colors you will. Not to mention the fact that you're all Madison has now. You want to see her wearing a 'Property' tag? Because she will if you keep going."

Nathan's shoulders slumped and he rubbed his face vigorously. "I know, I know. I don't want her anywhere near this shit, but I don't know how else to protect her from the people my father pissed off. You know who he was. You know who he dealt with." When he spoke, his voice shook.

"That's part of my problem, Nathan. I don't know who he's dealing with lately. Listen, you leave the protecting your sister part to us. We can help you keep her safe, but the first step to doing that is getting the Voleurs off this island. At the end of the day, the choice is yours, but you need to make damn sure it's the right one for the right reasons." She put her card on the table. "Keep this. You hear anything at all that I can use, you call me." She waved Alyssa over. "Go ahead and let him go this time. Have a good night, Nathan. And thank you."

❖

The next day, Bo opted to watch as Sergeant Gill tried her best to block out Topher's monotonous tirade about how he would have done something or other better than whoever it was that had done it in the first place because even though he didn't do it *personally*, the other person obviously didn't do it the best and most efficient way possible: Topher's way. *Why. Did. We. Hire. Him?* Judging from the beginning of their conversation, he had come into her office to tell her something about something that the narcotics officers found from the Voleurs, but obviously that conversation had veered off between the time she got a cup of coffee and the time she'd come back. "Topher, please for the love of God—"

Bo saved her from having to tell him to shut up by knocking softly on her open door.

"Hey, you got a second? I want to run something by you." Bo stared blatantly at Topher and added, "Privately." She waited for him to get the message and Paige breathed a sigh of relief when Bo shut the door behind him.

"This time it was a marathon. Attwater ran his marathon wrong. Attwater. Ran his damn *marathon* wrong."

Bo snorted. "Hey, Topher's mile isn't that bad." When Paige glared at her she simply said, "Sorry."

"What's up, Bo?"

"You never got back to me on what LT said about posting an officer at Classic Auto. I hate to say this, but I think Topher's right about the drug thing."

Paige choked on her coffee and Bo calmly handed her a napkin that was sitting on her desk. "How'd those words taste coming out? You had to say that when I had coffee in my mouth?"

"It's more fun that way. And it sucks, but still, I think he's right. We pulled in Marcus Sindel's son this morning, and he said that while he can't say exactly what it is that they're doing, his father was in contact with someone named Diablo talking about needing the proper equipment and chemicals to get the job done. He specifically mentioned acetone, and that's a big part of meth manufacturing. He knows that they'll move their operation after the shootout, but he doesn't know where, and said they never needed any heavy equipment rentals, so following that trail might be a dead end. I'm hoping that if Cass is moving something through her dealership, I'll be able to figure out the major players if I have an officer there."

"Well," Paige said, her eyebrows raised in surprise, "I can already tell you one of your players. You mentioned Johnny Garcia and the Demons, right? Diablo is the nickname for one of their captains, Richard Henderson. Guy's a real piece of work. He's one of the FBI's most wanted, and if the Voleurs are talking to him, then yeah, they're working with the Demons."

"So, what does that mean for us? Where do I go from here?"

"LT said he wanted more solid evidence about Classic before we put a permanent man there, so I want you and Topher to take turns running a train on Halliburton. I want names and faces so we know who to start looking for. I'll talk to Topher about it and I'll tell him he also needs to lay down hard on Port to make sure they work with us instead of freezing us out like they've tried to do in the past. You mentioned you had some street sources that would still talk?"

Bo nodded, already working out a plan.

"Keep talking to them. See if they can get a bead on why the Voleurs are rounding up the pimps. It might be completely unrelated; it might not be. Either way, I want to know every avenue we have to explore. Right now, we've got screws. Those are going to be great for holding all this together, but we need steel and concrete if we're going to build a bridge strong enough for the DA to stand on. Got it?"

"Fuck yeah." Bo walked out feeling the adrenaline running through her, making her heart race. This was going to be a career making case and she was leading the hunt. This was going to be so much fucking fun.

Chapter Seven

We need to be extremely careful how we proceed from here. GPD is ramping up their investigation, and if they're not out in the parking lot I'm pretty sure I'm about to have an officer posted in my lobby. Or else they'll be directly in my office."

Daniel Halliburton's deep sigh wasn't something Cass wanted to hear. "I thought I told you to distract her, Cassidy?"

"She's not the type of person to be distracted by petty dalliances. I'm working on getting some information about her past that could be used against her, but on the surface she's squeaky clean." Cass knew that was a lie even before the image of Bo with her hands all over Tiffany popped into her mind. Detective Alexander was anything *but* squeaky clean.

"Then perhaps you should make your association with her more than simply a *petty dalliance*, to use your own ten-dollar word. You have skills, Cassidy, and you've never hesitated to use them to get what you wanted before. If this woman's dick operates anything like mine, I'm sure you could find a way to turn her head."

Cass couldn't stop herself from throwing up in her mouth just a little.

"You were put in charge of this for a reason. Make sure I don't regret my decision, Cassidy."

He hung up the phone rather forcefully, and it left Cass feeling sick inside. She hated that he absolutely had a point, and she hated even more that she was considering listening to him. She closed her eyes to settle herself, listening to the sound of the waves only a few yards from her front door. She might have missed the trees of East Texas, but having this house right on the water certainly served its purpose. Only a few weeks into the new purchase and she was thoroughly enjoying the perks of living right off the beach. Hot women constantly running by, calming waves when she was feeling anxious or when her stepfather decided to be a dick. A seagull here and there.

She wondered for a moment if this was the kind of place she would live if she had the choice. What her life would be if she could walk away from the Voleurs. She frowned when detective Alexander's face popped into her head, and she forcefully shook the image away. That bitch was *not* going to ruin the serenity of her home.

Her plans to derail Detective Alexander were cut short, however, when she opened her front door to find a delivery of roses taking up an unreasonable amount of her front porch. She looked around warily but didn't see anyone close enough to be the delivery person. Still scanning the surrounding area, she reached for the card attached to the flowers.

Hey there. We had so much fun the last time we were together. I kept waiting for you to call, but you never did. Not nice to leave a girl like me waiting. I finally had to do some really naughty things to track down your address. See you soon, lover.
Sav

Cass stared into space trying to figure out who in the hell Sav was. When she remembered the redhead from Nikki's place the first time she'd seen Bo out on the town, she couldn't help but roll her eyes. They had shared one wild night full of really great sex, but Cass had made it clear one night was all it would ever be. Obviously, Sav hadn't gotten the memo.

A prickly feeling at the back of Cass's neck made her look around once again. She'd thought nothing of it when Sav had called the first time—citing a business card haphazardly thrown around at

Nikki's Place as the source of the ungiven phone number—but she certainly didn't have her home address on that business card.

Sav's card said she had to do naughty things to get the address. Now Cass was thinking that's how she got her phone number, too. Not that it mattered. She would contact Sav and let her know, in no uncertain terms, that their relationship, while fun, would not extend past their one night. She threw the roses into the garbage can beside her porch and told Max to be "On guard." The usually docile dog would simply corner an intruder on a normal day, but now if anyone other than Cass tried to get in, they would be mauled before the door shut. That particular trick had taken Max a very long time to learn, but damn if the boy wasn't eager to please.

By the time Cass reached Classic Auto, noticing an officer she thought she recognized in her parking lot, she had relaxed just a little. At least, until she saw the flaming red hair sticking out from the top of her chair. Her brand-new chair. As she leaned over to look at the desk clerk, she tried for a smile.

"James, honey, who's in my chair?" *My brand new, super comfortable, goes up and down and has a built-in back massager, previously unsoiled chair.*

James blinked repeatedly. "She—she said—she said she was your—your girlfriend."

Cass smiled tightly. "For future reference, I don't have one of those."

As she stepped into her office, she gently closed the door behind her and cleared her throat. "Miss Sav. Thank you for the flowers, they were a very nice surprise. How can I help you, ma'am?"

She tried for a neutral expression as Sav leaned back in the chair—her brand-new chair—let out a high-pitched giggle, turned around, and stood up.

"Oh, stop being so silly, baby. You know I'm only here to see you." She pranced around the desk and tried to plant a kiss on Cass's cheek. Cass was able to sidestep her, but Sav simply grinned and tried again.

When Cass avoided the second kiss as well, Sav pouted. "Why won't you kiss me, baby? I've really missed you. You haven't called or anything. I've been by the bar every night since you left me all alone in that hotel room, but you never came back to see me."

Cass stared at her before stepping back again and crossing her arms. "I'm sorry, Sav, but I thought I made it perfectly clear that the night you and I had was going to be our only night. I didn't even give you my phone number. Not that that stopped you," she muttered.

Sav giggled. "I know you like to play hard to get, baby, but you know I'll always get you."

As much as she hated to admit it, Cass was beginning to get a little worried. She'd been with crazy before, but this one looked a little more bat shit than usual. "Please refrain from calling me baby. I don't even know your last name, so obviously we aren't close enough for that."

As Sav began moving around the office picking things up and examining them, Cass explored the possibility that she might get violent. *That's what these bitches do in the movies, right?*

"It's Williams. Sav Williams. Of course, you should already know that, Sarah Cassidy Halliburton."

Cass felt her blood run cold. The only people in the world who knew she had been born Sarah were either dead or not talking. She might have been born with that name, but she'd gone by Cass her whole life, and it had been changed before she even graduated high school. Information like that would have taken a lot of digging. "Who the fuck are you, and how do you know my name?"

Sav gave her a look of placating exasperation, throwing her hands up in a seemingly playful gesture. "I know everything about you, baby. I love you."

"Okay, well." Cass began fumbling behind her for the doorknob, intent on putting as much space between her and this psycho as possible. "I don't love you, and the only thing I know about you is that you seem a little obsessive. That being said, I'd really appreciate it if you would leave now and don't contact me again."

The change in Sav's demeanor was so sudden, it made Cass's breath catch. Where before she'd been a laughing—albeit crazy— harmless woman, now she was someone with zero emotion in her eyes. Cass had faced down hardened criminals with the best of them, but this woman took the prize.

"I would genuinely appreciate it if you stopped trying to get rid of me, Cassidy."

"Look, I don't know what I did or what I said—"

"You shared your body with me." As Sav spoke, she moved closer until she had Cass pressed against the door. "Don't you understand that when you share your body with someone that your body makes a promise to that person? You made a promise to me, Cassidy. A promise I intend to make sure you keep." She leaned in and gently kissed Cass on the cheek and it was all Cass could do not to flinch. "Or else I might just have to get between you and whatever else is keeping you from me. Maybe your father?" She lowered her voice to a whisper. "Or maybe Max?"

Cass snarled and pushed Sav off her. "Don't be so naive as to threaten my father. As for threatening Max, what makes you think I won't have you killed before you even try?"

The smiling woman was back. "Because, silly goose, you don't want anything happening right now that will ruin what you're doing with the Voleurs on the island, right?" Another fucking giggle. "I told you, I know everything about you. I'll see you later, baby."

She waited, obviously wanting Cass to step aside. Cass debated the merits of killing Sav where she stood but decided it probably wasn't the best idea in such a public space. She moved away from the door while making sure she kept her eyes on the redheaded psychopath. She knew way too much about things she shouldn't, and that meant she had been in places she shouldn't have. Without being seen.

"Toodles, my love."

When Cass was sure Sav was gone, she picked up her phone. Maybe she could work this to her advantage.

❖

For Bo to say that she was surprised when she got the call that she was needed at Classic Auto would probably be an understatement.

When she got there and was directed straight to Cass Halliburton's office, surprised became the understatement of the century. Even more so when she stepped into the office and saw the woman in question looking less calm than usual. If Bo wasn't mistaken, she'd almost think Cass looked upset. Whatever she had been called for, it wasn't for Cass's amusement.

She sat in an uncomfortable chair in front of Cass's desk and took a notepad out of her jacket pocket. "Miss Halliburton, how can I help you?"

Instead of responding, Cass stood up and closed the door behind Bo. That little bit of movement seemed to take all her effort, and Bo watched in amazement as Cass simply closed her eyes and laid her forehead on the door. Her entire body seemed to be shaking, and Bo was flummoxed.

For the first time, the woman in front of her wasn't the volatile crime lord that the FBI called "ruthless, power hungry, and bloodthirsty," but a wounded, scared woman who looked completely vulnerable. The fact that the woman beneath the facade was strikingly beautiful unnerved Bo more than just a little.

When Cass turned to look at Bo her expression was guarded, but there was too much pain for her to hide.

"How can I help you, Miss Halliburton?" This time, Bo spoke more softly.

Cass walked back to her seat and steepled her hands in front of her. Her face might have been a mask, but her eyes were swirling pools of turmoil. "I need you to know, first and foremost, that the only reason I called you, Detective, is because she threatened my dog."

Bo nodded and gestured to the notepad she had set on the desk. "Do you mind if I take notes?"

Cass shook her head and waited for Bo to open up to a blank page before she continued. "Her name is Sav Williams. Or at least, that's the name she gave me. Whether or not it's real, I don't know, but I'm inclined to believe her. She's roughly five foot seven, and she's got really freaking red hair and giant tits." When Bo glanced up from her notepad, Cass just shrugged and said, "You'll forgive me if I wasn't exactly pinning her for a lineup. I went out to Nikki's

Place and I met her there. She said she had just gotten off and wanted to…well. Get off. Before you ask, I don't think she was a bartender at Nikki's, but you're more than welcome to ask your friend."

Bo didn't bother to question how Cass knew she and Nikki were friends; she just let Cass keep talking.

"I agreed to the idea, and we were going to go back to my place, but we didn't make it that far. When we were done, I didn't give her my number and I made it very clear that I didn't want to see her again."

Bo stopped writing. "I take it she didn't get the memo?"

Cass nodded. "When she called me the first time, she said she found my number on a business card, and I took it at face value. I entertained her for a couple of days, but her text messages were vulgar and explicit, and frankly, I just got tired of it. I changed my number."

"Can I ask why you didn't call the police right away?"

Cass scoffed. "What for? 'There's a woman texting me sexually explicit messages and I don't like it'? What good would that have done? Besides, once I changed my number, she stopped texting and I just assumed it was over."

"I'm guessing that's changed now?"

Cass seemed to look over Bo's shoulder at someplace far off. "When I left my house this morning, there were so many roses on my porch I could barely make it through the door to grab the card. They were from her and the card said she missed me and had to do 'naughty' things to get my address. I don't know what that means. When I got to work, she was here sitting in my chair. She was going on and on about how she was in love with me and she knew everything about me and basically that I was her soulmate because we slept together. I tried to explain that she was mistaken, and all of a sudden she was telling me it was either her or Max."

Bo sighed softly and rubbed her temples against a sudden headache. "I have to ask, Miss Halliburton, though I obviously don't support this…don't you have people who work for you that take care of this exact type of thing?" She blinked in surprise when Cass handed her two Advil.

"Yes, I do. But contrary to popular belief, I don't enjoy people *hypothetically* dying because of me, and I get the feeling that might, *hypothetically*, have happened if I had told one of my boys."

Bo couldn't help but smile at the fact that Cass had just blatantly admitted to her people being murderers in a way that was one hundred percent inadmissible in court.

"Besides," Cass continued, "a body with my name on it would surely sully my good reputation around here."

"So why me? Why not another detective?"

Cass looked momentarily serious again. "Because unlike your counterparts, you actually believe in the job you do. Because I don't think you'd let this go simply because of who I am. Max might be super dog, but even he can't dodge a bullet, Detective."

A cloud of emotion swept over Cass's face and Bo waited, because she knew in her gut that whatever was going on was going to change the direction of her investigation. *Which* investigation remained to be seen.

"His sire was my mom's dog. He's the only thing I have left of her. And I know from our previous encounters that when you get a case, you're like a dog with a bone. That's what I need right now."

Her usual demeanor was back, and Bo tried another tack. "Care to elaborate on any of those previous encounters? Throw me another bone to chase?"

Cass stood and Bo followed. "Your only concern when it comes to me is catching this maniac before she hurts my boy. Can you do that?"

Bo shrugged. "I don't see why not. Besides, Chubby has a crush on him. There are a few legal steps we need to follow though, you understand. The first thing I have to do is file a report, and once that's done, I'll most likely need you to file a restraining order. I can look into this woman, but without an official paper trail there's not much I can do."

Cass looked contemplative. "Fine. But I don't want it getting out. I wasn't lying when I said I didn't want someone hypothetically dying on my behalf."

"I wouldn't dream of it. Tell your dog Chubby says hi."

Cass laughed, a genuine laugh, and Bo couldn't help but smile as she walked out. "Good-bye, Detective."

Two weeks later, Bo was scrolling diligently through screen after screen of police reports, news articles, and lease agreements looking for a way to pin down one Sav Williams. The more she dug, the more entranced she became. How this woman had managed to sneak up on Cass Halliburton was a mystery, but it was obvious that it wasn't a mistake. Sav, as it turned out, was in town as the biker bunny of one of the Demons who had just been arrested consorting with the Voleurs. Bo dug a little deeper and found more connections to mafia dons, cartel leaders, and low level drug dealers. Those connections explained how she kept her hands clean enough to be one of the top networkers of a computer company Bo had only read about once in *Fortune* magazine.

The fact that Bo could make the connections meant it had only been a matter of time before she was caught for the blood trail she left in her wake, but this woman was not someone to be fucked with. Point-blank, she was fucking clinical.

"Is this for the Halliburton case?" Gerald Guthrie asked her as he walked up behind her desk.

Bo jumped slightly and nodded. "Yes, but not the one you're thinking of."

Gerald frowned as he looked at her screen. "Who is Sav Williams? She's not a Voleur, is she?"

Bo shook her head. "No. This is the case *for* Cass Halliburton, not against her. I'm hoping we might be able to use this woman to our advantage, though."

Gerald was silent for a moment. "Then why the hell are you still here, Bo? You were supposed to be off at five."

Bo finally stopped typing and looked at him. "Why wouldn't I be here? I'm almost done, and when I'm done with this, I'll have an arrest warrant. We could press this woman for info on Halliburton."

Bo knew in her gut that was a complete lie, but she didn't like the way Gerald was looking at her.

"Yeah, but…it's *for* Cass Halliburton."

"And? What difference does that make?"

Gerald sighed and shook his head. "She's a criminal, Bo. Don't you think maybe she deserves a little bit of this? Who gives a damn if someone is stalking her?"

Bo narrowed her eyes. "I give a damn. That's a very dangerous line of thinking, Gerald. Our badge doesn't make us any better or any worse than anyone else out there. It means we protect, and we serve. At the end of the day, Cass Halliburton is still a person and she's just as deserving as anyone else. Not to mention stalkers tend to have a nasty habit of being dangerous."

Gerald seemed to just barely avoid rolling his eyes. "Whatever you say, Bo. Have a good night."

Bo turned back to her screen to continue putting together her file for the warrant on Sav Williams, but in the back of her mind, she still heard the conviction in Gerald's voice, and she didn't like it.

Two days later, she was knocking on Cass Halliburton's office door again. "Are you busy?"

Cass looked up and shot Bo a Cheshire grin. "For you, Detective? Never."

Bo smiled slightly and set a sheet of paper on the massive oak desk, sliding it across to Cass. "The booking sheet for Sav Michelle Williams. It's slightly unorthodox, but I figured you might want to see it. Max is safe, Miss Halliburton."

The relief on Cass's face was evident. "Did she say anything? Why did she do this? What's wrong with her? Don't sugarcoat it, Detective."

Bo sighed and nodded. "Okay. She's a black widow and then some. There's evidence of her doing this to at least three other people in three other states, and that's only the departments that are big enough to access the national database. There's a record of her staying in a few other areas as well."

"So, she what? Sleeps with people and then kills their pets?"

"Not…exactly."

"I told you not to sugarcoat it."

"Sav bounces from drug lord to drug lord. She was in town hanging on to the back of one of the Demons you seem to suddenly not mind." Cass's eyes flashed and Bo smiled. "Her name wasn't on a single report. The only reason I even found a thread to pull was because I couldn't for the life of me figure out who would be so stupid to threaten your dog. I ended up finding a picture of her in an old arrest report filed in Houston a couple of years back. I started there and found a string of random accidents and unexplained deaths that all seemed to happen right around the time a big power move was being made. Now, you have to understand this is just my connecting the dots and it's all circumstantial, but from what I can put together, whoever Sav was *really* with would send her as a distraction to the opposing side of the deal."

Cass shook her head. "Let me guess. She pretends to be obsessed and make threats to force people to do what she wants. If she's with a Demon I'm guessing that the people she was threatening weren't the type to call the police. Which means that she had to be shacked up with some pretty fucking powerful people to avoid being killed."

"Exactly. And if the deal went their way, Sav moved on. If it didn't, the threats were carried out. In all the cases I found, there wasn't much time between a report about a deal going south and another report of an unexplained accident or someone dying randomly of a heart attack or blah blah blah. Usually someone or something really close to the person Sav set her sights on."

Cass frowned. "In my case, Max."

"Right. The only thing in the world you care about, I assume. In two of the other cases, it was also a pet. One was a mother. A few siblings. You get the idea."

Cass's eyes were the size of dinner plates. "Then how the hell hasn't she been caught yet?"

Bo sighed wearily and looked down, shaking her head. As much as she loved being a cop, sometimes she hated the system just as much as the people who got screwed by it. "That's one of the less fortunate things about police work. If things aren't immediate or direly important, usually they're forgotten. In all of the cases I was able to put together, there was only a vague report of a woman matching Sav's description filed by someone *other* than the actual victim, and then so much time had passed between the initial meeting and the murder of the pet or other party that the two weren't put together. The two pet killings were blamed on the neighbors, and the human deaths were blamed on faulty brakes, bad heart, random break-in. In each case, however, only a couple of weeks after the initial death, the person who was being stalked was also found dead in a sudden accident. Every one of those deaths were blamed on the gang member Sav was with."

Cass ran her hand through her hair. "Holy shit. This bitch was good at what she did. I don't understand, though. Why not just come right out and say she wanted the people to do something? Why the elaborate charade?"

Bo shrugged. "I don't know, honestly. Best I can figure is that if she did that, she'd be more vulnerable without the protection of whoever she was working for. If she makes it look like she's just your friendly neighborhood stalker who's smart enough to get places she shouldn't without getting hurt, then people are less likely to shoot first."

"So what you're saying is she was just fucking psycho." She looked like she was about to say more when she glanced up and locked eyes with Bo. "What? What else is there?"

"When we went to her apartment to arrest her, there were pictures of you all over the place and there were steaks in the fridge stuffed full of rat poison and antifreeze. Did…did Max find any random treats or pieces of meat in the last two days?"

Cass nodded, wide-eyed. "I had to pull him away from a steak on the outside of my garbage can. I thought someone had just tried to use my trash and missed."

Bo didn't have to say out loud what they were both thinking: Max got damn lucky.

"She's going to jail for a long time, Miss Halliburton. Your boy is safe."

Cass stood and shook Bo's hand. "Thank you, Detective. I know helping me probably wasn't high on your to-do list."

Bo shook her head. "Who you are makes no difference to me, Miss Halliburton. But you should know that me helping you on this makes no difference, either. I might have started looking into Sav to help you, but what I found was pretty damn eye-opening. Either she sought you out as a power move or, more likely, she was being used to blackmail you into doing something big. She wasn't just used in every day bullshit, and the fact that she came here with a Demon tells me that you were a target. I'm still going to investigate you, I'm still going to have an officer here every day, and I'm still going to take you down."

Cass just shrugged. "Whatever you say, Detective."

CHAPTER EIGHT

A week later, Bo received a phone call from one very angry Cass Halliburton. In the time that passed since she had helped Cass make sure Max was safe, she was only able to make it to Classic Auto a couple of times. Topher, along with a few volunteer officers, was the one who had taken primary on making sure they could get a good rundown of all the major players coming in and out of the dealership because Bo's hands had been tied with a random court case from the shootout at the mechanic shop. If the list of names they had were any indication, their theory that the Voleurs were now working with the Demons was completely correct. Unfortunately, Topher wasn't the kind of guy to get along with criminal types, and that seemed to be exactly why Bo's ear was ringing from the screaming coming out of the receiver.

"Miss—Miss Halliburton. A little lower, please, I honestly can't understand you."

"Get. Over. Here. Now, Detective. Understand that?"

Bo sighed deeply. "What is this about?"

"It's about the fact that while I appreciate that I can't stop you from putting a car in my parking lot, you need to come put your pig in a fucking kennel!"

"Miss Halliburton—"

"You either get here now or your officer is dead."

The *click* signaling she'd hung up made Bo close her eyes and count to ten. It didn't work. Obviously, Cass seemed to think their shared moment meant she could order Bo around, and Bo sought to correct that severe mistake immediately.

It didn't take long to see the reason for the prompted call. A man named Robbie Notaro, ranking member of the Nevada Demons, was nursing a bloody nose, and Topher seemed to have a pretty gnarly shiner coming on.

Bo took in the scene. "Topher…what the fuck, man?"

Topher shrugged and didn't seem particularly inclined to talk. When Bo got in his face, his eyes widened. "Are you trying to screw up this investigation, Topher? What the fuck happened? And I swear if you don't answer I will personally make sure you lose your gold shield."

Bo might not have been a supervisor like Topher, but she had been there longer, and he knew she had the connections to make good on her promise. "He came in, he slammed his shoulder into mine, and he called me a pig. I told him to repeat himself and he turned around and said it again. I threw a punch because he fucking deserved it."

"And at no point did you think to simply put him in handcuffs and take him to the station so that we could interrogate him and maybe get some information out of him? Instead you decide to fight him in front of a room full of people who can verify he was only defending himself? What the fuck are you thinking?"

"I'm a man, Zander. I know you may not understand, but when a man puts his hands on another man, a man has to stand up for himself."

I know he did not *just*—Bo took a deep breath. "You're not a man, Topher, you're a fucking cop. You're wearing a goddamned uniform and you just punched someone in the face in the middle of my goddamned investigation and now I have to put out the fire with—"

"Detective Alexander."

"Speaking of Satan." When Bo turned to face Cass, it was obvious that she was barely managing to keep her fury under control.

"I don't care what his excuse is, I don't care that Robbie touched him first. I want him gone. In fact," she held up a finger to emphasize her point, "I want all of you gone. If I see another badge in my *parking lot*—even if they're buying a car after work—I will personally sue your entire department so hard your chief's grandma will have to pay. Do I make myself perfectly clear? God fucking help you if one of you makes it into my lobby. You want to talk to me? Fine. You and you alone haven't fucked up so bad I want to kill you."

Bo grabbed Topher's arm to walk him out. "You can expect me, then." She paused, and just to stoke the fire, she pointed at the man currently holding a bag of ice on his nose and a phone to his ear. Before she could speak, he held out the phone. "My lawyer. He isn't too happy that your officer assaulted me. You want to talk to him? Remember I have witnesses."

Bo snarled. "If you ever lay a finger on one of my officers again it'll be the last thing you do as a free man. Consider this your one free pass."

"Detective—"

Bo didn't hear the rest because she was already out the door.

Three days later, Bo found herself being ushered straight back to Cass's office. She had opted to stay in her car in the parking lot for the better part of that week so that she could make notes of who was talking to whom, and she felt she had a pretty good rundown of the hierarchy of the people making deals at Classic Auto. Her only problem was that while she could easily name names, she had absolutely no idea what deals were going on behind closed doors.

She had specifically made it a point to *not* go inside to bother Cass's patrons, though, so she was unclear as to why Cass seemed to have a problem now.

Cass began speaking as soon as the door was shut. "Detective," she began, her head resting against her chair, her eyes closed, "is there any particular reason you feel the need to spend every waking moment in my parking lot? Surely you aren't learning anything new. Don't you have anyone at home waiting on you to keep them company? I seem to remember a gorgeous pit bull who was very fond of you. How does she feel about the amount of time you're spending here? I bet she's jealous and that sucks because I'm quite fond of her. You're ruining my chances."

"How do you know Chubby hasn't been with me?"

Cass opened her eyes and looked up at Bo without saying anything.

"You're hiding something, Miss Halliburton. To answer your question, I actually have learned quite a bit sitting out in your parking lot, and I intend to keep staying there until I figure out what it is you're doing to defile my island."

Cass smiled and stood, stretching her body in a way Bo knew purposely pressed her breasts out. She walked over to stand beside Bo, and she couldn't help but notice the way her T-shirt fit quite perfectly.

"Did you ever stop to think," she said as she gently laid a hand on Bo's chest, "that maybe I'm here simply because I want to be?" She let her hand trail over Bo's shoulder as she moved behind her. "That maybe I just want to enjoy myself?" She leaned down and whispered in Bo's ear, "And maybe enjoy someone else, too?"

Bo shot up, barely missing hitting Cass in the chin. "You're exasperating!"

"Maybe, but that doesn't mean you ain't enjoying this little game of cat and mouse we have going."

A slow smile spread across Cass's face as she stepped close enough that Bo could feel the entire length of her body and smell her sweet, subtle perfume.

"In fact, Detective," she spoke in a low, honey-soaked timbre, "if you're good, I may even let you be the cat."

Bo couldn't help the hard swallow that followed, and Cass's wicked grin let her know she had purposely caught Bo off guard. She placed something small in Bo's hand and said, "If you want to see something, meet me here tonight." She seemed to debate her next words but smiled as she leaned up and bit down on Bo's ear. "I promise it'll be worth it." She turned and sat down, and Bo growled as she composed herself before storming out, clutching the business card in her hand.

A little past eleven o'clock that night, Bo stood in front of her full-length mirror, buttoning the last few buttons on her shirt. Chubby sat beside her and whined, so Bo knelt and rubbed her behind the ears.

"This is a trap, isn't it? I'm going to get in trouble, huh?"

Chubby leaned in and touched her nose to Bo's.

"I know, baby girl, but I have to go. I don't think she's going to try anything too stupid in a public place like this, and I've got to see if I can find anything out while I'm there. Got to follow the breadcrumbs, Chubster."

Chubby's response was to lick Bo from her chin to her forehead, and Bo laughed while she rubbed Chubby's bulky body all over.

"I'll be home in just a little while, okay? I promise. Be a good girl while I'm gone."

Chubby jumped up on the bed and seemed to smile at Bo as she lay down.

Too soon, Bo was standing in front of Heartbreakers, one of the most longstanding gentlemen's clubs in the county, just off the freeway on the mainland. When she walked in, a bouncer was waiting to check IDs, but he handed Bo a green wristband.

"The boss says this is yours. She wants you taken care of tonight."

Bo raised her eyebrows in surprise, and his cocky grin said that's exactly what she was in for, but for lack of better options, she simply took the band and put it on, cussing silently when it pulled out some of the little hairs on her arm.

When she sat at the bar, the bartender set a Tennessee Honey on the rocks in front of her. "You have got to be kidding me."

He shook his head. "The boss says to take care of you tonight." He spoke with significantly less sarcasm than the bouncer.

"I don't suppose I can have one of those Wednesday night free steaks, then?" She might as well eat since she was here.

He nodded and she gave him her order before he went back to what she assumed was the kitchen while Bo nursed her drink and looked around.

The women gyrating on the stage in the cavernous room barely seemed legal age, even with the massive amounts of makeup. Bo had worked in the area long enough to know that they were, but it still turned her stomach to see grown ass men ogling young women on stage. She was thankful that the steak set in front of her gave her an excuse to turn around. She hadn't made it a couple of bites in when the hairs on the back of her neck rose and she had to fight the urge to turn around.

She had completed the steak and two more tumblers of whiskey without a single trace of Cass Halliburton. She was offered another drink but turned it down because she didn't want to risk getting buzzed on the off-chance Cass had something planned. She strained to see through the smoke filling the room but couldn't place any faces she knew. Here and there she noticed the telltale red and gold but couldn't see anyone long enough to check out where they were disappearing to. She moved to stand, deciding she had sat still long enough, but was quickly stopped by a tap on her shoulder.

"Follow me."

She whipped around, but the voice could have belonged to any of the women around her carrying drinks. Once again feeling eyes on her, she looked to her right and saw someone walking toward the VIP section. She couldn't be sure, but her gut told her to follow. She was quickly seated and a curtain was pulled, leaving her alone in the darkness. Just when she would have reached for her gun, she felt a familiar caress on the back of her shoulders.

"I'm glad you made it, Detective."

"Miss Halliburton." She would never admit it, but she was mildly unnerved being in the near total darkness with Cass. It was almost intimate, and that felt wrong. She nearly jumped when a hand brushed the inside of her thigh.

A small light came on, casting the room in a warm glow, and Cass sat in the seat beside her. "I wanted to give you a taste of exactly what it is I'm doing here."

Bo shook her head. "Absolutely not. I'm leaving."

"Sit down, Detective." Cass's tone left no room for argument, and for reasons she couldn't explain, Bo was inclined to listen. The lights dimmed again and a woman stepped through the curtain as a song about dancing in the night began to play from a hidden speaker.

"What—"

"Don't be rude, Detective. Hannah is here just for you. I promise you don't want to disappoint her." The woman in question began by dropping to her knees, her hands tracing the inside seam of Bo's pants.

Cass stood and moved behind Bo, her hands on Bo's shoulders as Hannah stood and turned, moving her hips in rhythm to the music, her hand exploring her own body, squeezing her breasts and teasing mercilessly. "You see, Detective," Cass whispered in Bo's ear, "I've noticed that many of our clubs are sorely lacking in diverse clientele."

Bo didn't want to stay, but she couldn't make herself move. The music was booming, and the smell of Cass's vanilla perfume was intoxicating. Hannah lowered herself and began grinding against Bo, her legs on either side of Bo's thighs. She was on fire and Bo could feel it in every fiber of her body.

"That's it, Detective." Cass's voice had dropped to a husky timbre. "Just let Hannah do her job. Relax." Bo tried not to groan. Tried to keep her head and listen to what Cass was telling her. "I came down here to make sure I fixed that diversity problem. Of course, the women we usually employ have been told that their job is to service the men. Hannah is one of many who will be dancing for us on our *special* nights."

Hannah grabbed Bo's hands and wrapped them around her own breasts as her hips moved and pressed into Bo's. The song was reaching the crescendo, and Bo could feel a matching twist in her stomach as Hannah pressed harder into her. "Feels good, doesn't it? The Demons just happen to have a lot of experience in that area. It was my idea to bring them in. See? Nothing more than a simple," she nipped the skin at the base of Bo's shoulders and Bo gasped, "lap dance. Just an extension of our already lucrative business. Nothing illegal. No reason for you to continue to be such a persistent presence."

"What are the Demons getting out of it?" Bo's voice sounded strained, and she moved to shove Hannah off, only to have her hands stopped by Cass.

"Touching the girls is illegal, Detective. Don't make me have to ban you from the club."

And suddenly it made sense. Bo felt the fires in her belly cool as the song ended. Hannah seemed poised to go again, but Bo held up her hand, purposely not touching her. Get her alone, get under her skin. Give her a lap dance she didn't want and then get her banned from the club for shoving the girl off of her. Once again, it was something that would get her taken off the investigation, and Bo had walked right into it. She stood and moved so close to Cass that their lips were only inches apart. "I don't think so, sweetheart. This shit might work on a rookie, but it won't work on me. What are the Demons getting out of this?"

Cass stared at her but didn't answer.

"That's what I thought. You played your hand too early, Miss Halliburton. Try harder next time."

She turned and left the VIP room, making note of all the people wearing red and gold sitting in the bar. Whatever Cass was doing, at least part of it was happening in this club, and it didn't have anything to do with the girls dancing on the stage. As she walked out of the club, tossing the green wristband to the side, she went over what she had so far. What did a strip club, a car dealership, and a mechanic shop all have in common? What could all three locations be used for that was big enough that the Halliburtons would come down to check on it? And why was Cass suddenly so happy to get hands-on to turn Bo's head?

When she got home, Bo needed to talk and get her thoughts out while they were fresh in her mind, and Chubby was a rapt audience. Nikki's bar wouldn't even close until two, and God only knew how long it would take her to actually close everything down, so calling the girls wasn't an option. Gerald wasn't answering his phone so Chubby would have to do.

"Using a club I wasn't even investigating as a distraction doesn't make any sense whatsoever, unless the entire point was to prove that she could get under my skin. Not that she did," Bo was quick to clarify. "She's trying too hard to distract me, and that tells me there's something to look at. What am I missing, Chubby? All of this ties together somehow, I can feel it. I just don't know how. The Demons, the Voleurs, the girls, the money. Hell, I'm willing to hedge my bets and say Topher is even right about Classic Auto being involved. I just can't find the link that ties it all together. Is it really as simple as expanding their business? If that's the case, then what the hell were they doing in the mechanic shop? You can't run a worldwide prostitution business out of a mechanic shop."

Chubby growled softly but offered no further wisdom.

"Then again..." Bo pondered as she grabbed Chubby's face and stared into her eyes, "What if that's exactly it?"

"Boof." Chubby licked her face.

"Exactly. Worldwide. The Voleurs have chapters in almost every country in the world. But there are still major areas of those countries they don't or can't control. What if that's what this is? What if they're moving..." She felt sick to her stomach and didn't want to finish her sentence. "What if they're moving the women into places they don't control yet? That would make a truce with the Demons plausible." She tugged on her boot and fell backward on the bed, allowing Chubby to rest her blocky head on her chest. "It makes sense that since I *am* laying it on so hard at Classic, she decided to throw me off by doing this whole dance routine, knowing all the while that it would push me harder toward Classic so that she could move the bulk of her business to the club where I'm not going to look because she told me to look there by telling me not to look there?"

Chubby just stared at her.

"You're right, that's pretty convoluted, even for me."

"Boof."

"Okay, let me try again. Wouldn't it make sense that she draws my attention to the club because they're using Classic Auto to move something? It's the only thing that makes sense. If they're moving girls—and I'm not saying they are, but *if* they are—then they could be using Classic as a front for the money. They bring more pimps in to control more women, they bring in the Demons to get more area and eliminate the competition. Goddamn it. That still doesn't explain why they needed the mechanic shop. We went through all of the boxes, but it was nothing but stolen parts. I seriously doubt Halliburton would have shown up just for that. Okay, so if it's not girls, then what is it? Damn it, I've got to get out in front of this, Chubby. Before it gets so big that it takes all of us down with it." She managed to finish getting undressed and fell back into bed, her head swimming and the scent of Cass's perfume haunting her dreams.

When her alarm clock went off at five in the evening, she was immeasurably glad she had told Paige she wouldn't be in until late. Her plan was to wait until later in the evening to go back to Heartbreakers and see if maybe she couldn't weasel her way into Cass's office in that building the way she had at Classic Auto. If for nothing else than to see if she could find the puzzle piece that made the whole picture start to take shape. She could only assume that since Cass had invited her there in the first place, it wasn't going to be hard to get in to search without needing a warrant.

She wasn't sure how she was going to get into Cass's office once she entered the club, assaulted by a cloud of smoke and the smell of stale beer, but this time it only took two glasses of Coke for Cass to find her, so she didn't have time to work it out.

"Detective. See anything you're interested in?"

Bo turned to face Cass, smiling. "You mean there's more here for sale than just the alcohol on tap?"

"Well, of course," Cass answered without pause. "We have the beer that's not on tap, too. We also have really good steaks." Cass wiggled her eyebrows and Bo couldn't help but laugh. Then Cass sobered and asked, "What do you want, Detective? Surely, you're not here for another lap dance? I'm afraid that was a one-time deal."

Bo surprised herself—and it appeared Cass, too—when she answered honestly. "Pity. I kind of liked hearing your voice while your friend rode my lap. I was hoping I could convince you to hop on this time. Then again, I'm sure more than a few of the men here have already propositioned you for that."

"My body is not for the enjoyment of men." Something dark passed through Cass's eyes as she responded without humor.

They regarded each other in silence before Bo finally said, "I'm here because I was hoping to snoop around your club without you pulling me in for a lap dance, but you seem to have read my mind."

Cass smiled around the thumb she was biting and said, "Lucky guess." She swept her arm toward the club. "Look wherever you'd like, Detective. I promise I won't get in your way." As she moved to walk away, she stopped to lean over Bo's shoulder, "And if I ever catch you snooping in my club without my permission, it won't be the Voleurs you have to worry about." As she spoke, she reached down to Bo's waist and gently fingered the badge clipped to her belt.

Bo waited for the smell of her subtle perfume to leave before making her way around the club until she found the door to the back offices. While she wasn't surprised that it was unlocked, she *was* surprised to find absolutely no one else there. All of the employees, it seemed, were working in different spots around the club. The fact that Cass let her in so easily meant she was unlikely to find anything of use, but it didn't hurt to check. Sometimes bad guys got cocky and missed things.

She moved from room to room but didn't stop to sit down until she came to the one that obviously belonged to whomever ran the club. She went through all of the papers but didn't find anything that looked off. Nothing but shipping manifests for various household chemicals and dyes. To the naked eye, Heartbreakers was exactly what it seemed—a gentlemen's club. She was set to put the papers back when she noticed acetone on the list. She couldn't be certain, but she was pretty sure that wasn't a chemical used in typical bar cleaning, so she took a photo with her phone.

Just as she was about to leave, Bo noticed a door partially hidden behind a curtain and tried to open it, only to find that it was locked. She was about to begin searching for a key when she heard someone coming in behind her.

"It's a closet."

Bo turned and Cass handed her a beer.

"I can give you the key if you don't believe me."

Bo took a drink from the bottle and waited. Cass just laughed and rolled her eyes before handing Bo a silver key from the top drawer of the desk she had just been sitting at. As it turned out, she wasn't lying; it really was just a broom closet. "I keep it locked because when I first got down here and took a look around the place to see how Marcus was running it, I found about twenty beer bottles in there from staff who were sneaking away to have a drink during their shifts."

Bo sighed in frustration and took a long drink of beer.

Cass laughed. "Detective, what exactly were you expecting to find here? A marijuana operation? I assure you, if I was running something out of this club, it wouldn't be brought down by something as simple as a stray bud or bad paperwork. Not to mention I royally suck at gardening so it would probably be dead before it ever had a chance to bloom."

Bo threw her bottle away and pointed a finger at her. "You're up to something."

Cass was obviously trying not to laugh again. "So you keep saying, and yet you've been at this how long with no proof? Surely you don't think I'm just that good?"

"What is the acetone for?"

Cass laughed again, but there was an obvious edge to it. "Excuse me?"

"The acetone." Bo held up the photo on her phone. "You gave me permission to look around so I decided to keep a copy of this manifest. What's the acetone for?"

"It's...a degreaser." Cass made it sound like Bo should have known that, but she wasn't one to take the easy answer.

Bo smiled. "You mean to tell me you're using industrial strength acetone to degrease your kitchen?"

"I mean to tell you that until you come back with a warrant for my private thoughts, what I am or am not using in my kitchen is none of your fucking business. Try again next time then, Detective."

With that, she turned and walked out leaving Bo feeling mildly exhilarated. Acetone almost made sense at the mechanic shop because Cass was right, it was a degreaser. It was not, however, something to be found in a kitchen or a bar, as far as Bo knew. She would have to look up all the uses, but she was pretty sure the acetone was definitely a piece of the puzzle.

Chapter Nine

Cass watched as the giant man she had told to come see her made his way through her dealership. He was big and mean looking enough that even her less-than-legal patrons gave him a wide berth. When he walked into her office and closed the door behind him, he had to duck his head to make it into the room. He was going to be her new captain since Marcus had decided to expire early. For the life of her, though, she couldn't remember his name. *It starts with a B.*

"Miss Halliburton."

She frowned and shook her head. "No, don't call me that." *That's what Detective Alexander calls me. Not that* that *matters. Billy. His name is Billy.* She sighed and looked at him and realized she'd missed whatever he'd continued to say. "I'm sorry, Billy, could you repeat that? I wasn't listening."

He frowned but repeated himself, nonetheless. "I was telling you that we're ready to begin moving the product. Everything is set. We just need your go-ahead."

Cass chewed her lip, momentarily lost in thought. "We have a problem, Billy. Detective Alexander was going through some of my paperwork last night and managed to find a shipping manifest that didn't belong to Heartbreakers. Thankfully, nothing *too* important was on it, but I need you to find out who was in charge of filing the manifests and have them brought to me. I absolutely refuse to be caught unawares like that again."

"Yes, ma'am. I'll have the name to you within the hour."

"I like you, Billy. You want to know why? You don't ask questions and you're not a loudmouth." She looked up at him completely. She had made her previous statement without thinking, and she suddenly felt a little too exposed. "Marcus Sindel was a loudmouth and now he's dead. See how that works?" He visibly paled, but to his credit, he stayed standing at the modified parade rest he had adopted when he first entered. "You can have my go-ahead. To move product when you give me the name of the man who almost fucked shit up for me."

She looked down to continue working on the paperwork in front of her, but when he didn't move, she looked back up. "Is there something else, Billy?"

"I don't like the cop on our payroll, ma'am. Being this close. It makes me nervous, and I don't trust that we see everything the cop is doing."

Cass smiled slightly at his refusal to name "the cop." Keeping names out of things was an old habit, and one she liked. "It's a necessary evil, I'm afraid." When he didn't leave, she said effectively, "You're dismissed." She watched him follow the same path back that he had taken in, and then for a moment, she allowed herself to relax as she watched the sun glisten off the Gulf. She could almost feel the warmth on her cheeks as she closed her eyes, and it reminded her of when her father would bring everyone to the beach for their family days. She and her sister would build sand castles while Daniel and their mother lounged on beach towels. It was a simpler time, a simpler life. It was a life she lived when her dreams had been of going to school and making a name for herself that didn't ride on her father's coattails. A name that didn't involve the Voleurs. She brought her thoughts back to Bo Alexander and sighed deeply. How easy would it have been to just tell the detective exactly what she was doing on the island and get it over with? Bo didn't wear a camera and Cass had never been read her rights so any lawyer the Voleurs employed would be able to clear her of all charges. Of course, being free from the weight of the patch also meant being free from the protection it offered her. She wondered what the persistent detective would try this week. She hoped in a small, small part of the very back of her mind that whatever it was included her being able to put her hands on that gorgeous body again. *Again, not that* that *matters.*

"Have you heard about the new club they just opened up in Houston? Pearl Bar or something like that. I think it might be spelled differently."

Bo was still lying in bed with her eyes closed. She had planned on using her day off to sleep in, but apparently Nikki had different plans. "There are quite a lot of bars in Houston. Why would I care about this one at nine in the morning on my day off?"

"Because it's a lesbian bar and today is their grand reopening," Nikki stated matter-of-factly, as if Bo obviously should have known this already.

"Nik, there are—again—a lot of gay bars in Houston."

"Bo, I'm coming over. Get out of bed."

The click on the other end of the line made it clear Bo didn't have a choice. She sighed deeply, exhaling her very soul into the air around her in an attempt to lull herself back to sleep, then headed to the bathroom to begin her morning routine.

"Pearl Bar," Nikki explained as Bo—still in pajama pants and brushing her teeth—sat bleary eyed in front of her, "is spelled normally." In response, Bo simply continued to brush her teeth. "It is also not just a *gay* bar, which you would know if you went out to more than my club."

Bo spit out her toothpaste and rinsed the toothbrush while contemplating if going back to sleep was a valid reason for homicide.

"It's a bar that caters specifically to the female crowd. Rumor has it that they don't mind the kind of activities I refuse in my bar. Like sex."

"Sex in any public place is illegal so I highly doubt that's true, but is there any particular reason you're trying to pimp me out?"

"I want you to go check out my competition. Because my beautiful wife is forcing me to go out of town to visit her parents this weekend so that I don't sully my own reputation by crashing their grand reopening party."

Bo couldn't help but laugh as she rubbed the remaining sleep from her eyes. "Why didn't you just say that in the first place?"

Nikki shrugged, genuinely innocent. "I didn't think you'd walk away from work for such a silly reason. But I really want the info."

Bo smiled at Nikki affectionately. "Nik, I love you, and I was going to take today to rest, anyway. We're making headway on the who's who with the Halliburton case, but until we can get some solid evidence of them moving legitimate product, there's nothing I'm going to be able to do except continue to stake out Cass and possibly the older buildings in the medical district. I don't mind having a little fun today."

A big kiss on the lips was Bo's reward and she laughed as Nikki hugged her tightly.

"Thank you, thank you, thank you!"

"Is there a dress code or anything like that for this?"

Nikki shook her head. "Nope. Just dress to impress." She grinned.

"Don't I always?"

They spent the morning catching up, and Bo decided she was looking forward to checking out the new club. Her life had become a blur of Voleurs and questions, and it would be good to get away from it for a while.

Cass cussed out loud as one of the spare parts she had set up in the garage fell on her head.

"Well, now. That's not very ladylike."

Cass dropped the wrench and stood up to step into the arms that were held out for her. "Big Mama! How the hell are you?"

The large woman returned the hug in spades, picking Cass up and spinning her around like a rag doll before setting her back on the ground. "A hell of a lot better than you, I reckon. What fell?"

Cass pointed to the front end of the old carburetor she had set up on the shelf. "I accidentally sat back against the wall and that front end hit my head."

"Well, don't do that then, Baby Girl." Anyone else calling her by the nickname given to her when she joined the Voleurs and Cass might have taken offence, but Big Mama had taken Cass under her wing when she first started riding under the red and gold colors and had for a long time been someone Cass looked up to. That respect wasn't going anywhere anytime soon.

Cass felt a warmth inside her that she hadn't felt in a very long time. "No one has called me that since Daniel took over."

"Yeah, well, I'm too old to let you forget where you came from. Hand me a wrench and let's get this new carb put on while you tell me what's been going on here lately. I hear that son of mine has been stirring up all kinds of trouble."

Cass laughed and rolled her eyes as she knelt back down, careful not to bump into the shelf wall again. "Pigsty is Pigsty. He always has been and probably always will be." Cass held her hand out and wasn't surprised when the correct part was handed to her automatically. She might have been the only female Voleur in existence, but most Proud Voleur Old Ladies like Big Mama knew their way around motorcycles just as well as most of the men who worked for Cass.

"Well, maybe if he had someone like you straightening him out at home it wouldn't be such an issue, Baby Girl."

"Big Mama, don't start. You know I'm not into men like that, and even if I were, Sty isn't my type."

"Well, a mother can only wish for the best, right?"

"Yeah, yeah. Are you going to help me with this carb or not?"

Big Mama just laughed and scooted the new front end over to Cass. "I've missed you, Baby Girl. How has everything been going? Really."

Cass shrugged and set the carb back into its proper place on her bike. "Everything is the same as it's always been. I'm sure you've heard about everything the boys are doing down here on the island? Lord knows you've got ears everywhere."

A dark look passed over Big Mama's face as she nodded. "Yeah, and I hear it got the Judge laid up in a coma in the hospital. You had better be careful, Baby Girl. I'd hate to have to shoot somebody."

"Dusky got put in a coma because the bullet exacerbated some sort of condition he didn't know he had, but I understand. Trust me, I'm not taking any chances. My father has his panties in a wad over the whole thing and, as usual, likes to blame everything on me." She'd never have said that to anyone else she worked with, but Big Mama knew her father, and she'd know exactly what Cass meant. It felt good to say it out loud.

"Maybe it's time you thought about making your way out, then."

The comment was so out of left field Cass gasped, but before she could form a response Big Mama clapped a hand on Cass's shoulder as she stood and wiped her hands on her jeans. "Well, look. I came down here because I heard you were back in town and it felt like I gave you enough time to settle in without bugging you. Now I'm thinking maybe it's a good thing I stopped by because a friend of mine just reopened her club, Pearl Bar, out in Houston. It's completely on the up-and-up and caters to the ladies. Maybe it's just what you need to get away for a night, huh? It's the grand reopening, after all."

Cass laughed and shook her head as she once again stepped into a massive bear hug and for a moment, let herself melt into the woman who had been a surrogate mother to her for years. "I really have missed you, Big Mama. You need to make yourself available more often."

"Oh, well, now you know us PVOLs ain't allowed anywhere near y'all and your business."

"Yeah, well, just the same. And maybe I will check this club out tonight. What did you say it was called again?"

Bo turned up her radio and tried to nod to the music she had playing at full blast, but even the thunderous booming of Kid Rock's "Cocky" through her custom subwoofer—something that usually got her pumped up for anything—couldn't seem to break through the haze in her mind. After her conversation with Nikki, she had opted to find herself a date for the night to take with her to Pearl

Bar, but she was thinking maybe it would have been better to just go by herself. She was on her way to Saltgrass Steakhouse to meet up with the woman Nikki had set her up with, but for the first time in her life, she wasn't looking forward to meeting with a supposedly beautiful woman.

Just the same, she made it to the restaurant and forced herself to smile as she got out. When she made it to the front door, it wasn't hard to pick her date out from the crowd waiting to get a seat. Thank God for Landry's Select Club, Bo thought as she reached to pull out the card that would allow her to jump the line of people waiting.

The woman was just south of six feet tall in her shiny black heels. The red dress she sported hugged every curve on her body and made her naturally tan skin seem that much more beautiful. When she turned and caught Bo's eye, her thousand-watt smile made it impossible for Bo not to smile back. She seemed to be exactly what she'd been described as—a gorgeous woman who absolutely wouldn't mind having sex with Bo, if the hungry look in her eyes as she watched Bo approach was any indication.

When Bo reached her, she leaned in and kissed her cheek gently. "I really hope you're Elizabeth Perez because if you're not I'm going to have to ditch her so that I can fight off your date, and I'm really not dressed for fighting."

The woman laughed just a little too loudly and looped her arm through Bo's, sliding close. "As a matter of fact, I am. However, if I weren't, I have no doubt you could kick my date's ass just fine in anything you wore."

"Well, in that case, allow me to escort you inside, Miss Hal—" Bo coughed. "Miss Perez." Bo mentally berated herself for the stumble but refused to dwell on it.

Elizabeth looked mildly confused but smiled just the same. "Absolutely. I went ahead and asked about the wait time. I hope you don't mind?"

"Of course not. I don't suppose you asked about the Landry's Select Club wait?"

She laughed and shook her head. "I'm afraid it didn't cross my mind. I've never been privy to those *exclusive* memberships."

Bo laughed along with her. "Luckily for you, I am." They pushed through the crowd to the hostess and Bo was pleasantly surprised that her "cut in line" card was actually useful this time. Twenty-five dollars for the chance to cut an hour and a half wait time seemed extremely worth it now. They were at a table within minutes and they both ordered a water when the waitress came around.

"So, Bo, tell me. What exactly is the point of this select club card?"

Bo gestured to their table. "This right here. Honestly, though, this is probably only the first or second time that it's actually come in handy. The point is supposed to be VIP seating, meaning I get moved to the head of the line behind the next waiting card member. Usually everyone in line is also a card member, though, so it might only take ten minutes or so off the wait time. We got lucky tonight."

Elizabeth giggled softly behind a hand over her mouth, and Bo noticed just how cute she really was. Her long black hair had fallen over her exposed shoulder, giving her an almost innocent quality. Something Cass Halliburton seemed almost desperate to avoid. *Not that I'm thinking of Cass right now.* She looked up and realized her date was staring at her with an expectant look.

"I'm sorry, what did you say?"

"I asked whether or not I met your expectations?"

"Oh!" Bo felt the heat rising in her cheeks as she stuttered for an answer, suddenly unable to speak English. "Very pretty. Nice. Extremely nice."

A shy but polite laugh had her rolling her eyes at herself.

"I'm sorry, I just wasn't expecting that. You're gorgeous, Elizabeth. I have to admit, though, I didn't get much of a description other than...well, exactly that." The silence that followed her comment had her second-guessing herself. "Oh, God, don't tell me I fell short?"

Elizabeth looked surprised. "No, of course not! I'm so sorry, I'm just...well, you're not what I was expecting, I'm not going to lie to you."

Bo's brows furrowed slightly, but she cocked her head with a smile. "Is that a bad thing?"

"No." Elizabeth smiled warmly. "I was told you were roguishly charming with a wild streak that might scare me. Someone else simply said 'hot as hell.'"

Bo laughed out loud at that. "Oh, man. Well, I guess I should be flattered. I'm a little worried I'm not what you expected, though. How would you describe me, if 'hot as hell' doesn't fit?"

Elizabeth seemed to ponder the question and then a brilliant smile lit her face. "I would call you exquisite."

Bo choked on the water that she had taken a sip of, drawing a laugh from Elizabeth. "Sorry," she coughed, "I don't think I've ever heard quite that type of word used to describe me."

"That's a shame." Elizabeth reached over the table and gently placed her hand on top of Bo's. "Someone has been selling you short if they've described you as anything but. Honestly, though, there is one thing that disappoints me."

"Oh?" Bo moved her hand under the guise of grabbing another drink of water. She didn't look too closely at why she didn't want Elizabeth touching her hand, but something about the whole night felt off in the pit of her stomach. "What disappointed you?"

"I am ridiculously overdressed."

They shared a hearty laugh, and when Bo felt she could speak she asked, "I wanted to ask you about that, but I didn't want to offend you. Why the hell are you wearing Louis Vuitton heels and a knockout dress like that to Saltgrass Steakhouse? I mean I could maybe understand Perry's or something even more high class, but here?" Elizabeth seemed embarrassed, so Bo didn't continue.

"Yes, well, unfortunately I have never been to this steakhouse. I was simply told it was fancy and that I should dress nice. For me, this is dressing nice."

Bo snorted before she could stop herself. "Let me guess. That came through the grapevine from Nikki, right?"

"I believe so, yes."

"Never ever believe a single word that woman tells you through the grapevine. She likes to exaggerate so that by the time the word gets to its intended target, it's been watered down and still sounds outrageous."

"I take it that didn't happen this time?"

"Apparently not," Bo said, still chuckling.

"Well, maybe next time I'll just have to ask you directly, won't I?"

Bo knew she should respond, but the only thing she could think of to say was that she wasn't interested in a next time. She couldn't pinpoint why, only that something about this woman seemed off and made her mildly uncomfortable, so she simply nodded and smiled.

Elizabeth seemed to accept that as she picked up the menu and began looking through it. "Is there anything you would recommend? I'm very peculiar when it comes to steak, but if you say they're good I'll trust you."

"Actually, the filet mignon is really good. As long as you like bleu cheese, because it comes with an amazing bleu cheese dressing gravy thing on it."

Elizabeth looked up at her over the menu, an amused grin crinkling the corners of her eyes. "That sounds delicious. In fact, bleu cheese dressing gravy things are my favorite."

Bo laughed and apologized. When the waitress came to take their order, they both ordered the filet mignon, and Elizabeth was very specific that she wanted the bleu cheese dressing gravy thing, much to the waitress's confusion.

"So, Bo. Tell me something about yourself. What made you want to be a cop?"

"Damn. Go right for the tough hitting questions, why don't you?"

Elizabeth shrugged. "I could just ask you your favorite color."

"Periwinkle. You?"

She laughed and shook her head. "Not periwinkle, that's for sure. I'm quite fond of royal blue, though."

"Royal blue is a very...regal color."

"And this is why I didn't ask what your favorite color is." Elizabeth laughed. "It's much better for conversation if I ask the hard-hitting questions."

Bo sighed in mock exaggeration. "I'm not going to get out of this, am I?"

"You can always refuse to answer, but then I'm just going to have to assume that you became a cop because it was easier than being a drug dealer."

Bo flinched. How was Elizabeth to know just how close to home her statement hit?

"I'm sorry if it's a tough subject. I really didn't mean to offend you."

Bo jerked her head up, realizing she had once again let herself get lost in thought. "No, no, it's my fault, I'm sorry. I just had some family issues that dealt with drugs that led to me taking up the badge. I figured maybe someone who knew how shitty life can be would understand better. Be a better cop." She wasn't about to go into her sister's death and her part in it. She wasn't in this for the long haul, just for some fun. And sharing her past wasn't fun.

"I completely understand. I was lucky enough to get away from a bad family situation when I was younger. I'm eternally grateful that I was able to make it on my own. I know the rest of my family hasn't been so lucky."

Their steaks came out, giving Bo time to breathe and push away old memories. She watched the plates being set in front of them and waited for their waitress to refill their water glasses before she allowed herself to continue the conversation, trying her hardest not to wiggle in her seat as the urge to run grew.

"I take it that means you had it pretty rough as a kid, too?"

Elizabeth tilted her hand side to side. "Somewhat. My father protected me from the worst of it. He, unfortunately, decided to leave before I was old enough to follow, so I had to deal with a lot of my mother's…let's say insecurities, before I was old enough to move out. When I did finally leave, I begged my little brother to come with me, but he refused so I stayed with my father for a few years while I saved up to move out on my own. I managed to become a self-made millionaire and last I heard, my mother was driving a bus and my brother was literally robbing graves. My father has been dead for three years."

Yeah. Sharing didn't make for light-hearted conversation. Bo's stomach dropped when she clued in on the name, and she had to fight the almost overwhelming fury that rose as she remembered the young boy she had bought groceries for a couple of weeks prior. He'd been brought into the station and she couldn't help but notice the defeated look in his eyes. The cop who had brought him in had let him go with a warning, and Bo had followed him out, curious about his story. After talking for a while she'd bought him groceries and sent him home. "Perez. You're Hector Perez's sister. The one who has refused to help him and his mother get by, even though she can't work anymore. There can't be too many Perez boys running around robbing graves so I'm going to assume I'm right?"

The light left Elizabeth's eyes and was replaced by something hard and cold. "I guess it shouldn't surprise me you know that side of my family story."

"But there's always two sides?"

Elizabeth nodded emphatically. "Yes, absolutely. Like I said, when I left my mother's house, I begged him to come with me. I wanted to take care of him, he just didn't want to leave my whore of a mother alone." Bo's eyebrows shot up and Elizabeth held up placating hands. "I'm sorry, I'm sorry, that was harsh."

"Hector seemed to think that your father beat your mother and that's why they split."

"He did. I'm not going to lie and say he didn't, but at the time, to me at least, the truth was a lot grayer than it was black and white. He slapped my mother a few times because she refused to do anything he asked of her and my father was raised that a woman's place is subservient to the man. While I might not agree with that, I also don't agree with the fact that instead of standing up for herself, she took her anger with him out on me. Every time my father beat her, she turned around and beat me. Eventually, I got to the point where I didn't even hate him for hitting her because I saw it as revenge for hitting me. It was only after I moved out that I realized how wrong I was."

"But you moved in with him just the same? Why not go to a friend's house? Or hell, why not call the damn cops? That's kind of what we're here for."

Elizabeth sighed softly. "Like I said, I didn't realize the error of my ways until after I moved out. While I was with both of them, he treated me like a princess. He would hit her for yelling at me, he would hit her for not giving me what I wanted. He would hit her for not giving him what he wanted. Before he moved out, I thought he was my protector. Even when she turned her anger on me, it made it that much worse for her later because I would tell him Mama spanked me or slapped me. That's why I say to me the truth was a gray area. Once I moved out, though, I saw the truth for what it was. He never hit me, but he did get very angry with me, sometimes for the littlest things, and he scared me a lot. I moved out on my own very shortly after moving in with him. I tried to get my brother away from my mom but, surprise, she never touched him, and he can't remember ever witnessing her hitting me. I made peace with the fact that he was staying with her to help her, but I can't in good conscience help her get by. I just can't. When my brother called me to ask for help when she got hurt, I offered one more time to have him come stay with me and he not only refused, he screamed at me about being a selfish lying bitch. I think we're beyond being anything to each other at this point."

Bo took a while to digest what she was told. It didn't really clash with anything Hector had told her, and honestly, she couldn't blame Elizabeth for her actions. Still, she didn't think she could stomach letting this night continue.

Elizabeth seemed to sense the change in the atmosphere around her. "I completely ruined this, didn't I?"

Bo smiled softly and shook her head. "No, not entirely. I just think maybe the night isn't going to go as planned."

"Is this date salvageable at all? With the risk of sounding absurdly easy, I really wouldn't mind going home with you, Bo. Regardless of our differences, I think you and I could be really good together. Or at least really fun. I'd like to explore that."

Bo laughed quietly and took Elizabeth's hand in her own, kissing her knuckles gently. "Would you believe me if I said it isn't you?"

"So, this is the 'it's not you, it's me' thing?"

"Sort of. I just never intended for this night to get serious because honestly, I don't have time for that, and unfortunately, it has. I can't take you out dancing and then take you home and still be okay leaving it at that."

"Ah. Yes, I've been there. Still, I think we could have some fun. I promise I don't expect anything from you but that. If you're willing?"

Bo sighed softly and shook her head. "No, I'm not. Like I said, we're past that point. I know too much about you to make tonight completely casual."

Elizabeth nodded and they finished their dinner in amicable silence before parting ways in the parking lot. Bo climbed into her truck and aimed for the mainland, hoping to shake off whatever the hell had made her so melancholy even before the date had gone south.

Cass slowly made her way through the pulsating crowd on the dance floor to the massive and unusually comfortable couches on the side wall. She'd had a meeting with her higher-ups that morning at Heartbreakers and she'd had to put up with enough mansplaining and over-exaggerations to last a lifetime. Product was moving, deals were being made, and everyone was happy. Now she wanted a break.

The recommendation from Big Mama couldn't have come at a better time. As much as she loved the water and the smell of the ocean at her place, the meeting had ruined the serenity walking on the beach could usually provide. It was meetings like that one that reminded her that she really hated people with penises. Obviously, a hot new lesbian club as far away from Heartbreakers as she could get while being available in an emergency was the answer to her problems.

Now, she was simply enjoying a crowd of lust-filled women grinding to the music slamming through the speakers; one of those women was currently walking toward her with a look that left no doubt as to what her intentions were. Cass smiled and stood, meeting the woman on the edge of the dance floor. "Care to dance?" the woman asked breathlessly, sweat glistening on her face from the heat of the bodies surrounding them. Cass nodded and took the outstretched hand, letting herself be pulled onto the floor. Tonight, she was just another woman in a crowd, and the Halliburton name meant nothing. It was perfectly freeing.

The dark room, lit only by flashing strobe lights, gave them plenty of shadows to hide in among the dancing crowd, and she closed her eyes as the woman pressed close to her, letting her hands roam all over Cass's body. Cass felt a welcome warming in her stomach as the stranger's hands moved over her breasts, squeezing gently as she felt the woman's body pressing into her back. A tingle started between her legs as the hands working her over began a slow, steady tugging on her already turgid nipples as she felt a slight thrusting into her ass.

She moaned softly, unable to help herself as she pressed into the body behind her. As the woman's hands moved lower, she was almost able to forget she was in public. God, how long had it been since she'd gotten laid? She bit her lip, feeling the familiar stirrings of lust spreading through her. She opened her eyes to turn around but stopped when she caught sight of a familiar face in the crowd.

Bo had her arms around a gorgeous brunette, her hips snug against the woman's ass and her mouth kissing and biting every spare inch of the woman's neck. If Cass hadn't been paying close attention, they would have looked like any of the other couples in the raucous mass, but she was paying rapt attention and she could see the way the brunette's too-short dress was lifted just slightly. She could see the way the detective's hips were thrusting just so, and she could see how the woman's hand, stretched back behind her to tug and pull at Bo's hair, pulled tighter as she begged silently, "Harder."

Obviously, the detective hadn't come just to dance any more than Cass had, and Cass had seen enough to know she was packing more than just her gun tonight. *This* looked like a party she wanted to crash. She pulled away from the now forgotten woman behind her, ignoring the irritated, "What the fuck," as she made a beeline for the only woman on her mind now.

❖

Bo was so very close to the release her body craved, and she groaned as she felt another hot body press against her back, new hands reaching around to squeeze her breasts as she moved her hips harder into the cleft of the woman's ass in front of her. She thrust harder, grunting as the hilt of the strap-on slammed into her clit. She was poised to burst when the soft, subtle smell of perfume and vanilla filled her senses. She snarled and whipped around, oblivious to the brunette's cries of frustration as she yelled over the music, while quickly tucking herself back into her jeans, "What the fuck are you doing here?"

Cass pressed flush against Bo's body, spreading her legs just enough for Bo's hard length to fit between them. Bo could barely stop her eyes from rolling back in her head as Cass rocked her hips suggestively. "The same thing you are, I'd imagine. Drinking, dancing, trying to get laid." She reached down and squeezed Bo through her pants, jerking her cock just slightly. "How close are you to coming, Detective?" she said throatily in Bo's ear. "Do you want me to get you off right now? I could, you know."

"Stop." Bo meant it as a warning, but it came out a guttural groan, and this time she couldn't stop her eyes from closing.

Cass licked up her neck and bit down soundly on the soft skin of her earlobe. "I don't think so. I want you to scream for me."

Bo's knees buckled just enough to make her lean over, and her chest heaved as she gasped for breath, fighting against the sensations coursing through her body.

Bo turned to storm off through the oblivious crowd surrounding them, but she heard Cass yell out from behind her, "Think of me when you make yourself come tonight, Detective." She leaned against the wall as she got outside and closed her eyes tight. "That's not going to fucking happen." She kept the words to herself because anyone else would have known it was a lie.

❖

Bo slammed the door behind her before slamming her fist into the wall. The crack she felt in her knuckle didn't clear the red haze in her head, but the soft whimper she heard from behind her did. She turned around to see Chubby belly crawling to her, her floppy white and brown ears laid completely back and a quiet, steady whine coming from her. Bo closed her eyes before bending down and picking Chubby up like a baby. "I'm sorry, honey."

Chubby's response was to cover Bo's face in frantic doggy kisses.

"I know. I love you too, baby girl. I'm sorry I scared you." She sat on the floor, still holding the big dog in her arms as she contemplated her night. "I have to find a way to get around this woman. I haven't had to deal with someone this hell-bent on screwing with me since high school. She knows she's pissing me off, too, and that's a problem."

Chubby, once again, seemed to be hanging on Bo's every word.

"Okay, Chubby. Tell me what I know for certain."

The Great White Whale said nothing, simply wagging her tail—seemingly content to be held on her back and listen.

"You're right. We have a lot of pieces to this puzzle but still no solid outline. I know the trafficking is a good angle, but honestly, Chubs, it just doesn't feel right in my gut. Port Police aren't being cooperative, so I can't even check shipping crates from Halliburton Industries to see if I can find anything. Cass Halliburton is a steel trap, and I get the feeling she won't lay off me even if I back off her, not that I would. I'm just going to have to find a way around her for the time being."

"Boof."

"You're right, sorry, I can't go around her without a warrant, and to get that I need more than breadcrumbs. My bad. What else, though? The acetone is important. I know it is, but there's no way they can keep hiding their tracks this good setting up an entire fucking manufacturing ring in the middle of the island, regardless of what Topher says." She sighed deeply. "Where's my files?"

She set Chubby down and changed into a comfortable pair of pajamas before heading to the living room and grabbing the stack of files on her bookshelf. She had already gone through them a few times, but she kept hoping one minor detail would stand out. She was just about to close the files again when she noticed the personal effects sheet for one of the Demons who had been recently arrested. His saddle bags had been searched, and the arresting officer found one thousand dollars in tens, half a pound of crystal meth, and a couple of joints. Bo knew from her time in the narcotics unit that acetone was an ingredient used in manufacturing meth and wondered whether Topher really had been on to something when he suggested the Voleurs were cutting out the middleman.

They would need somewhere to hide the chemicals, and most of the ingredients used wouldn't stick out in a mechanic shop. The ingredients that *would* look out of place could easily be hidden in a back room somewhere. *Or even in a fucking medicine cabinet in the bathroom.* And unless she found absolute solid proof that all the chemicals were being used to manufacture, no judge would sign off on a warrant to look for things like cough syrup and acetone. She turned to Chubby. "I need to find more than just pieces. I need a giant chunk of the puzzle to start fitting the pieces together. What the hell am I missing?" She gave up and went to sleep, her dreams full of women writhing against her. By the time she was up and headed for the office, she was horny and cranky and ready for a distraction.

Later that morning, Gerald found Bo leaning back in her seat at her desk with her eyes closed, a steaming cup of coffee in her hand resting on the armrest. "What can I do you for, Detective?"

She cracked one eye open and then opened both eyes and sat up, taking a sip of her coffee and grimacing. "I need to think of a way to get eyes on Cass Halliburton's boys and what she's doing here without her blocking me at every turn."

He chewed the inside of his cheek and then cocked his head and asked, "How is she blocking you?"

"Kind of hard to pay attention when a woman's got her hand on your dick, Gerald. Even if you don't want it there."

He blushed bright red and she laughed. "No, I mean how is she getting the drop on you?"

Bo, still chuckling, shrugged. "She knows I'm coming most of the time and so she has ample time to prepare for an attack, I suppose. She knows she won't goad me into a fight, so the next best thing is to just make me so uncomfortable I leave. Unfortunately, it works, and I wouldn't know if there's something to see or not because I'm too busy trying to get *away* from her instead of going after her. The few times I have been on the offense she's clammed up and told me if I don't have a warrant I need to leave. We both know I can't get that without something solid so I'm kind of stuck right now. I know where I need to be, but I can't get there legally."

He thought for a few minutes while Bo sipped her coffee. Then he said, "What if you distracted her, first? You know, so she can't get the jump on you. It would at least give you enough time to get a look around and try to see what's going on, right?"

"Detective Guthrie, are you suggesting I use sex to get close to Cass Halliburton?"

She didn't think it was possible for his face to get any redder than it already had, but she was wrong.

"N—no, I just...well, I thought—"

"I'm kidding, I understand what you meant. It's not a bad idea, actually. She's already made it clear she apparently thinks I'm hot so maybe I can use that against her. Really go on the attack instead."

He sat beside her. "How is that going to help us get a smoking gun, though? You might be able to get a better idea of who exactly is moving what, since we already know the players, but that's not going to help us unless we know which warehouse down on East End to check out specifically. We can't look at the wrong one or else they'll spook again. And forgive me for saying so, but no matter how good you are in bed, she's not going to spill about her operation to a cop."

"I was thinking about that on the way up here, actually. I have a friend in the Coast Guard who owes me a favor. I was thinking that since Topher doesn't seem to be getting anywhere with the guys at the Port, I could cut them out completely and have my buddy run a random on some of the shipping containers we know are coming from Halliburton International. Maybe he'll get lucky and find something worthwhile. We know the Demons are running the port so if we can track a bad shipment back to them, maybe they'll roll over on the Voleurs on the island and we'll know exactly where to look in the medical district and exactly what we're looking for, since I've got threads pulling me in a couple of different directions. Maybe it'll give me a better idea which direction to follow."

"That's not going to make Topher or Sergeant Gill very happy."

Bo waived dismissively. "I don't care about making Topher happy, and Sergeant Gill will understand. This is *our* investigation, after all. Cutting Topher out doesn't mean shit. Let me give my buddy a call and then I'll get ready to go out tonight and see if I can't find Cass. I don't know for sure where she'll be, but I know she's been at Heartbreakers a few times so I'll check there first. Maybe I'll get lucky."

"That's a lot of maybes."

"Well, maybe it'll work."

Bo felt the thrill course through her like a shot of pure adrenaline. She could feel it in her bones: something was about to break, and when it did, she was going to be damn sure she was there. Otherwise it could cost her a whole lot more than just an investigation.

CHAPTER TEN

When Bo walked into Heartbreakers that night, it was with the knowledge that she was the hunter, and her prey was hunting her back. The tight black T-shirt she wore showed off almost all of the tattoos on her arm, and the tight pants hugged and accentuated every curve she had. Her ears glinted silver with all the piercings she had accumulated in her life, as did her right eyebrow. For a moment, she remembered what it felt like to go undercover in the narcotics unit, and how close that was to who she had been in the past. She wasn't planning on gaining any information straight from Cass, but she knew that what she could see could be just as important as what she heard, and seeing the underground of the club in action had been something she hadn't yet managed to do. Her Coastie friend was already running searches on various shipping manifests, trying to find the right load to hit for her and she was eagerly awaiting his call.

She knew there was a chance that Cass wasn't in this club tonight, but she had a gut feeling and she had learned over the years to listen to that feeling. She sat at the bar between four other people, her back to the counter. She didn't question it when the bartender simply handed her a beer. She took in the large number of Demons she could see shifting around in the shadows. The girls who were working the crowd seemed awfully familiar, too. No one seemed to be exchanging anything other than cold hard cash, though, so she couldn't do anything about it except make a mental note of the fact that the Demons who were taking women into the back room seemed to be coming out with cash in hand, instead of the opposite way around. *Maybe the Demons are the prostitutes now. Yes, Bo. Because* that *makes sense.* Still, it was one more oddity to add to her collection. Pimps. Acetone. Meth. Backwards cash transactions. She thought of the thousand dollars the Demon in her file had been caught with and added that to her mental list as well.

She had almost finished her beer when she spotted the all too familiar head of wild blond hair. The crowd was thick tonight, and that made it extremely easy to follow her target without being seen. She watched Cass talk to a bouncer—or what Bo could only assume was a bouncer—before nodding to him and gesturing toward the rooms Bo had seen the Demons going in and out of. She waited for him to leave before mingling with the crowd, intent on getting Cass's eyes on her so that she could have a moment to look into those back hallways. Even a glimpse of someone she could bring in would help.

Bo made her way through the throng of people and pressed her body against Cass's back. When Cass stiffened and would have turned around, Bo growled and gripped her hips hard, pulling Cass back against her chest as she started a slow grinding motion against her ass. Cass pressed into her, and she knew she wasn't imagining the way Cass arched her body when Bo bit down on her neck before licking around her ear and whispering, "You aren't the only one who knows how to play, Miss Halliburton."

Cass seemed to shake her head clear and tried to grind back into Bo, but Bo shoved her around, pressing into her front and yanking her head back with a fist full of hair. She could feel Cass's body shake as she placed slow, wet kisses down Cass's neck.

"Detective, to what do I owe the pleasure?" Her voice shook when she spoke, and Bo grinned to herself.

"I'm tired of being caught with my pants down. I figured it was about time I returned the favor. You didn't seem to mind the other night."

Cass gripped Bo between her legs and Bo stiffened. Cass gave a sultry laugh. "I certainly don't mind. In fact, I was really hoping you would let me finish you off the other night." She stopped long enough for Bo to look down into her eyes and she smiled. "I know how ready you were. I almost made myself come thinking about that look in your eyes."

Movement caught Bo's eye and she looked toward the back room, and Cass took the opportunity to bite down hard on her earlobe, making Bo grunt in surprise. She shook her head and tried to look back into the hallway, but Cass grabbed her chin and pulled her back, pulling Bo within inches of her own face. "Would you have liked that? Would you have come hard for me? I bet you would have screamed, huh? I want to know what it sounds like when you scream, Detective."

Bo looked up and watched as the bouncer from before led Tiffany into a room in the back. She moved to follow, but Cass grabbed her shirt roughly. "That's a VIP section, Detective, and I'm positive you don't have a membership. Now, don't tell me you came all the way to the mainland just to tease me?"

Bo pulled Cass against her and bit down again on her neck, drawing a soft gasp as she used the weight of her own body to push Cass back toward the hallway where Tiffany reemerged and assimilated into the crowd. She turned to follow the path the bouncer had led Tiffany down, but Cass put a hand on her chest. "I won't tell you again. That's for VIP guests only. Do I need to have you removed from my club?" She sounded breathless, but her eyes were fierce.

"All due respect, Miss Halliburton, go fuck yourself. This is a public establishment and I'll go where I want."

Cass smiled coyly. "You're right. I'll let you go anywhere your warrant says you can go. Otherwise, I'll state it a third time. VIP only." Bo glared at her and she laughed softly. "That's what I thought. Good night, Detective. You know where the door is." She walked away and Bo left the club, if for no other reason than to avoid being thrown out. She pulled out her cell phone.

"Gerald? Listen I didn't get to stay long in the club because Halliburton threatened to throw me out, but your idea worked and now I think I might have a lead." She hung up on his voice mail and started formulating a plan to lay out for her sergeant.

❖

On Monday, Bo pulled Guthrie into Sergeant Gill's office and closed the door. When Paige said, "How can I help the two of you?" her tone of voice didn't give away any irritation with Bo having commandeered her time without permission, but her raised eyebrows said more than her words did.

"I wanted to update both of you at the same time. I was at one of the Voleurs' clubs Friday and I saw a woman being led into one of their back rooms. You remember the street source I mentioned a while back? She's a prostitute."

"Please explain how a prostitute in a Voleur club is a thing, Detective."

"I've known this woman for a very long time. She may be a prostitute, but she doesn't work for the Voleurs and she doesn't trick in clubs. She thinks it's too dangerous and there aren't enough sober witnesses."

Paige shrugged. "Can't fault her for that. So, what do you plan to do with this information?"

"My contact doesn't work the streets every night, but I can't pull her from her day job or show up at her apartment without raising suspicion. I didn't see her Saturday so I was thinking next Friday when I know she'll be out on the street I could—"

A loud knock on the door was followed by Topher swinging the office door wide and stepping inside. "Oh, good. You guys are all here. That saves me the trouble of going to find you. I just got word from one of my sources inside the Voleurs that they're going to be moving new product through their club Heartbreakers on Friday."

Paige matched the unamused look Bo gave him.

"Sergeant Dusek, while I appreciate the fact that you are our liaison and have been a great help in our Halliburton case, that does not negate the fact that you are not a part of my unit and as such are not necessarily privileged to all of the information that is exchanged behind my door. That said, why is this big news? The Voleurs move product, they always have."

He ignored her rebuke. "Because when I say *new* product, I mean like they're supposed to be letting people sample the shit that they're making themselves. Trying to cut out the cartel, exactly like I said. They make a new product, give some samples, make money. They use the money to get more ingredients for more new products, and before you know it they're employing their own fucking pharmaceutical company to make everything the cartel supplies."

She raised her eyebrows. "Are you able to get any of your guys in the club to track who's delivering the so-called new product? Bo can get in there, but they already know she's a cop. If what you're saying is true they'll be on her like white on rice the second she walks through the door."

He had the decency to blush as he shook his head. "Unfortunately, the only Voleurs allowed near the clubs Friday are high ranking members and their lower level distributors. None of my narco guys have done enough for the club to make it past probi status. That's why we're coming to you."

Bo grinned. "They may know I'm a cop, but that's not enough of a reason for them to ban me from coming in. I also know what to look for. I'll go back to Heartbreakers on Friday and talk to Tiffany later. Do we have any way for you guys to listen in or have another officer in the club with me?"

Paige nodded. "We can fit you with a wire and have a small camera clipped to you. Based on Topher's info, we won't be able to have cops crawling around inside." She glanced over at Topher and he voiced his agreement. "So we'll have some officers outside listening in should you need backup to make an arrest. Topher, since this is most likely to turn up narcotics, can you provide some of your officers for this who aren't undercover? They're most likely to handle the evidence properly."

"Yeah, that's fine. I can get them together for you."

"It'll be the usual setup, Bo. We can hear you, but we'll keep ourselves muted and call you if we need anything so you won't be talking to yourself." Bo nodded. "You let us know the second you have anything we can make an arrest on. If we can nab the distributors, that'll be the next step to getting this damn thing shut down, since we couldn't stop it from getting started."

"You know I will, Sarge. Plus side, I get the feeling they've come to expect me on Friday nights. The Voleurs might be controlling which members come in, but they won't be closing their club to the public, so I won't have any issue getting inside to look around again. And if I have video, it'll give us that solid proof we've been looking for."

❖

"Back again, Detective?"

Bo smiled and nodded. "What can I say? It's becoming a habit." The bartender poured her a glass of honey whiskey and handed it to her. She sipped the drink without thinking, her back against the bar, eyes roaming, taking in everything and everyone. After an hour, she hadn't even seen one Voleur or Demon, and she was beginning to question Topher's intel. She had only been planning on having the one drink but gave in and tapped her glass on the bar behind her. She left her hand in place and brought it to her lips when the bartender put the glass back in it.

She ignored the slightly bitter taste at the first sip and instead groaned appreciatively at the burn as the top shelf liquor went down her throat. She didn't even want to think how much she was probably paying for one glass, let alone two. She'd just make sure to file it under work expenses at the end of the year. She chuckled to herself and reached for her phone when it vibrated.

"Alexander."

"What are you wearing?"

"Absolutely nothing under my clothes."

There was an audible gasp. "Slut."

Bo laughed and said, "What's up, Sarge?"

"I just called to check on you. We're not hearing anything of substance from you. Have you made any progress?"

Bo downed the remainder of her whiskey and shook her head. "I ain't seen shit. This placed is packed and I haven't even seen a peep show. You'd think there would at least be a hand down someone's pants somewhere. I don't know...something's not right here, Paige. I'm not sure Topher's intel was good."

"I bet if you got out on the dance floor, you'd see a lot more of that kind of action."

Bo frowned and wiped the trickling sweat off her forehead. She could feel a buzz kicking in, but that didn't make sense after only two drinks. *Must have been damn good whiskey.* "What does being out on the dance floor have to do with anything? I can see perfectly fine from where I'm sitting."

"They're probably watching you, Bo. They know what you look like and they know what you are. A predatory woman in a strip club not touching the girls or dancing is going to scream 'I'm a cop on duty.' Not to mention if they're going to be giving out samples, it's going to be in the middle of the floor where no one can see anything."

Bo could feel her temperature rising but shook it off. "So, you're saying I need to go get a lap dance? Get my rocks off while I'm watching people trade rocks off?"

"I'm going to kill you, Zander."

"That's not a bad idea. I'll keep you posted."

She hung up the phone and slowly made her way toward the seething mass of bodies jumping and twisting in front of her on the dance floor. Maybe dancing really *wouldn't* be a bad idea, after all.

She melted into the crowd and grabbed the hips of a small female form in front of her. She grinned as the woman pressed back into her. She let the music move her, and soon, she was moving to the rhythm of the swarm surrounding her, clit throbbing with the bass pounding in her ears, her mind dancing with the hypnotic display of lights swirling around her head.

The music changed and a woman began crooning about being vicious and making pain her mistress. Any thought of keeping an eye out was gone and she paid no attention to the camera on her chest or the wire recording her every sound as a warm hand snaked its way up her back. She almost moaned at the sensation of nails scratching skin. She turned, running her lips up the soft neck in front of her, groaning out loud when a hand reached down and began squeezing her through her already too-tight jeans. A hand grabbed her shoulder, nails digging in, pinning her in place.

"Bite me."

She obliged and sank her teeth into the burning skin, her tongue snaking out to catch a bead of sweat. Her stomach clenched painfully at the small gasp she elicited, the hand squeezing harder.

"I know you want me, Detective," a voice whispered in her ear.

Bo tried to process the feeling of klaxons blaring through the pounding in her body and the weird haze in her mind, but the mouth possessing her and the hand squeezing harder and harder made it difficult. "I've got a pulse. Squeeze harder."

Whiskey soaked laughter filled her mind as hard nails scratched long marks down her back. She slammed Cass into the nearest wall and pressed against her hand.

Two drinks. Too high for only two drinks. She tried to pull away, tried to clear her mind, but the world was lost in a lust-soaked dream.

Cass's hand moved faster and faster. She unzipped her zipper. Nails broke the skin on her back.

Bo groaned, losing control. She could feel it building in her stomach. *Warning bells! Clang, clang, motherfucker!* She was hot. So fucking hot. *High. Too high.* Such a bitter taste. Whiskey isn't bitter. *God, it feels so fucking good.*

Cass used her free hand to squeeze Bo's painfully hard nipple through her shirt. "Tell me what you want, Detective."

"Get the fuck out of there, Alexander, something is wrong!"

They spiked my drink.

Bo snarled and pushed away from the woman panting in front of her. She had to get out. Had to get away. Something had gone wrong, but she couldn't make sense of it. She could hear Cass's laughter echoing in her head as she stumbled and pushed through the crowd. She slumped against the wall outside, gulping in the cold night air. It helped, but not enough. Shaking, barely able to focus, she called a ride to the only safe relief she could think of.

❖

Bo stalked toward her, her movements calculated, predatory. She was on the hunt and Tiffany was on the menu. Bo's breathing was hard, fast, shallow. Her dark T-shirt was soaked through with sweat and the zipper of her jeans was stretched tight over a thick strap-on that rubbed her higher with every step toward her goal.

Tiffany gasped as Bo shoved her back against the wall, quickly pressing against her hard enough for Tiffany to feel the thick prominence between her legs. She moaned and arched into Bo, rocking her hips into it.

A part of Bo wanted to run, wanted to get away, but she growled deeply and closed her eyes against it. "Open my pants. Take it out. Now." Tiffany did as she was told, one hand gripping the stiff cock as her other dug into Bo's shoulder.

Bo's entire body twitched as Tiffany began a rapid up and down motion on the strap-on, her hands firmly planted on the wall on either side of Tiffany's head as she leaned down and captured Tiffany's mouth—her tongue exploring, plundering, owning. She heard the soft whimper of pain but couldn't make herself stop. She reached down with one hand to push Tiffany's barely-there skirt up, shoving her panties aside as she thrust her fingers deep inside, claiming her there even as her tongue claimed Tiffany's mouth. She kissed her way frantically up Tiffany's jaw and whispered hoarsely in her ear, "Let me in here, Tiff. Let me fuck you here. How I want. Say yes, Tiff." *Say no! Make me stop!*

Bo's voice was like gravel to her own ears, and a distant memory of drug fueled agony surfaced as Tiffany gasped her acquiescence, moaning as Bo forcefully turned her and reached down to spread her ass, sliding a finger in there as the thick head of the strap-on replaced her other fingers.

"Fuck yourself on my cock. Let me watch you." She'd said those words before. She thought she was done with that.

Tiffany moaned and threw her head back as she shoved herself back, filling herself with Bo before pulling almost all the way off and slamming back down again. She muffled a scream by biting her lip as Bo dug fingertips into her hips to stop her movements before she thrust completely inside, fingers and cock, at the same time as she bit down on the sensitive skin on the side of Tiffany's neck. She could feel the skin breaking under her teeth as she started fucking Tiffany in earnest.

"You're going too slow to make me come, Tiff. You know what I need. Now give it to me."

She could feel her thrusts growing more frantic as she tried to fuck away the memories of the past and present blending together in a maelstrom of pain and confusion.

"Come on, Bo, fuck me harder, baby. Make it hurt when I come. Make me scream!"

Bo groaned gutturally and yanked her back to meet her hard thrusts while slamming her into the wall in front of her, her hand clenched around Tiffany's throat. "Come. Now!"

Tiffany screamed as they both came, and Bo tried her hardest to push the face of the beautiful blonde out of her head.

Cass breathed deeply and shook herself, trying to act as best she could like the encounter with the detective hadn't affected her just as badly as it had Bo. She'd known when she told the bartender to slip Bo some Molly that it would make her more receptive to Cass's advances, but just how receptive she would have never guessed. Bo's body had been so strong, so powerful. The way her hips had moved against Cass's hand, and she smelled *so fucking good*. Would it have been just as good without the Molly? Would Bo have been as receptive? The slip had been a calculated move to ensure the detective was easily pliable and wouldn't notice her surroundings but... *Damn. Cass* almost wished she would have stayed and let Cass make her come, and Cass had no doubt she could have. No doubt at all. She had been so ready when Cass opened her pants. For a moment, Cass once again let herself get swept away in the fantasy of another life. What if she caved and gave the detective what she wanted? What if she wasn't a Voleur at all? *What if she had let me touch her? So hot and wet and—*

"Miss Halliburton."

Cass looked up at Billy, who was currently acting as a bouncer to ensure that anyone who caused trouble while moving their product was swiftly removed. Her inside source at the PD had ensured no undercover officers would be staking out their business and had been sure to mention that Bo would be there watching, as usual. Billy was there to help with the less than savory patrons and to be her eyes when she wasn't there. For the moment, she was inordinately glad that the low lights in the club ensured he couldn't see that he had startled her.

"Yes, Billy. How can I help you?" Even to her own ears Cass's voice sounded distant and distracted.

He looked as if he were going to comment on something that was completely not his business. Instead, he simply said, "I just wanted to let you know that everything went according to plan. Sty's information was correct and all eyes were on Heartbreakers tonight. They didn't see shit. The Demons have held up their part and our product is where it belongs. The first phase is complete and if we're correct and they cross Heartbreakers off their watch list, we can proceed to phase two."

"Good. That's perfect. Now we can start moving through Classic. Have the boys get ready to sell some cars." When he didn't move, she looked up at him. "Yes, Billy?"

"I was just going to suggest, ma'am, that if you needed to… relax, there might be a back room available." She eyed him sharply, but didn't say anything, so he continued, "There's a really pretty brunette that's been eyeing you all night."

"No!" She could tell by the look on his face that she had startled him with her vehemence. "No, sorry. I'm not really into brunettes. You're right, though. I could use some stress relief. Find me a blonde and have her meet me in room three. Thanks, Billy." With that, she turned on her heels and stormed into the shadows. She was getting tired of the hiding and tired of the games. She wanted to be free from the weight this whole operation had put on her shoulders. Maybe a good fuck was all she needed.

❖

A bull dancing the flamenco on Bo's head woke her up the next morning. It only took three hits of a nonexistent snooze button for her to realize that her alarm was actually a ringing phone. She moved through the sludge of a drug induced hangover to answer it and hold it to her ear. "Zander."

"Detective, this is Barri Holt. I'm a friend of Alyssa's." Bo opted for a grunt in lieu of a response, so the young woman on the other end of the line continued. "Anyway, Alyssa told me that you were looking for anyone coming in connected to the Voleurs, right?"

Bo groaned, still not willing to open her eyes. "Who did you find?"

"I, uh, found a girl. A woman. I found a woman. Well, she's eighteen." It was obvious by the jailer's lack of conviction in her response that she was both extremely new and completely unsure of whether or not calling the lead detective on a major investigation was, in fact, a good idea.

Bo risked opening one eye to glance at the clock and was surprised that she had slept in until past ten. "Why does this concern me?"

"She's an eighteen-year-old girl from Nigeria who barely speaks English, but I specifically understood the words, 'Detective Alexander' and 'Voleurs.' I figured at that point it was best to call you in case something important popped up in an interview."

Bo slid her legs out of bed and slowly rolled to a sitting position. Nausea from the hangover battled with the fury at having been so fucking preoccupied she'd allowed herself to be taken advantage of. What a fucking rookie move. She took a deep breath to restrain her temper and then said, "How long can you hold her for?"

"Probably not very long. It's Mardi Gras and she didn't do anything except solicit an officer."

"I'll be there in thirty minutes. Make sure no one else talks to her."

"Yes, ma'am."

She hung up the phone only for it to immediately ring again.

"What?"

"Try again, Alexander."

Bo took another steadying breath before gritting her teeth together and muttering, "Yes, ma'am, Sergeant?"

"The bartender from last night has been arrested and Cass's club has been fined. She denies all knowledge of his intentions and he corroborates her story. His reasoning is asinine at best. He says he chose a random drink, which means we can't touch her. I'm not so stupid that I would have forced you to write a report last night, but I need one now just to make the charges on this guy stick. The gloves are coming off, Zander. Our guard is up, and our hackles are raised, and I want this bitch off my island now. We didn't see shit last night at Heartbreakers so I'm about to take Topher to task for his faulty info getting one of my officers in a bad way."

She hung up without needing a word from Bo, and Bo continued getting dressed. When she saw her truck, she realized with a start she had no idea how she got home the night before. That was a problem for future Bo.

When Bo arrived at the county jail, she had to fight not to keep her sunglasses on when the fluorescent glare hit her eyes. The Molly had exacerbated the dehydration from the whiskey, and she was paying the price with her sanity. The interrogation room wasn't any better, but she put on her game face when she stepped in and faced a young woman who may have been only eighteen but had the poise and presence of an African queen. Bo cocked her head slightly and said calmly, "Comment t'appelles-tu?" *What is your name. Thank God for high school French.*

The young woman smiled. "My name is Grace Njikeu. You do not have to speak French to me, though I appreciate your consideration." It may have been accented, but her English was perfect.

Bo took a seat in front of Grace as she spoke. "I apologize. I was under the impression that you didn't speak English very well."

"It has been my impression with police officers that unless you give them something very specific to work with, they will not give you what you want."

Bo had to stop herself from laughing at the grunt of offense from the deputy keeping guard on the door behind Grace. "I understand, Miss Njikeu. Can I ask why you specifically requested to speak to me, though? As I understand, you aren't in much trouble."

Grace drew herself up taller and tilted her chin up as she spoke. "Tonight, I had sex with a man I did not know so that I could make money to survive. When he was done with me, he forced me to stand out on a street and give my body to any other man who asked. I was not allowed to keep the money the other men gave me."

Bo felt the contents of her stomach turn sour and remembered talking to Chubby about the possibility that the Voleurs were getting into the trafficking game. She took a deep breath and then said, "How did you come by my name?"

"There was another woman on the street, Tiffany. She asked if I had been on that road before and I told her the truth, that tonight was my first time seeing America from anything other than a van or a window. She told me that I should find a police officer and ask for you."

Bo understood. Grace hadn't been soliciting a police officer, she had been asking to go to the police station. "Grace—may I call you Grace?" The young woman nodded, and Bo continued. "How did you come into contact with the man who forced you to be on the streets tonight?"

"It is not as if I could make money some other way. The man who took my money, he has not given me any other way to survive."

Bo shook her head slightly. "Let me rephrase my question. How did you get here, Grace? To America."

She laughed then, as if Bo had just asked her the most stupid question in the world. "It is not obvious? I have seen enough of your American television to know that the same methods seem to apply to everyone. Someone comes to my village. They pretend they are there to help, to teach us their language, to teach us their customs. They pull us aside and they promise a new life if we want to come with them, that we will be able to send money to our families."

"And then you're theirs and you're trapped." Grace nodded. "So, then you must know that talking to me will put your life in danger."

"I am aware, but I am no one's slave. I would rather be dead." Her jaw clenched and though tears filled her eyes, she seemed adamant they would not fall. "This is not the life I want. My ancestors would be ashamed."

Bo ran her hands through her hair and sighed deeply. "Can you give me a description of anyone? Anything that could help me?"

Grace shook her head sadly. "No. All I know is that one wore the Voleurs on their back and the others were Demons, the ones who came for me. Tiffany said that was important to you."

Tiffany was right. If they could identify the Voleur, they could bring him in for questioning. It could lead somewhere. "The Voleur. Can you tell me if it was a man or a woman? Long hair, short hair? Tattoos or scars? Any little detail could help."

"It was a man. They did not exchange names, and the Voleur wore a mask around me, but the Voleur man said, 'The boss will be pissed if this doesn't work.' His voice was unremarkable. As for the Demons, well, they all look the same, no? Nothing remarkable about them either."

Bo frowned and wondered what "this" was and how it fit into her investigation. "Okay, Grace. I just have a couple more questions."

"May I have a glass of water?"

Bo nodded at the deputy who grabbed a glass for her. Once she had downed the contents, she motioned for Bo to continue.

"How many girls came with you from your village? And do you know the names of anyone who brought you here?"

Grace shook her head. "I could give you names, but they would be of no help. John Smith. John Doe. I know enough of your customs to know these were probably fake. And as for how many? They only brought four of us. The one, the Voleur, he said that as long as everything went right this time that there would be more next time."

Jesus Christ. That answered that question. The Voleurs were using the Demons' connections to bring in women from other countries and force them into the sex trade. "Okay, thank you so much, Grace. Let me ask you…do you want to go back home, or do you want to stay here in protective custody? I can also recommend a women's shelter that I have some contacts at, but that's going to involve a lot of paperwork because you didn't come here legally. That's not something we're inclined to hold against you, just so you're aware."

"I would rather see the sunlight from my own prison. I will go home."

Bo nodded and told the deputy to cut her loose. One thing was damn certain, she needed to call the sergeant. Topher may have gotten intel on drug manufacturing, but he seemed to have missed the big picture.

She went home to try to sleep off the remainder of her headache, but she couldn't get comfortable. Her sleep was fitful and plagued by dreams she didn't want to be having. She couldn't stop thinking of the way Cass's body had molded to hers, the way Cass's hand had felt in her pants. She had been so close to coming it hurt, and when she had Cass against the wall, thrusting into her, Cass's moans had filled her every thought until she couldn't have stopped if she tried.

No, it wasn't Cass's body she had pressed against the wall, it was Tiffany's. Tiffany had been the one she had taken her rage out on, and Tiffany would certainly have known she was high and definitely deserved an apology. Regardless of Tiffany's chosen profession, Bo refused to be someone who simply used a woman just to get off, especially considering they had a past.

She sighed as she once again rolled out of bed and waited for the room to stop spinning before she stood up and straightened the clothes she had fallen asleep in. She glanced at the clock and realized she had slept longer than she thought, so Tiffany should be out on the streets now. As she walked out of her house, she contemplated the ramifications of being drugged. The bartender had freely admitted to it, which was something. The question was why. She couldn't be certain, but she was almost sure that there were no drugs moving through the club last night, and the officers outside said the same thing: no one important came in or out. That meant that whoever had given Topher the intel was wrong, and he needed to be looked at. If all that was true, though, why go through the trouble of drugging her? Just to prove they could? Just so Cass Halliburton could... She closed her eyes against the onslaught of images and feelings. There was no way. Of course, if there was a dirty cop feeding them information to make them turn the other way, her being drugged would go a long way toward her not being sure she hadn't seen anything. She scratched at a peculiar feeling in the pit of her stomach. She had a feeling she was on the right track and she didn't like it.

She also didn't like that her immediate reaction had been to run to Tiffany. She'd thought that part of her life was over.

CHAPTER ELEVEN

The streetlights were harsh and made Bo's headache worse, but she found Tiffany standing around in the same spot she usually frequented. Tiffany saw her immediately. The look on her face told Bo she had been expected, and the open palm slap laid across her face told her she was late.

"I don't mind sleeping with you, Bo, you know that. I never have. But I refuse to be used by someone who was high as a kite last night without so much as a hello. Especially when you promised you would never touch that shit again." The tears rolling down her face, and the fact that she obviously didn't mind them being out in the open, were a testament to how hurt she was. "And you know what the worst part is?" As she spoke, her voice cracked. "You didn't just promise me. You promised Kelly, too. And—"

"And that's a promise I would never break, Tiffany. They drugged me!" Bo tried to stop the rant, but Tiffany wouldn't have it.

"And you think that gives you an excuse, Bo? You came here completely out of your mind, fucked me blind, and then left. How do you think that made me feel, Bo?"

Bo ran her hands down her face and shook her head. "There's nothing I can do to make it right. I'm so sorry, Tiff. I was blasted and the only thing I could think of was—"

"Was getting off. I get it, Bo, I do. But why the hell did you come to me? Why didn't you offer me an explanation?"

"I went to the club on duty and they spiked my drink, and then Cass Halliburton got me on the dance floor and…well. You're my safe place, and I saw you at the club last week…" She faltered, not knowing how else to explain it.

"I get it. I was already on your mind."

"That doesn't make what I did right, but that's what happened. And then I guess I was too ashamed to stick around because I ended up at home."

"You're a dick, you know that? You ended up at home because I drove you there after you almost passed out on top of me. I was too scared to let you drive yourself home."

Bo stayed silent. It was true, and she was pissed at herself for the whole mess.

"God, I hate you sometimes. Why are you here now? Other than to apologize."

"I still need to know what you were doing in the club that night, Tiff. I took advantage of you and that makes me far worse than Cass, but I have to do my job, too."

Tiffany took a deep breath and gently laid her hand on Bo's chest. "Are you okay? I'm sure it couldn't have been easy for you, going through that again."

Bo took her hand and held it there. "It wasn't exactly a painful experience."

Tiffany smiled and shook her head. "No, I'm sure it wasn't. I can't talk you out of this, can I? Even if I told you that it's so much bigger than you think?"

Bo shook her head. This was what she needed, and a break in the case wouldn't make everything worth it, but it might make it feel better.

Tiffany leaned closer. "There are rumors, Bo. A lot of money changing a lot of hands and some powerful people coming in. People even Cass—"

"Well, well, well. Detective Alexander, I have to say I never thought I would see someone like you slumming it down here on the East End. Not again, anyway."

Bo stood up straight and turned around to face Cass, trying to push Tiffany behind her to hide her if possible. "I'm a cop. I have every reason to be here, as you well know. You, on the other hand, seem entirely out of place, so I might just ask you what the hell you're doing here. Come to exchange money with your drug dealers, perhaps? Pick up some company for the night?"

"If I wanted company, I'd just ask you. You almost begged for it last night." Cass smirked and winked, and then put a faux sympathetic frown on her face. "No, Detective, I was just coming back to check on my good friend Tiffany, here. See, I came by last night to say hello and catch up and I saw some drugged-crazed cop sexually assaulting her." As she spoke, she moved around Bo to stand beside Tiffany and placed her hand on Tiffany's neck, effectively forcing Bo to take a step back.

"Imagine my surprise when I come back and see that same cop talking to Tiffany again. Obviously, I was worried because I know my friend wouldn't be talking to the police voluntarily." To emphasize her last words, she squeezed the back of Tiffany's neck, her eyes giving the warning she hadn't spoken out loud.

"Get your hands off her, you soulless fucking bitch." Bo punctuated every word with a finger pointed in Cass's face.

Cass's eyebrows shot up in surprise. "I've been accused of a lot of things, Detective, but I don't think soulless has ever been one of them. I actually think I find it mildly offensive."

Bo laughed harshly. "How can you think you have a soul when you're forcing girls young enough to be in high school to work the streets for you?"

"I assure you, Detective, if I were to dabble in something as," she tilted her head thoughtfully, "soulless as prostitution, I would think I'd be the type of mistress who would have her escorts free to come and go as they pleased, so long as they remained loyal." She gave Tiffany's neck a squeeze, eliciting a small gasp.

Bo scoffed. "Oh, yeah, they're so free when you have your boys yank them from their home countries and force them to sell their bodies without giving them any hope for a better future. You kidnap them and then force them into the sex trade. What's next, you going to move them all around the country and make them give blow jobs to priests? Free to go, my ass. That's what all you people say."

Cass pinned her with a hard stare, and for the second time since they'd met, she seemed slightly off balance. "And maybe, Detective, just maybe, some of those people," she spat out the word, "mean exactly what they say." She dropped her hand from Tiffany's neck and stormed off, leaving Bo and Tiffany standing in shock.

"What the fuck was that?"

Tiffany shrugged. "I have no idea. To be perfectly honest with you, I didn't think that woman was capable of anything but sarcasm and spite. She certainly doesn't seem the type to just run off." She took a shaky breath. "But I know she's capable of snapping my neck."

Bo flashed back to Cass's expression when Sav had threatened to kill her dog. She shook her head. "To be perfectly honest with you, I'm not sure what that woman is capable of anymore." She turned to face Tiffany and grabbed her hand gently. "I still need to know, Tiff. What were you doing in Heartbreakers last night?"

Tiffany shook her head adamantly. "For your own protection, I'm not telling you. You can arrest me, you can shove me against the wall, you can do whatever you want, I don't care. I'm not giving you the key to your own damn suicide mission, Bo. Let it go." She held out her hands for Bo's cuffs, and then turned and left Bo with only her thoughts.

Cass couldn't think of a single reason that made any logical sense for her to be standing where she was. It had been almost a week with zero contact from Detective Alexander or any of her police department counterparts, so why in God's name had she decided that poking the bear was a good idea? In her heart, she knew, but her heart wasn't what was on the line if her plan should backfire.

She almost changed her mind, but the rapping of her knuckles on the wood door seemed to negate that. She could play ding-dong ditch, her rational mind said, but the door opened too soon for her to make a clean getaway.

"Miss Halliburton." Bo's face was a mask of stone, but her voice gave away her obvious confusion. Cass pushed past her before she could stop herself and turned to watch Bo slowly closing the door.

"We need to talk. Don't get me started on how unorthodox this is, but we need to talk." She started pacing the floor but stopped when the dog, Chubby, came up to her, tail wagging. She knelt and nuzzled the big dog until a throat clearing from above her made her look up.

"Miss Halliburton, it appears I must ask you for a second time, what the hell are you doing in my house?"

Cass stood and faced Bo, looking up slightly to meet her eyes. "Like I said, we need to talk. You made some comments that I'm not entirely comfortable with." As she spoke, Cass went to sit on the surprisingly comfortable sofa that dominated most of the wall to the right of the door. Chubby came to lay beside her, but Bo, she noticed, kept an eye on every move she made.

"Look, Detective, your dog trusts me. Why can't you?"

Bo gave her an incredulous look that almost made her laugh and retorted sharply, "Besides the obvious? My dog is clearly a traitor, and if you don't answer my question, I'm going to force you out. Painfully. Now, for the third time—"

"Yeah, yeah. I already said we needed to talk. Take a seat, you're making me nervous."

Bo's eyes got even wider, but Cass simply raised an eyebrow and gestured to a well-used recliner, not lowering her hand until Bo threw her hands in the air and sat, looking too much like a petulant child for Cass not to laugh just a little. At the glare thrown her way, Cass stopped and coughed.

"Speak. Now."

The situation required a deep breath to stop the bubbling laughter again when Chubby, ever faithful, woofed just slightly and Bo rolled her eyes.

"What is it exactly that you think I'm doing here? On the island, I mean. With the Voleurs. Why do you think I'm here?"

Bo shook her head firmly. "What my investigation has turned up is none of your business. Why the hell would you think I'd tell you anything?"

Cass smiled just slightly. "That's not exactly true, but okay. Here's the deal. The comments you made the other night are way off base. You seem to be under the impression that I'm orchestrating some kind of prostitution ring here, and I need to tell you you're wrong. I'm not going to lie to you, Detective, I have a reason for being here. And yes, the Voleurs do employ ladies to enjoy their company from time to time, regardless of how that company is enjoyed. How and when the ladies work for the Voleurs, however, is on their own morality scale, not ours. They're free to come and go as they please."

"Then how do you explain the young woman who came to me telling me a Voleur brought her from her home country and forced her to sell her body? How do you explain a woman I know very well being forced to have sex with one of your bodyguards in the back room of Heartbreakers?"

Cass was very quiet for a moment, trying to collect her thoughts as she processed what Bo had told her. It was obvious the display of information had been to get a reaction out of Cass and it had, but not for the reasons she might think. It could have been any of the girls Cass employed lying to get the Voleurs in trouble, but there were much easier and less convoluted ways to do that if they really wanted. There would be absolutely no reason for anyone to lie about something like that, especially if it meant they could be killed for it. Cass sighed and then said softly, "Can I ask you a question?"

"Yes?" It was obvious from the force of her response that Bo had been expecting Cass to continue the argument with a monumental denial.

Cass glanced up from the floor where she had been staring and Bo raised her hands in apology. She repeated herself in a more docile way and Cass asked, "Are you absolutely sure she was having sex in the back room?"

She stood and paced in frustration, running her hand through her hair. "No. You've got her trained well and she's fucking scared, so she wouldn't tell me shit. But tell me this; if she wasn't having sex, then what was she doing?"

Cass smiled just barely. "That's for you to find out. But I can tell you this, I may have done some illegal things in my life, but I have never and will never force a woman to do unspeakable things to survive. I would never force a woman to share her body, regardless of how many men in my organization might want me to. I certainly would never tear an innocent young girl from her home and force her into sex slavery for my own benefit. I am *never* going to allow my organization to participate in human trafficking or forced prostitution, Detective. I'm a businesswoman in lots of other ways, but I'm not evil."

Bo opened her mouth to respond, but Cass cut her off. "I don't know anything about this young woman claiming she was taken from her home, but I will do my best to find out."

"Why are you telling me this? Why should I believe you?"

Cass stood, smiling as Bo stiffened. "I'm going to be honest with you, Detective. I'm telling you because I like you." She watched as the storm of emotions crossed over Bo's face—surprise, happiness, confusion. "You're not easily bought, you stand up for what you believe in, and I'm sure you're the type to own up to your mistakes. You're also ridiculously attractive. I feel like if I let you believe this about me, our relationship might be a little rockier than it already has been, and I just can't have that. I've done some things I'm not proud of in the name of the Voleurs, and even some things I have been proud of, but I refuse to have someone sully my character with such impunity. Especially if they're doing it behind my back. Remember, it's the south, Detective. Even criminals have a code."

Bo walked to the door and opened it, looking at Cass pointedly. "I'll take what you've said under advisement, but you'll forgive me if I don't take your word at face value."

Cass simply shrugged and made her way toward the door. "Think whatever you want, Detective. Just not that."

As she left, Cass mentally kicked herself. Code or not, she could have just as easily let the detective go off on a wild goose chase and it would have made her life so much easier. *No, not that. Anything but that, and I would have.* The question now became, if the woman who ratted to Bo wasn't lying, and Cass didn't think she was, then who the hell was the Voleur involved? Obviously, they were using the Demons' connections at the port, which could mean a few things. Either someone was playing both sides of the fence and not telling the Voleurs about it, or she had purposely been kept in the dark about this and everyone but her knew. Either way, it wasn't a situation she wanted to be in, and she needed to find out what the hell was going on.

She couldn't help but wonder if her father knew. She couldn't risk asking him on the off chance that he would have her killed for sticking her nose where it didn't belong, and she had no doubt he would. Struck with a feeling of vulnerability, Cass jogged back to her bike. This operation was turning out to be a total shit storm, and fighting both sides of the thin blue line was getting very tiring.

❖

Bo couldn't get dreams of subtle perfume and vanilla spice mingled with deep moans and hands all over her body out of her head, so she found herself in Sergeant Gill's office, looking for anything to bring the case to a quick close. "Look, Sarge, you know I'm usually pretty damn good at this kind of shit, but this investigation is going in a thousand different directions at once. Topher's narco dicks are telling us to look for drug manufacturing, Port Police is completely refusing to cooperate because they would know if something was going on, so fuck us, I guess, I've got a woman telling me she's been trafficked from Africa but can't mention any names, and to be quite frank, the only thing I'm seeing in Heartbreakers is the possibility of the Demons running girls in and out of there, and I'm not even sure that's really happening."

Paige looked mildly surprised. "You came up with all that and haven't said anything to me before now?"

"I've been working things through with my dog first. Sarge, I don't know what's real and what's not. Every time I get something that's supposed to be solid, my eyes tell me something different. Every time my eyes tell me to follow something, that thread only leads to more questions that I can't answer. If I pull the wrong string the whole thing will unravel and we'll be fucked."

"What are your street sources saying? Trafficking from Africa is pretty fucking serious and we could easily pull in the FBI on that or invoke RICO and round up every Voleur on the island."

Bo thought about the look on Cass Halliburton's face when she had accused her of human trafficking in front of Tiffany. She thought about how seriously she had stated her convictions. *I may not be innocent, but I'm not evil.*

"Bo?"

She jumped, realizing she had been lost in thought. "Other than a quick slap to the face? No. I've got some other sources asking around about the trafficking, but I haven't seen any other evidence of it and neither have they. Without names on that we'll be fielding complaints until we're dead if we try to invoke RICO on the entire gang, and you know damn well the FBI isn't going to help without solid proof."

"I need you to stay ahead of that, Bo. If it's really happening, get me the fucking proof now. What about the manufacturing? Topher's guys are positive it's happening, and they're just not being allowed to see."

"The one chance I had to get intel on that got fucked up. I can't be sure of anything at all, but honestly, Sarge, I really don't think anything was going on. The bartender drugged me, sure, but I really don't think there was anything to hide. I think they did it to fuck with me on principle."

Paige narrowed her eyes. "I really don't like that answer, Bo."

Bo shook her head. "Trust me. A probi having faulty intel and a bartender with balls of steel is the lesser of two evils. I don't know which way to go at this point. I put in a call to my friend in the Coast Guard, but he—" She looked down at a shrill ring of her phone and smirked. "Speaking of Satan." She answered the phone and put it on speaker, setting it in the middle of the desk.

"Derek! I was just talking to my sergeant about you. What have you got for me?"

"Well, Bo, I'm honestly not sure you'd believe me if I told you."

Bo spared a glance at Paige, who was looking right back at her, waiting for the shoe to drop. "Try me."

"Are you sitting down?"

"Yes."

"I found a plate."

Bo's shoulder's slumped, and she could almost feel the moment her soul left her body. "Why the hell are you calling me for a plate? It's fucking dishware, man."

Paige simply went back to her laptop.

"No, no. Not a dish plate, dumbass. A printing plate. Like to print money."

Paige slammed her laptop closed and was suddenly paying rapt attention. "Derek, this is Sergeant Paige Gill. I need you to tell me exactly where and how you found this plate. Don't leave anything out."

"Of course, Sarge. Bo called me a few weeks ago to let me know that you guys have been looking into the Voleurs for manufacturing drugs, so me and my crew have been doing random inspections of some of Halliburton International's crates, and one of my boys accidentally knocked over one of their parts boxes and out it fell."

"You have got to be kidding me." Bo almost couldn't believe what she was hearing.

"Nope. It was in a box with a custom exhaust kit. There wasn't anything else that shouldn't be in that box, so I'm almost positive it was left there on accident."

"Yeah, no shit. Does the bill of lading say where it came from, specifically?"

"Well, I know the box was marked from one of the Galveston warehouses in the port, but the guy who loaded it was actually arrested a while ago and is now being held by the FBI under lock and key. They won't even let us touch him."

"Goddamn it." Paige slammed her fist on the table. "Derek, has there been any sign of drug movement coming out of the port that you've seen?"

They could hear something that sounded like a beard scratching the mic of his phone before he said, "No, ma'am. Obviously, we find some every now and then, but everything we've found on the randos has been the same shit we always find. Stamped from the cartel and hidden in random statues and rice containers and shit. No Voleurs stuff."

Bo frowned and cocked her head. "What about…people?"

"Are you fucking kidding me, Bo?" he asked. "Do you really think I wouldn't have started with that if I found fucking humans in a shipping container with Halliburton's name on it?"

Bo sighed. "Sorry, you're right. All right, thanks, Derek. Let me know if you find anything else, okay? And I wasn't kidding about that people thing. I've got sources giving me questions that need answers. Keep your eyes peeled."

"Sure thing." He hung up without saying good-bye.

"Okay." Bo started ticking things off on her fingers. "We've got narco telling us there's rumors of manufacturing, which would explain the Demons, but we've got no drugs coming out that aren't already stamped from the cartels, and we can't find any warehouse that might have that kind of operation going. We've got a woman claiming to be trafficked from Africa, but no signs of human trafficking and no other women claiming the same story. Now all of a sudden we've got a random ass printing plate that at some point has passed through a Halliburton warehouse on the island but whose apparent shipper has been arrested. We're pretty sure Heartbreakers and the car rental place are fronts, but we don't actually know for what. Did I miss anything?" She left out the fact that Cass had drugged her and then shown up at her house the next day. No need for more complications.

Paige shook her head.

"So, what the fuck is going on? What the hell do I do now?" Bo tried not to yell, but it was damn hard.

"I think you should go get some clarification from Topher on exactly what it is his boys are hearing."

"Why can't you do it?"

"Because I'm the boss and I don't want to talk to him."

"But—"

"Good-bye, Zander."

Chapter Twelve

Bo found Topher sitting at his desk around three in the afternoon, illuminated only by a single lamp on the corner of his desk. *Funny thing about narcs, you can always find them in the dark.*

"Detective Alexander," he breathed, sounding mildly irritated at her very presence. "How can I help you?"

"I need to know exactly why it is that you're so adamant that the Voleurs are manufacturing drugs on the island. And I need to know why you guys in narcotics aren't trying to take it down right now instead of just keeping tabs and funneling information to us."

He seemed momentarily taken aback. "Excuse me?"

Bo decided the toddler treatment was warranted. "Why. Are. You. Adamant. About. Manufacturing? And why aren't y'all going after it? Why are you sending us? I was cool with it at first because you told me your probis couldn't get good intel, but you've been pushing this story for a while now and I've got no return on my investment. So, what the fuck is going on?"

Something in her tone must have registered with him, because for the first time, he didn't pull his usual *I am man hear me roar* bullshit. If anything, he looked almost unsure of himself. He took a deep breath and let it out loudly. Judging by the look on his face, she could only assume he was calculating the risk of letting someone not exactly on his team in on the secrets of the undercover workers. They might have both been on the blue line, but even then cops were notoriously secretive when it came to the people they worked with directly versus the people they shared a badge with.

"I already told you, my boys are probis. Yeah sure, some of them are ready and willing to do whatever it takes to get their patches and go deep undercover, but none of them have yet. They work security, they move boxes, they fetch the fucking paper. None of us could get deep enough to actually get anything solid enough to move on. That's why I decided it would be good to work together. My boys are certain, but nothing they've told me can be corroborated as anything other than hearsay. We needed you to go in guns blazing and shake shit up. Get you in place to get under Cass's skin and keep their eyes on you instead of on my probis. I mean, one of my guys said she was messing around with one of her crew, letting him get her off but she wouldn't return the favor. But I figure you still had a chance."

"So what you're saying is you fucking used me and my team without any certainty that what we were chasing was real?"

"No. I'm saying I used you to get evidence I couldn't, because I already knew what I'm saying was real." His smile was smug. "You were bait, a diversion. You played your part."

"So why drugs? Why not human trafficking and the like?"

His bright blue eyes grew dark and his face took on a look Bo couldn't decipher. "They're doing something, and they're doing something big. Maybe it includes shit like that, I don't know. My guys are still on the inside and maybe they'll get lucky and overhear something, or move up a rank. But you'll have to do some work too."

As Bo walked away, she could feel her fury rising but couldn't pinpoint exactly why she was so mad. So what if Cass lied? She was a criminal, and that's what criminals did. But she could picture Cass's expression, the way her eyes had narrowed and how irritated she'd been at the thought of the sex trafficking. It didn't fit. And Topher... Bo couldn't shake the feeling he was holding out, that he knew more than he was saying. But why would he? They wanted the same end game, right? Was it just that he wanted credit if they managed to bring the whole damn thing crashing down? Although she wouldn't put it past him, that didn't feel quite right either.

She pulled her phone out as soon as she was in the harsh fluorescent light illuminating the rest of the department and dialed Gerald Guthrie's number. When he answered, she spoke without preamble. "Gerald, are you off yet?"

"No, ma'am, how can I help you?"

"There's a prostitute hanging around East End somewhere named Grace. Grace Njikeu. I need you to pick her up for me."

"You need me to pick up a random prostitute named Grace? Okay."

She barely resisted the urge to put her hand to her forehead. "She's African. Very…" She paused, searching for exactly the right word to describe the young woman, "Regal. You'll know her, I promise. She's got a French accent. If you can find a tall, slender Black woman named Tiffany near the old abandoned grocery store, she can tell you where to find Grace. If you can't find her then let me know because she might not be safe."

"Got it, Zander. Is there any reason you need this particular woman?"

"Yes, actually, but I don't want to say too much over the phone. I want you to bring her to the station so you and I can talk to her."

"Yes, ma'am. Anything else?"

"Yes. Bring some donuts because I promise you, she probably hasn't eaten and we're going to disrupt her dinner hour."

She waited patiently, and just under an hour later, Gerald paged her to the interrogation room. If she didn't know better, she would think Grace's eyes lit up when she saw Bo.

"Hey there, Grace. How have you been since we last spoke?"

Grace finished the glazed donut she was working on before answering. "I have been well, Detective. I hope you can say the same?"

Bo smiled but shook her head. "Unfortunately, no, Grace, I can't. You see, I'm in the middle of what could be a massive investigation, and I've got a whole bunch of tiny pieces that really don't fit together at all, including you. That makes for a very messy situation and I was hoping maybe you could clean it up a little for me."

Grace only stared at her. When she said nothing, Bo continued. "You said there was a Voleur who was working with the Demons when you came here, right?" Grace nodded. "Was there ever *another* Voleur that dealt with you? A woman with long blond hair?"

Grace frowned hard at this. "No, there has never been a woman. Only the man with the beady eyes."

"He had beady eyes?"

"Yes. And when I arrived the Demons did not like him, but they do now."

Gerald perked up. "You saw him again? What did he look like?"

Grace shook her head. "No, only his eyes through the mask. He kept his face hidden. I do not know why. The Demons did not hide, but they had no reason to. They are smart enough to know I would not tell you their names and I am smart enough to make that statement true."

"Can you give me any descriptive information at all? Please, Grace. Anything."

"*Non.* As I have told you before they are all unremarkable. Some with dark skin, some with white, all with dark hair. They wore long sleeves, so I didn't see any tattoos."

Bo sighed. "That's probably because they didn't want anyone easily identifiable working with anyone who could be picked up by the police. Okay. How did you get here, Grace? Was it on a big boat? Did you have a room?" Bo knew these were questions she should have already asked, but her head had still been reeling from the drugs during their last meeting and she hadn't been thinking clearly.

This time, she nodded. "Yes, I had a room. It was a very nice boat. The man who took me off the boat, he has been in my hotel room sometimes. He says that the boss is pleased and will arrange a bigger boat for more girls next time. How I wished I could have hit him then."

"And have you met the boss?"

Grace once again shook her head. "No, but I have heard his voice when one of the men was speaking to him on the phone. He said his Demons were doing a very good job. His voice was…what is the word? Rough. He did not give his name."

Bo frowned and she and Guthrie looked at each other before looking back at Grace. "Grace, you said the boss mentioned 'his' Demons. Did he ever say anything about the Voleur?" Guthrie asked.

"No, the Voleur, he is alone. I do not know anyone else."

Only one. Bo felt a puzzle piece about to slide into place. "Grace, has the Voleur ever given you any drugs?"

If looks could kill, Bo was fairly certain she would be dead from the glare Grace gave her. "How dare you! I may be forced to sell my body, but I will never *sully* my body as a mongrel!"

Bo held up her hands in defense. "I'm sorry, that came out wrong. What I meant to say was have they ever given you drugs to give to someone else? Have you ever been asked to transport drugs for them?"

"The way you phrase your questions is very important. You would do well to remember that should we ever need to speak again, Detective Alexander. Do not mistake me for a peasant simply because I wished to make a better life for myself than what was offered in my village."

"I'm sorry, Miss Njikeu. I'm sorry. But have they ever made you transport drugs for them?"

"No. I have seen the drugs you speak of, but I was never asked to do anything with them. They came from the boat just like I did, and they were moved somewhere else."

"You're sure they came from the same boat as you? They weren't put on the boat after you got off?"

Finally, Grace sighed, an irritated sound. "Detective, is there a reason you keep questioning my answers? The boat stopped once before we got off, somewhere on the water. There were men on another boat in the water and they gave the Demons the drugs. We came to this island and they went somewhere else."

"They never had you give anything to anyone, other than sex?"

She frowned and bit her lip and then looked up again. "Money."

"Money?"

She nodded. "Yes. One time the Voleur, he took me and a group of other women to a place with loud music and we were to give money to the Demons."

"Money. Okay. Did this happen a lot? Do you know what place it was with loud music?"

"No, only that there were more Voleurs there. We were handed envelopes of money told to take it to the various men. It didn't matter who. I don't know why they couldn't just hand it over themselves." She shrugged. "It wasn't my place to ask. And before you ask again, no, I couldn't tell you anything about the men there. I kept my eyes down and did what I had to."

"Do you know if the place with loud music was on the island?"

Grace shook her head. "I do not think so. I could barely see out of the windows, but I am certain we went over a bridge."

"Did you see any names?"

"No, I am sorry. We were only there for a short time before we were taken back to a different place to sleep."

"Okay. Thank you, Grace. If there's anything at all that comes up, give me a call, okay? Anything that you think would help. Detective Guthrie is going to bring you home now."

"Yes, okay."

They left and Bo scratched the back of her head as the kernel of an idea started forming. She had all the pieces, she thought, she just needed to figure out how they fit together. As she contemplated, a plan began forming and though she wasn't sure it was going to work, she knew she was going to need Cass Halliburton's help, and that was going to require telling her what she had learned today.

After making the rounds and talking to all of the other Friday night regulars at the Pearl Bar, Cass sat on the back couch and closed her eyes. To say the least, it had been an extremely stressful week. Her father was going absolutely bat shit over the fact that the Coast Guard had recently begun inspecting his crates and he seemed to think it was her fault. Because she controlled the fucking Coast Guard. *Right.* At the moment, she was simply content to enjoy the potent buzz brought on by all the free drinks that had been given to her. Perks of the East Texas accent, she thought to herself.

It was almost like there was a shift in the energy, and Cass could feel her. When the couch dipped beside her, she didn't have to open her eyes to see who it was. When a subtle cologne, dark and spicy, drifted across, she had to bite her lip to keep from moaning out loud. She had been dreaming about that cologne. And the body it covered. Not that she would ever admit that to anyone.

"Miss Halliburton, I believe you and I need to have another conversation."

Cass smiled and leaned in slightly without opening her eyes. "Detective, if I didn't know any better, I'd think you were stalking me."

"Maybe you don't know any better."

The words were spoken in a low, quiet voice, and Cass had to lean in close to hear them. She inhaled sharply when her breast brushed against Bo's arm. She was buzzed, she was pissed at her father, and suddenly, she did not give one single damn about minding the rules. *Fuck it.*

She pressed against Bo's side and kissed down her neck, filling her senses with the smell and taste of her. *So good...* She was about to move to straddle Bo's lap when a firm grip stopped her, forcing her eyes open.

"Miss Halliburton, we need to talk."

Cass took the time to study the detective's face. Even through the alcohol induced haze, there was a cold fury burning there that made Cass's breath stop. She was angry, and for the life of her, Cass couldn't figure out why. To her knowledge, the Voleurs hadn't been causing havoc around town, and she certainly hadn't been messing with the detective, much as she might have wanted to.

"Is this because I broke into your house again? Wait, no, you let me in, so that's not it." Bo's expression remained the same. Her face was a glacier, cold and unmoving, but her eyes were angry. *So very angry.* The air around her felt like barely controlled chaos, and in that moment, Cass desperately wanted that control to break. "What's wrong, Detective?"

"I don't appreciate being lied to, Miss Halliburton. I understand it's an occupational hazard, but for once in your life you seemed to be telling the truth and I believed you. And if you *are* telling the truth, then it's even worse because that means that you're completely fucking clueless about what's going on in your own organization."

Cass shook her head and tried to clear her thoughts, but Bo still wasn't making any sense. "Try that…one more time."

"I'm coming for you. I'm coming for you and every other Voleur on my island. I'm going to bring you down so far that not even Satan himself—"

Cass slapped her hand over Bo's mouth. "Shut up and stop talking. You're not making any sense, and you're ruining my buzz talking about church in the middle of a bar. Listen, you know the 13-Mile Road beach access?"

Bo's eyebrows furrowed, and she glanced down at Cass's hand, but she nodded just the same.

"This bar closes at two. It's currently one. I am going to use that hour to sober up and then I am going to drive back to the island, and you are going to meet me at the 13-Mile Road beach access point and we are going to continue this discussion when I'm sober. Understand?"

Bo glared at her and yanked her head away. "Yeah."

"Okay. Good. Now unless you plan on doing something very naughty to me right now, please leave me alone." She settled back into the couch and tried not to acknowledge the fact that she missed the warm body beside her as soon as it left.

Bo pulled into the parking lot and backed in beside the now familiar black Harley Roadster, the telltale vest lying over the seat, marking the bike as property of a Voleur. She tried for what seemed like the umpteenth time to figure out why she was listening to Cass Halliburton instead of forcing this meeting to go her own way, but she couldn't come up with a reason. Not a good reason, anyway. Not a reason that didn't involve the smell of subtle perfume and vanilla.

It would be a good thing, she reasoned with herself, if Cass was telling the truth. It would mean that young girls weren't being shuffled through her city and being used for nefarious purposes. *At least not that she knows of.* Her rational mind argued that there was no way Grace was lying with as involved of a story as she gave. Somehow, someway, there was at least one Voleur that was trying to set up a human trafficking ring in Galveston. The only question was whether or not Cass was aware of it, or if she was, as she intimated, completely unaware and unsupportive. Bo sincerely hoped that was the case because it was the one detail her entire plan rode on. She made a decision and got out of her truck, then walked down the wooden access ramp to the water.

She saw Cass before Cass saw her and Bo took the time to study her. She was standing in a pose that radiated complete ease with her back to the entrance of the beach. Bo could only assume one of two things: either this was a trap, or Cass was absolutely, one hundred percent comfortable with this particular spot. Either scenario was likely, and Bo scanned her surroundings as she slowly approached. This late—or early—at night, there was no one else around, and the houses that lined the sand had all their lights out. Even if they didn't, they were far enough back that two people on the beach wouldn't be seen very well unless there were binoculars involved. Again, Bo scanned for a glint in the windows just to make sure.

As she drew closer, she could tell that where she first thought Cass's arms were simply at her side, her hands were actually in the pockets of her shorts, and she seemed lost in the ebb and flow of the nighttime tide. The moon reflected brightly off the waves, and Bo had to admit it was a beautiful sight. Any other time and she might have been tempted to stand and watch beside Cass, but this wasn't any other time.

She cleared her throat softly as she finally stepped beside Cass. "I didn't think Voleurs were allowed to leave their patches lying around like that, Miss Halliburton."

Cass turned to look at Bo and smiled gently. "When you're as high ranking as I am, you can pretty much do whatever the hell you want. If you don't care about the consequences."

"And do you?"

The smile faltered. "I won't be here long enough for someone to see it. Hello, by the way. How are you, Detective?"

"I'm wondering why I'm here."

Cass kept her smile as she turned, and Bo sighed as she began walking down the beach. When Bo caught up, she said again, "Miss Halliburton, please. Why am I here?"

"Well, I would assume you're here because I asked you to be."

"And why would you do that?"

Cass gestured to the expanse of sand in front of them. "Because, Detective. You obviously had something important to talk to me about, and this beach is one of the few places on this island I have found where, for the most part, I can be completely alone, free from prying eyes and people following me."

"Do you usually have a problem with that?" The answer was obvious, but Bo still asked.

Cass laughed harshly. "Only the entirety of the Galveston Voleurs, GPD, and now the Demons."

"And I'm going to take a wild guess that you definitely have a problem with GPD watching you, right?"

Cass stopped so suddenly that Bo almost ran into her, but she managed to stop just in time. "Only when they interfere with my business."

"Oh, your drug dealing business?"

"Can't we just be friends?"

Cass laughed and shook her head as she resumed her stroll, but when a crunch sounded under Bo's foot, Bo pointed down without looking. "Not if that had a live animal in it." She waited until the look of consternation passed and realization of a joke dawned on Cass's face before she continued. "I'm not going to deny that you have a very engaging personality when you want to, Miss Halliburton, and I do enjoy talking to you when you're not trying to mess with my head. However, you're still a criminal and I'm still a cop, and my job is not to be friends with you. I do, however, have very important business to talk about with you."

Cass stopped again and tilted her head. She looked Bo up and down. "Do I mess with your head often, Detective?" she said, obviously not inclined to talk business.

Bo remembered the feel of Cass's hand, squeezing between her legs, and the image hit home. Hard. She worked to control her breathing. "Yes. You do."

A knowing smile spread over Cass's face. "Well, maybe I should work on that."

"Miss Halliburton, are you going to tell me why you asked me to come out here? Other than it's private? If you're not going to let me tell you what I have to say, then I'm not sure why I'm here."

Cass closed the distance between them and slowly, as if waiting for Bo to rebuke her, pressed the length of her body against Bo's. "Did you ever think, Detective, that maybe I just wanted to get you somewhere private? Somewhere I could have you all to myself?" When she spoke into Bo's ear, her voice was an octave lower than usual.

She ran her hand through the back of Bo's hair as she spoke, and Bo closed her eyes, trying her best not to think about what Cass would do if Bo let her. "Miss Halliburton, while I sincerely appreciate the boost to my ego, your advances aren't going to work. I don't make it a habit to be affected by straight women." *You are such a fucking liar.*

Cass seemed genuinely confused and laughed as she continued to massage the back of Bo's neck. "Detective, just in case it's escaped your notice, I am anything but straight. I took Sav home, remember?"

What she remembered was making it harder and harder to ignore the burning in her belly, and Cass's expression said she could tell. Bo gripped her shoulders and pushed her back, giving herself space she should *not* have needed. She was here for the truth, and whether or not that came from the woman in front of her remained to be seen.

"Regardless of whether you are or are not straight, and even if you weren't a drug dealer, I refuse to associate with someone who treats women as nothing but objects to be spread around for money."

Cass's eyes went hard, and if Bo didn't know any better, she'd say Cass barely held back a snarl.

"That's right. You said you don't believe me about the human trafficking thing. First off, where the hell did that even come from? Last I knew, that wasn't even on the table in the investigation."

"And you know this how?"

"None of your business. Answer my question, Detective. What the hell makes you think I'm suddenly breaking into the skin business?"

"I have my sources."

"Who? I want to know who."

They'd begun mentally circling each other again, neither willing to take a step back, but neither wanting to take a step forward, either. Bo was silent as she calculated the risks of revealing what was told to her. If what Topher told her was true, she risked outing an inside informant and that could mean death for her fellow officer. If what he said wasn't true, though…

And for no reason she could explain, Bo believed her.

"In a roundabout way, I was told a story. There was a party during which you and a member of your crew decided to go in a back room and get busy. You allowed him to pleasure you, but refused to return the favor, citing the fact that you had something better coming that would get him off. At first, we assumed it was drugs because we already know the Voleurs are heavy in the drug trade. Add to that the fact that I've had a young woman, who will remain nameless, tell me that a Voleur is working with the Demons to bring her and other women from her village into the city through the port. That's two very different sources telling me the exact same story, Miss Halliburton, so you'll forgive me if I'm skeptical."

If it were possible for eyes to glow red, Cass's would have, and Bo fought the urge to lean back. "Detective, I'm going to tell you this one time and one time only, so listen good because I have a feeling what I'm about to say will set the precedent for any of our future conversations. I have never willingly slept with a man, nor will I *ever* willingly sleep with a man. I am a lesbian. I thoroughly enjoy the female body and I have thoroughly enjoyed many a female body and will continue to do so for as long as I am able." She took a deep breath.

"That having been said, every woman I have ever slept with has been one hundred and ten percent willing to do what I wanted, and had there been even a hint of a question I would have stopped. I told you before, I may not be innocent, and I may not be on your side of right and wrong, but damn it, I am *not* evil. Wherever you heard this bullshit story from, they were lying."

She took a breath and Bo nodded once to let her know she still had her attention. "The girl. Who is she?"

Bo shook her head, refusing to be the reason a young girl's life was put in danger.

"Detective, please."

Damn it, if she didn't look sincere. Bo sighed. "Miss Halliburton, I can't. Even if I did believe you, I can't be the one who gets her killed."

"What makes you think I have anything to do with her, Detective? I think I've been crystal clear that I do not and will not participate in that kind of activity."

"She mentioned specifically that there was a Voleur that met the Demons when they docked. Very *specifically* a Voleur, although according to her, she's only ever seen the one, not the crew. Even if you're not a participant you expect me to believe you'll protect someone you don't know over the club you've pledged your life and loyalty to?"

Cass was so still Bo didn't think she was breathing anymore. There was obviously a lot going through her mind.

"I have absolutely no part in that, but make no mistake, I will find out who does, and they will pay heavily." She spoke with lethal authority in her voice.

Bo let out a deep breath. "I don't know why but I believe you."

"Maybe because I'm telling the truth." She smiled again, but this time it didn't reach her eyes. In fact, she looked almost sad.

"I believe you. But that doesn't change the fact that you and the rest of the Voleurs are doing something here on the island that is very illegal. This just gives me one more thing to investigate you for, so unless you can find some way to help me out, you're still a massive part of this case."

The sad smile widened, and Cass's eyes sparkled again as she stepped closer, almost touching Bo but not quite, and said, "Oh, yeah?"

"Oh, yeah."

Cass licked her lips and placed her hands gently on Bo's chest as she stood on her toes and pressed fully against her. "Good luck then, Detective," she whispered.

Bo's breath caught in her throat, and Cass didn't have to tell her it was obvious. This time, however, there was no malice in her expression. Only a matching heat that she didn't bother hiding before she turned and walked away.

Chapter Thirteen

The weather had been absolutely amazing for the last couple of nights, so Cass had been making it a habit to walk a few miles on the beach every night to clear her head and simply breathe in the salt air. The feeling of the sand between her toes was grounding and comforting, and at two in the morning, she could pretend like she was completely alone in the world. No one but her, the fish, and the seagulls. Also, those tiny little birds that ran really quick on the sand, but she didn't know what they were called.

She was just contemplating going for a nighttime swim when the screeching of her phone broke the pristine illusion, and Cass cursed herself silently for jumping. She answered without looking. "This is Cass."

"Cassidy. There's a problem at the warehouse. See that it gets fixed tonight."

He hung up before she could say anything, and she counted to ten before deciding that throwing her phone in the Gulf of Mexico probably wasn't the best solution. She debated taking her roadster, but then realized it would piss her father off even more if she took a few hours to get there, so she walked instead. She pulled a pair of boots out of her saddle bags and then made her way up the ramp to the parking lot to start her trek. She would be there before the sun was up. That meant it would be taken care of *tonight*, technically. Since someone had obviously decided to jump her in the chain of command and report directly to her father, she began to think there might be more than just rumors behind everything Detective Alexander had told her.

She had made it roughly halfway to her destination when she felt the first drop of moisture on her nose. She glanced up, noticing a seagull flying away from her general direction. "I swear to God if you just—" Her sentence was cut short by another drop, this one directly in her eye. She groaned in frustration, immediately regretting her decision to take a stroll. She made it only ten minutes further before the heavens let loose and soaked her completely through.

She might have enjoyed walking every night, but going in the rain to go take care of a business she wasn't even sure she wanted to be running was not her idea of a good time. She was seriously considering pulling out her phone when a large truck with tinted windows pulled up beside her and slowed to a stop. She slowly reached behind her back as the window began rolling down.

"I sure do hope you have a permit for whatever it is you're about to pull out of your pants." Detective Alexander grinned at her, illuminated in the blue lights of her dashboard. "Actually, scratch that. Go ahead and pull it out because if you don't have a permit, that's a felony and definitely something I won't mind arresting you for."

Cass rolled her eyes and reached for her wallet instead, holding it up. "All the licenses I need are right here, Detective. You want me to pull them out and show you?"

Bo shook her head. "No, I want you to get in."

Cass frowned. "You've got to be kidding me. I'm not getting in your truck."

"Miss Halliburton, it's pouring down rain and you're walking. I know for a fact you don't live in any of the houses in this area and even if you did, it's still too far to walk in the rain."

"Why are you doing this?"

A small smile touched the detective's lips as she said, "It's the south, Miss Halliburton. Even cops have a code. Besides," her voice perked up, "I have a gorgeous girl in here who is very excited to see you." Chubby chose that moment to pop her head up in the window, and Cass laughed as she stepped up on the running board to scratch her head. "Come on, get in. I promise to give you a one-time pass to not ask questions about wherever it is that I'm taking you. Within reason."

Cass tilted her head as Chubby began systematically cleaning her from one ear to the other. "What's within reason?"

"If there's a dead body, I might have to ask questions."

Cass bit back a smile as she opened the door and allowed Bo to shove Chubby to the back seat before she slid in, moaning gratefully at the heat that immediately enveloped her. "Might?"

Bo cocked her head in confusion as she pushed the shifter into gear to take off. "I beg your pardon?"

"You said if there's a dead body you *might* have to ask questions."

Bo laughed. "If there's a dead body, I most certainly will ask questions."

"I guess I'll have to make sure all my skeletons are in the closet then, won't I?"

Bo gave her a sidelong glance but didn't say anything about her skeletons. Instead, she simply asked, "Where am I taking you?"

"Not home." When Bo gave her a pointed stare, she gave an address close enough to the warehouse that she could comfortably walk without giving away the exact location. They sat in silence for a few minutes before Cass noticed the auxiliary cord hanging from the aftermarket radio in front of her. She reached for it and held it up with her phone. "Do you mind if I put on some music? I'm not a fan of quiet road trips."

The corners of Bo's mouth turned up as she shook her head. Cass plugged the cord into her phone and scrolled through her music before landing on "Anywhere but Here" by Safetysuit. When the song started, Bo's eyebrows rose, and she simply nodded in time to the music. Cass closed her eyes and leaned her head back against the worn leather seat, letting the music relax her.

The first verse and chorus came on without interruption, but as the second verse started, Cass picked up a slight change in the sound. She focused, trying to pinpoint what exactly was different, and then her eyes shot open and she looked over at Bo. The detective was singing softly, her voice in perfect harmony with one of Cass's favorite songs.

Cass couldn't help but watch her as she sang. Not only did she know every word of a song by a band most people probably didn't even know existed, but she had the voice of an angel. When the second chorus sounded, Bo's voice got a little louder and Cass felt her body grow warmer as she watched Bo singing unashamedly.

Cass watched her lips moving and remembered just what those lips felt like on her neck. So hot. So very soft. She wondered what they would feel like all over her body. How they would taste. What they would feel like on her own lips, kissing her, devouring her with the passion she knew very well that the detective was capable of.

She leaned in closer. She had to know what it felt like. She didn't think she could manage if she didn't. She moved farther to kiss Bo, only to accidentally change the song when she bumped the phone with her elbow. The change in Bo's manner was instant and she slammed her hand down on the volume knob, turning the music off completely.

"Hey," Cass said, more embarrassed at herself for what she had been about to do than anything, "that was a good song!" She was thankful that the darkness hid the blush she could feel rising up her cheeks.

"Yes," Bo said quietly, "it was a good song."

"So then why did you turn it off? Evanescence rocks."

"Because it was my sister's favorite song."

The use of past tense didn't escape Cass's notice. "Your sister? I wasn't aware you had a sister."

"You are not required to know every detail of my life, Miss Halliburton." Bo's tone made it clear the issue wasn't up for discussion.

Cass wracked her brain trying to figure out what she had done to piss her off. "You said...it *was* her favorite song." She had a sinking feeling in the pit of her stomach.

Bo was completely silent for a very long while. Cass was about to simply turn back to face the front of the truck when she finally said, "Her name was Kelly. She was five years younger than me."

Fuck. "Was. Again. You use the past tense when you talk about her."

"She was a really, really good kid. She got along with everyone, she was nice to everyone, she never did anything to hurt anyone. Her only vice was that she liked to party. Hard." Bo's face was a flurry of emotions as she faced down her own inner demons. "It was her seventeenth birthday. She was set to graduate in three months with honors and she wanted one last wild night before she buckled down for college. She had a full ride to A&M for their veterinary program. Damn, that kid loved horses. She would have been twenty-seven this year."

Cass was uncomfortable in the face of Bo's vulnerability, and she gently laid her hand on Bo's arm. Chubby seemed to notice the change in the atmosphere as she jumped into the front seat and lay on top of Cass, her nose just grazing Bo.

"May I ask what happened?" A tortured look crossed Bo's face, and suddenly Cass didn't want to know. Didn't want to hear it. "Never mind, I—"

"I was heavy into drugs at the time. I did a lot of X, and whenever she wanted to have fun, I could always get her some coke. I figured it was her last night of fun so why not make it a good night, right? We had been doing this for a few years, so what could go wrong?"

Cass's heart broke at the crack in Bo's voice, and she looked away, not wanting to see the tears she could hear.

"I don't think we ever actually planned on doing everything ourselves, but her friends never showed up, and we were too high to know better."

Oh, please, God no... Cass knew there were horror stories of highs gone wrong because of the drugs she sold, but she'd never had to come face to face with one like she was now. Never had to see the heartbreak her business caused. She could feel the grip of the patch on her back beginning to loosen.

"I woke up with a tube down my throat and no little sister. I had been in a medically induced coma for a week. I didn't leave the hospital in time to make her funeral, so I never got to say good-bye.

You wanted to know how I know Tiffany? That's how. She was Kelly's girlfriend. The first time we slept together was the one-year anniversary of her death. It was the only way either of us could find any semblance of peace for a very long time. Tiff ended up on the streets because she fell even deeper into the drug scene. I'm pretty sure she thought she could kill herself and be with Kelly again. I chose to go into law enforcement because I figured if I could stop even one kid from overdosing maybe it would ease my guilt. Fortunately, they didn't arrest me, so there was no drug conviction on my record. It gave me the choice and I took it."

Cass squeezed Bo's arm. "You can't think that was your fault."

"Whose fault is it? I'm the one who got the drugs, I'm the one who gave them to her. I was the adult. She was just a fucking kid, and I let her die." Bo pulled the truck over. "You want to know why I won't leave you alone? That's why. That's why I want the drugs out of my city and off my island. This is your stop, Cass."

Cass couldn't get out of the truck fast enough. She felt dirty. She felt sick. For the first time in her life, she felt like a bad person. She turned around. "Tomorrow. Meet me at the same place on the beach at three a.m. Can you do that?"

Bo nodded once and Cass slammed the door, waiting for her to drive away before she turned and dry heaved. Nothing came up, but that didn't make her feel any better. She went over everything Bo had told her. Her drug history alone was probably enough to get her fired, because something like that most certainly hadn't made it into her file. At best, it was covered up and at worst, it was completely omitted. It was enough to make any defense attorney worth their salt come in their pants over any future drug charges. They'd simply say she was biased because of her past. Add that to the fact that she'd obviously had an ongoing affair with Tiffany, a prostitute, and there was absolutely no way Bo would keep her badge if Cass turned her in.

All of that, and the only thing she could think about was the way Bo's voice sounded when she finally broke. All she felt was an intense sorrow, and with it came the full realization she'd been trying to push away for a long while now...

She didn't want to be a Voleur anymore.

Her entire adult life, the Voleurs had brought her nothing but sorrow and pain, and it was becoming increasingly obvious to her that they did the same for everyone around them. For years, she convinced herself that the illusion of power she held was enough, that being the second most powerful person in the baddest motherfucking biker club in the world was enough. It wasn't. Her body had been used and abused, her products brought death and chaos, and now her job was keeping her apart from a woman her heart was beating hard for. Not to mention it was clear her power was just that: an illusion. Someone was obviously running game behind her back and whether or not her father knew, she had no doubt he would support it if it brought him more money. It wasn't worth it anymore, but getting out wasn't going to be easy, or quick. She'd have to be careful and plan her exit, if she could find one that didn't include her dying. For now, she'd play the game at hand, but when it was done, she'd be gone.

Bo got to the beach first this time and watched Cass approach, backlit from the light of one of the streetlamps. She was a shadow in the darkness, but that did nothing to mask the sensuous way her hips swayed as she walked closer, or the soft swell of her breasts in a loose button-up when she was close enough for Bo to see her clothes. Bo couldn't help but notice how the soft blue of the shirt made her eyes pop, even in the low light.

"Detective, thank you for coming. Let's take a walk, shall we?"

Bo followed blindly away from the light, simply trusting at this point that she was safe. Cass led her farther into the shadows of the dunes before sitting in the sand and leaning against a large piece of driftwood, looking up at Bo expectantly. She obeyed and they sat in comfortable silence for a while as Cass drew figures in the sand with her surprisingly bare feet.

"I wanted to tell you I was sorry about your sister. I *am* sorry about your sister. I've been there and…it's not a good feeling. Losing someone that close to you, I mean. It hurts for a very long time."

"You couldn't have told me all of that while you were in my truck?"

Cass shook her head. "You know just as well as I do that you wanted me out of that truck as badly as I wanted to be out of it. It wasn't the right time for it. But I couldn't let it go without giving you my condolences. Besides, I had things I had to take care of for my father and I was already running late. If I had stayed and talked to you, I probably wouldn't have been able to concentrate."

Bo grinned. "Why, Miss Halliburton, don't tell me you find me distracting."

The ghost of a smile touched Cass's face and she shook her head just slightly. "Your story certainly was, if nothing else. You called me 'Cass' last night."

Bo frowned and looked down in embarrassment. She knew that Cass couldn't see the red in her cheeks, but she knew it was there and she tried her best to hide it. "Yes, I'm sorry that…that was unprofessional."

"I didn't mind. I liked it."

She went back to drawing in the sand, and Bo let her. She knew, somehow, that in this moment if she pushed, Cass would revert back to her usual, flippant, devil-may-care self. The current change was a breath of fresh air.

"I didn't always want to do this, you know. When I was younger, I used to think I would grow up and be a doctor or something. Sometimes I wonder about what would happen if I just quit and walked away. Decided to start over and do something completely different. I doubt my father would ever let that happen, though."

"He forces you to work for him?"

"Not forces, exactly. Everything I'm doing is by choice, for the most part, but sometimes I feel like the choice is more of an illusion than anything else. I'm almost positive that if I chose to leave, I wouldn't stay alive for very long. Not if I couldn't find a good place to hide. I know too much now. I have to say, though," she said, throwing a glance at Bo, "the straight and narrow does seem to have its perks sometimes."

Bo was content to sit and let her talk, so she simply stretched out and relaxed against the driftwood.

"I do wish you would lay off, though. Don't get me wrong, I don't mind having you around and if you repeat that I'll deny it, but you make it really hard to work. Especially considering the fact that you've told me that I have to figure out who's running a shadow operation out of my own damn organization. Add to that the issue that if I slip up, if I get caught doing something wrong, I'm dead. No questions asked. It makes it a little hard to breathe."

The surreal nature of their conversation wasn't lost on her, but she went with it. "That's one of those perks of the straight and narrow, Miss Halliburton. I don't have to lay off just because I make you uncomfortable or because I could mess up your operation. Though I would be upset if something were to happen to you. And if you repeat *that* I'll deny it."

Cass smiled. "You call it not laying off, I call it legal stalking."

Bo could tell she meant it as a joke, but there was now a slight edge to her voice that hadn't been there before. "The legality of what I'm doing has never been in question, Miss Halliburton. You, however, seem to completely revel in the illegitimate status of what you've got going on."

Cass shot up and stared at Bo, a look of utter disbelief plastered on her face. "Are you fucking kidding me? *Revel?* I've literally got pictures of you and Tiffany getting it on in a back alley. Granted, you might not have been fucking her that time, but I know that you have and don't even get me started on whether or not that even counted as consensual. Not to mention the fact that I've seen you having sex with someone on a very public dance floor. There's no telling what kind of shit you've done I haven't seen. So, I may *revel* in doing illegal shit, but you fucking get off on it."

Bo stood as well and pointed at Cass. "Having sex in no way, shape, or form compares to dealing drugs and whatever else it is that you're doing here. Don't try to say it does."

"Oh." Cass threw her hands in the air. "So you're saying that because what I do is inherently worse, that makes me the bad guy but you're okay because you're not the bad guy?"

"You're a criminal! I'm a cop! Your shit kills people! Yes, that makes you the bad guy!"

Cass growled in frustration and started pacing furiously. "Why do you keep saying that? You think because you've got some stupid fucking…sixty-dollar hunk of metal on your belt that that suddenly makes everything you do okay? If anything, *you're* the one fucking using women!"

"You're a dope dealer!"

"Oh, and I'm sure to you that says everything about me, right?" Cass laughed harshly. "All you want to fucking see is what I do to survive. You refuse to see anything else. I'm no different than your average street corner psychiatrist prescribing Xanax and Vicodin and God only knows what else to rich housewives who have nothing else to do to occupy their time than get high on pain killers and downers. Oh wait." She held up a finger. "He has a degree and took an oath, so that makes it okay. Prescription pain meds kill more people than any drug dealing I may have had a hand in, and that pharmacist isn't going to get murdered if he says no. But if one of his customers—because that's what they are, customers, not patients—dies of an overdose, he can hide behind that piece of paper on his wall and lament about how he always knew they were troubled and they must have just been ready to end it all and he helped all he could. But I sell something to a middleman and I'm the bad guy. My *customer's* customer dies and somehow, I'm the one at fault. One of your buddies kills someone or beats the shit out of them, they can just hide behind the 'we all go home' mantra and it makes it all okay? That's bullshit!"

"We are just trying to go home." Bo took the bait, Cass's logic infuriating. "Why can't you people see that? We don't want to kill anyone!"

"Are you very fucking sure about that?" They were standing toe to toe, and Cass took a deep breath to calm herself and ran her hand through her hair, looking into the distance. "Did you ever think for even a single moment that we do what we do so that we can go home, too? That I do what I do to go home? You think everyone who's ever been on the wrong side of the law woke up and decided to be a criminal? No. It was a decision made in a moment when there didn't seem to be any other choice. For me that choice was be a damn good criminal or risk being killed. Every day since I've made that choice I've had to make the same damn choice because I don't have another way out. You think that badge makes you different, but it doesn't. All it does is put you in some sort of parallel universe where the same things are happening to the same people for the same reason, but it looks different because you put a uniform on it. The fact of the matter is, it doesn't matter whether or not I enjoy what I do because you've already painted me as the villain."

Bo opened her mouth, but Cass held up her hand. "Let me paint you a picture. There's a new guy that just got the crap beat out of him by someone on the opposite side of the thin blue line. He decides that he can't be seen as someone who can't be taken seriously so the next time he gets in a fight, he beats the shit out of the guy. Puts him in the hospital, even. In the interview, when they asked him why he felt the need for such overkill, he says he was just trying to survive. Sound familiar?"

"It sounds like exactly what happened when your boy Stephenson was arrested for putting one of my officers in a coma."

Cass nodded. "It was also exactly what happened when your rookie officer put one of my very good friends six feet under a few years back. My friend was deaf and didn't understand the officer's orders to stop walking. 'I was just trying to survive. He kept moving so I kept shooting' is exactly what he said. It doesn't sound so different when you take the uniform off, does it? I'm not saying I enjoy what I do, even if I am good at it. But I am saying that you can't judge someone just because they sin differently than you." She looked like she was going to walk away, but then she sighed and put her hands on her hips. "We're not manufacturing drugs. I can't tell you what we are doing because I could get killed for it, and I'm sorry but you're not worth my life. I know what you're being told, though, and it's wrong. I wouldn't even be telling you, but like I said, I know what it's like to lose someone that close to you. You're barking up the wrong tree with that one." She bit her lip in an uncharacteristic show of vulnerability, and then she gently touched Bo's cheek.

"We're not that different, Bo. I really do wish you could see that." She started leaving, but before she got out of earshot, she yelled over her shoulder, "Stop harassing me, Detective. I would really hate to have to make a show of things just to save my own ass."

Long after Cass had left, Bo stood rooted to the spot, staring at the ebb and flow of the dark water of the Gulf. There were so many opinions on the water, it was ridiculous. Some people wouldn't swim in it because of horror stories of sharks and bacteria, and yet other people swam in it daily with absolutely no problem. To her, the water was something to be feared. To Nikki, it was something to be enjoyed. Try as she might, she couldn't understand how the same thing could be looked at from such drastically different viewpoints.

How could Cass have possibly just made being a drug dealer sound like it was nothing? A better question was probably how could she have just made being a cop sound so violent and uncaring? Subconsciously, Bo reached up to rub her chest where, years ago, the silver GPD shield had been pinned to her uniform for the first time. She couldn't explain the dull throbbing she felt. Cass would never shake her belief in right and wrong, in drugs wrecking lives. And the thought of it being a business like any other, with people who just wanted to go home to their families, was ludicrous. Wasn't it? Before she could stop herself, she touched her cheek where Cass's hand had been. She told herself she was imagining the tingling she felt there.

Chapter Fourteen

Cass groaned as she settled into the brand-new office chair that had arrived that morning. She finally broke down and ordered another new one after the first new one mysteriously caught fire. How was she supposed to know it wasn't flame proof when it was doused in gasoline? She had to suffer through an hour of customer service phone reps telling her how impossible it was that the electronics in the chair were so faulty as to cause a fire, but she figured that being forced to go back to the old chair this whole time while she waited for shipping was punishment enough for her pyromaniacal antics.

She was having a damn good day. She hadn't even been tempted to yell at any of her employees, legitimate or otherwise, and she fully believed it was because of the chair. She didn't think anything could ruin her mood, in fact, unless the chair broke. Then she would be pissed. She leaned back in said chair with her feet on her desk, her eyes closed as she let the built-in back massager—*ohh yeah*—do its job. She was starting to doze off when a knock at her door startled her awake. Without opening her eyes, she called for whoever it was to enter.

When she opened her eyes to see who her visitor was, the bright green eyes slowly and unabashedly perusing her body weren't what she expected to see. When those eyes met hers, she asked, "Detective Alexander, what can I do for you?" *A lot. A whole lot, I hope.*

"We're not done talking, Miss Halliburton. You don't seem to understand the gravity of the situation we find ourselves in. I have officers with years of experience telling me what to look for, and I've got street sources giving me inside information that I'm not chasing based solely on your word. If you want that to continue, you're going to have to give me a damn good reason because right now the only reason I'm not bringing you in on suspicion alone is because I can't find solid evidence yet."

Cass scowled and jumped up to shut the door quickly behind Bo. "What the hell makes you think anything I've told you so far is on an official record of any kind?"

Bo took a step forward, giving Cass the choice to either take a step back or let Bo's body press fully against hers. She chose the former. "Because if it's not, then I have no problem arresting you right now and letting the booking officer figure out the charges."

Cass sighed, growing tired of the game. "We both know that's not true. If it was you would have arrested me already."

Bo shrugged nonchalantly. "Maybe you're right. But think about it. Suspicion of human trafficking is a major thing and the Voleurs have already been put under watch for organized crime because of the RICO Act. Right now, I could round up every single person on this island flying the red and gold rockers and hold them indefinitely until I got more evidence to point me one way or another."

She leaned in closer and this time, Cass chose to stay still. *God, that cologne smells so damn good.*

"Maybe I'll do that. What do you say?"

"I say once again if you could have done that, you would have. So maybe you should just consider leaving me alone." It was a petulant answer, but she wasn't about to fall for such an empty threat just because she was seriously crushing on the person giving it.

"Give me a reason to, Miss Halliburton."

Cass grunted in frustration and pushed Bo back enough for her to walk around to her desk. "You understand that I don't like being backed into a corner, right?" She searched through her drawers for a yellow Post-it and scribbled a number on it before thrusting it in Bo's hand. "Before you ask, it's not another invitation for a lap dance. I will talk to you in one place and one place only, got it? I am under no obligation to help you. *At all.* Literally the only reason I'm going along with this is because I want to find out who brought those girls in just as badly as you do. This has nothing to do with what I'm doing here."

Bo glanced at the Post-it. "I need information, Miss Halliburton. I've got to come up with something to keep my official investigation going."

"That's not my problem. Take it or leave it, Detective. You already know I'm not going to help you bring down anything I might be involved in, so if you want my cooperation in finding out who's moving these girls you know where to find me." She waited for Bo to leave before slumping down in the chair.

Backed into a corner was right. Unfortunately, she had no doubt that if she didn't keep conversations with the detective going, Bo would eventually gather enough evidence about what Cass was *really* doing to put her away for a very long time. She watched out her office window as one of the Demons handed over a stack of cash to one of her Voleurs currently acting as a floor manager. The Demon would send someone to pick up whatever clunker car he just purchased and the money he gave would go into a bank account belonging to her father.

There, right in front of her, was the paper trail that could lead to her eventual demise if the detective got just the right piece of information. If Bo made good on her threat to find enough evidence to start filing RICO charges on the Voleurs, it would only be a matter of time before someone let something slip. Cass's only real decision at this point was whether to let everything continue and risk being arrested and killed in prison because she knew too much, or continue talking to the detective so that she could find out who decided to go past her and start their own endeavor in the human trafficking business so she could shut things down and regain control. Of course, there was always the option of making Bo disappear, but that wouldn't work for a number of reasons, the least of which being Cass didn't want her to disappear. Only one of those options involved an infuriatingly charming, handsome, and honest woman whose presence was quickly driving Cass insane. *In a good way.*

Cass picked up her phone and dialed Billy's number. When he shuffled into her office, she motioned for him to shut the door behind him. The decision she was making was spur-of-the-moment, but it felt right in her gut. "I need you to do something for me that might get you killed."

Billy looked surprised but he nodded just the same. "I'd gladly die for you, boss, you know that."

Cass shook her head and looked at him seriously. "Let me rephrase that. I need you to do something that could get both of us killed and a lot of people arrested. You're not doing it for the Voleurs, you're doing it for me. Can you do that?"

Billy leaned down to look her in the eyes and repeated his statement. "I don't work for the Voleurs. I work for you. I always have."

Cass chose not to dig into that statement. "There's someone running a shadow business from the island under our noses. Whoever it is, is dealing directly with some of the Demons and I can only assume he's trying to cut the Voleurs out of the loop because I haven't heard anything about it."

Billy grunted. "That doesn't sound like something that could get either of us killed, boss. The guy fucking up, maybe."

Cass ran her hand through her hair and sighed. "It's possible I'm the only one out of the loop. I can't be certain that my father doesn't know about it, and if he does then he left me out on purpose, and trying to stop it will get us targeted. I honestly shouldn't even be involving you, but something in my gut says I can trust you. I need you to figure out anything you can about someone on the island importing girls from Africa."

"Son of a bitch."

"Yeah. This ain't going to be pretty. At all."

Billy laid his hand over Cass's, startling her into looking straight up at him. "I promised your mother I would look after you if anything ever happened to her. I wasn't supposed to ever tell you, but it seems like this is a moment to break that promise." Before Cass could stutter out a response he walked out of her office.

She clicked the button to start the massage again. It didn't work. *The fucking chair broke.*

Bo made her way down the ramp to the now familiar invisible path to the driftwood where Cass was already sitting, eyes closed. She moved closer, taking the time to study her. She couldn't deny what her body was telling her; Cass was breathtaking. Her shirt was unbuttoned and falling to the side just enough to reveal the edges of a colorful bikini barely containing full, tanned breasts. Her Daisy Duke shorts were so tight, they probably would have been illegal in another country. Bo felt a tight pull in her groin and shook herself vehemently to clear her head.

She cleared her throat and focused.

Cass moved, her bright eyes open, a small, knowing smile on her face. "You should make more noise when you sneak up on someone, Detective. You might scare me next time."

"I definitely wouldn't want to scare you, lest you decide to shoot me."

Cass's smile grew as she patted the sand beside her. "No, shooting you would definitely not make me happy. Sit?"

Bo did as she was told and sat in the sand beside Cass. "You have something to tell me, Miss Halliburton?" She turned just slightly as she said, "Cass?"

The corners of Cass's eyes crinkled as she nodded. She turned to face Bo, pressing the outsides of their thighs together as she leaned one arm against the wood behind them. Bo was forced to turn too, and ended up leaning against the log, facing Cass with her arm outstretched to get comfortable.

"My father wasn't always a ruthless drug lord, you know."

Bo couldn't help but laugh at the randomness of that statement. "I have no idea what I expected from this, but I promise you that right there was nowhere near it."

"Maybe you should stop having expectations of these meetings, then, sweetie." There was a small silence between them before Cass spoke again. "He used to be a family man, believe it or not. I mean, he was never on what you might call the 'right' side of the law, at least not as far back as I can remember. He joined the Voleurs the day he turned eighteen, and from the stories I've been told, he worked his way up the ranks buying and selling drugs and other things—whatever it was his chapter was involved in at the time. By the time he married my mom, he had managed to work his way up to vice president, nationwide."

Bo did the math. "But he wasn't ruthless? He had to be what, thirty? Thirty-five? And he managed to work his way up that far that fast?"

"He saw drug dealing the same way I do. He was a businessman."

Bo chuckled and allowed herself to gently caress Cass's hand. "What exactly was this businessman's way of viewing drug dealing?"

"Someone is going to do it either way, and it's the best money you'll ever make. He negotiated deals, he didn't fight for them. Back then, that gained him a lot of respect. He used the money he was bringing home to take us on road trips, to buy me my first bike, to host massive neighborhood barbeques."

It was impossible not to see the happiness shining in her eyes. Whatever her view of Daniel now, it was clear to Bo that Cass had once genuinely looked up to the man her father used to be.

"So, what changed?"

"His position." The light slowly faded from her eyes and she pulled her arm away, crossing both arms in front of her chest in an unconscious effort to shield herself from whatever memories came next. "When he was voted in as El Presidente, worldwide, it was around the same time that a few major cartel leaders were being arrested. When those leaders left, that left the Mexican Militia to take over the drug industry. Whereas the cartels used to be run by men that were, at their core, businessmen like Daniel, now it's run by men who only speak violence. Who only understand violence."

"So…" Bo tried to understand. "So, he changed to keep up with them?"

Cass shook her head, and her eyes filled with such sadness that it was all Bo could do not to hug her tight. As it was, she opened her arms wide and Cass simply slid down, laying her head gently on Bo's chest. "He tried to stay the same, he really did. It worked for a short time, but when you're dealing with the scum of the earth, you can only go so long before you get dirty, too."

"What happened?" When Cass's breathing hitched, Bo tightened her grip. At that moment, the urge to protect her was overpowering any good sense she had.

"He was trying to make a deal with one of the head men of the cartels. He did what he always did, which was negotiate. When Daniel refused to budge on his prices, to the point that the man walked away from the deal, he simply assumed that the deal was gone and he would try again later."

"I take it that's not what happened?"

Cass shook her head and, seemingly without realizing it, ran her hand over the spot on Bo's chest where her heart was beating rapidly. "It was like you see in the movies. I was away with a friend. I think I was watching a movie or something. Daniel, my mom, and my little sister were going out to spend the day together. Daniel forgot his wallet inside, so he handed my mom the keys so she could start the Jeep."

Bo exhaled sharply and rubbed Cass's back as she pressed her forehead into Bo's chest. Her voice sounded so miserable, and Bo couldn't think of a single way to make it better.

"The blast hit him from behind and threw him against the door. The man from the cartel didn't even try to hide the fact that he did it. Why would he? He was untouchable. At least by the police."

"I'm guessing he wasn't safe from Daniel."

"No. And when he disappeared, it was like a switch flipped in Daniel. Everyone became a pawn, and as far as he was concerned, pawns were expendable so long as the king remained safe. The two of us were never the same, either. He made it a point for the longest time to remind me how much I looked like my mother. He told me the only thing I was good for was to remind him of what he lost."

"But you were his daughter, too."

Cass shook her head again. "I was his *adopted* daughter. My mom had already had me when they got married. The only thing I know about my real father is that he was a Voleur, too."

"So, when you told me you understood the pain..."

Cass sat up to look at Bo. "I meant I understood it. Like I said. Everyone became a pawn to him. Even the people who shared his last name."

"So, he forced you to work for him?"

"He...forced me to do a lot of things. Working for him was my escape. Once I realized that I could work my way up the ranks by selling more than *drugs*, I jumped at the chance." Tears slipped down Cass's cheeks.

As the pieces started clicking into place, Bo shook her head. "No. *No.* You were his family, Cass."

"That went out the window the day my mom and sister died. Make no mistake, we may share the last name, but any other connection we had died in that blast."

Bo took a chance and reached up, cupping Cass's face as she gently wiped a tear running down her face. She leaned in just slightly and Cass did the same. "You've been through so much. How could I possibly blame you for what you became?"

As tense as the moment had been before, it grew exponentially more so as Bo watched Cass's eyes darken. "What did I become, Detective?"

Bo leaned in just a little more and Cass's lips parted as her breathing grew harder. "A wild, crazy, ruthless...beautiful woman. How can you stand to let him use you like he has?"

Cass shook her head, her lips almost grazing Bo's. "I can't. I've thought so many times about leaving the life. I don't think I want to be this person anymore, but—" A twig snapped somewhere nearby and Cass shot up, almost knocking Bo backward as she did. She stayed silent and scanned the area for a long moment, but there wasn't another sound and so she kept talking. "Whether he's using me, or you are, I'm a pawn either way. I'd rather be a pawn for someone who wasn't planning on throwing me in jail to rot when they were done with me." Cass quickly brushed the sand from her shorts. "I've got someone looking into what you've told me. I'll keep you informed so you can make the arrest you're gunning for, but I'm not going to ask again, Bo. Leave me and my business alone." She turned and left, quickly swallowed up by the shadows.

Bo lay there for a long time, thinking about what Cass had told her. What would growing up with a crime lord father do to someone? Especially someone who saw money and nothing else? She couldn't imagine. Obviously, Cass was growing weary of the life she lived, but that didn't change anything between them because at the end of the day Bo was still a cop above all else. Knowing more of Cass's background, though, knowing what she went through growing up and what she did to survive…it definitely took away some of the sense of urgency Bo had been plagued with the entire investigation. It shouldn't have, but it did.

The next morning, Bo sat staring at a ten-dollar bill on her desk. She could once again feel the wheels turning in her head, but they were rusty, and there wasn't enough information to make them run smoothly. When Gerald tapped her on the shoulder, she jumped.

"You're going to stare a hole in that bill if you don't buy something with it."

She held it up for him to take. "It's a counterfeit."

"Oh, shit!" He threw it back at her like it was made of acid and she glared at him.

"It's a damn good counterfeit. From what I can tell, they took an old one-dollar bill, bleach-washed it, and then restamped it. It feels like real money because technically, it is. One of the Demons tried to use it to buy a Coke."

"Shouldn't we report this to the Secret Service? That's their territory, isn't it?"

"Normally, yes." She tapped on the report the ten had been sitting on. "But this isn't a normal situation. You remember I told you that my friend from the Coast Guard found a printing plate?"

He nodded.

"It was for a ten-dollar bill. This is the first evidence we've found that they actually used it."

"Oh."

She nodded, turning the retrieved bill over in her hands. "So yes, normally we would call the Secret Service simply to report a counterfeit. This time, however, I'm starting to get a feeling that maybe the operation is a little closer to home. I just have one issue."

"What's that?"

"Grace Njikeu. You were there when she mentioned the Voleurs using her to transport money. The issue is, number one, why did Grace say the Voleur got in trouble with the Demons for it if the Voleurs are apparently the ones who helped get her here? Number two, if there really is only one Voleur involved, it would mean him getting in trouble makes sense if the Demons are trying to keep it under wraps, but then where the hell does Grace fit into the picture? Who's the Voleur working with the Demons? And where in God's name do the Demons fit in to all this? I'm starting to feel like there's a whole lot going on and maybe the Voleurs aren't necessarily privy to all of it. That means that we're about to end up with an even bigger issue if we don't stop all of it. What do you think?"

He shrugged, eyes wide. "I have no clue. What about the manufacturing Topher is so sure is happening? Aren't his inside sources *positive* the Voleurs are manufacturing drugs?"

"Yeah, that's another issue. Like I said, the only drugs my buddy found were from the cartel. Wasn't that Topher's whole spiel, that the Demons were in town to buy drugs from the Voleurs and using the port to transport them?"

"Yeah, something like that."

"And yet none of my sources have heard anything about that and the one time we used our full resources to try to get hard evidence of it, on *his* word, none of us saw shit. The bottom line is none of this shit makes sense. There's a whole bunch of little pieces, but I can't figure out how they go together if I'm going off of Topher's word. It's like that moment when you get the border of a puzzle done and then you just sit there looking at it because nothing else looks like it fits anywhere? That's where we're at."

"So, what do we do now?"

Bo sighed. "I don't know, to be honest. It's like the more clues I find to what's going on the more convoluted the puzzle gets. I honestly think we're looking at three different puzzles."

"Three?"

"Grace, counterfeiting, and someone giving Topher unverified information. Most likely trying to rank up in narco, but that leaves us with our asses hanging out."

"Well, what if the Voleur who's helping the Demons is the one feeding Topher's inside guy their information? If he really is working both angles, it would make sense that he'd want to throw the Voleurs off his own tail, too."

She stared at him thoughtfully and then nodded. "That, my friend, is a very plausible idea. Again, only one issue."

"Which information is right and which information is wrong?"

"Exactly. Until we can find that out, we're still up shit creek without a paddle, and if the Demons really are trying to bring in more girls from overseas, our boat has a hole in it."

"Max! Fetch 'em up!" Cass's personal phone was ringing from somewhere back in her bedroom and she had no inclination to move to pick it up. A couple of seconds later, she laughed and petted the big Labrador on the head as he dropped her phone, covered with just a little slobber, on her chest. "Come on, big guy, jump up." She grunted as he lay down on top of her, and once he was settled, she answered the phone.

"Hello?"

"Hello, Miss Halliburton."

She rolled her eyes. "Somehow, I knew I was going to regret giving you this phone number." A low chuckle filled her ear and sent a shiver down her spine. She didn't know whether to be irritated or aroused.

"I need your help, Miss Halliburton."

"Yes, you always need something, Bo. What is it now?"

"I need you to fill in some pieces for me. I've got a puzzle in front of me that makes absolutely no sense."

"And why should I help you, Detective?"

"Because if you don't, I have about a hundred cops waiting on my phone call to round up every single member of your gang on this island. I get the sneaking suspicion that it would be a little hard to keep your organization going without anyone to run it."

Cass thought for a moment, and then decided to call her bluff. "That's the third time you've used that threat, Detective, so go for it. I'm not on the road and you have nothing solid on me. You pull my guys and I'll have another crew here by tomorrow ready to pick up where they left off." Another chuckle made up her mind about whether or not she was aroused and she shifted to ease the pressure of her jeans against her clit.

There was a moment's hesitation, and it was clear Bo knew Cass had called her bluff. "Truth? If I don't give my sergeant enough information to keep this investigation going locally, based on the pieces I have, she's going to be forced to call in the feds. I'm sure you don't want that to happen for obvious reasons, but I don't want to have to call them because I want to be the one to break this case, even if it's not the one I was originally investigating. I want to find justice for these girls more than anything else so if you want me off *your* back, I need help."

"What if I want you on my back?"

The other end of the line was momentarily silent. "Excuse me?"

"Nothing, nothing. Look, if you want information, I need to know that what I'm telling you isn't going to put me in jail. I don't... *want* to fight against you anymore, but I told you, if I'm going to be a pawn, it's going to be for the person who isn't going to take away my freedom, however little I have."

"I can keep GPD from arresting you, but I need the incentive to. You said you've got someone looking into the girls. Tell me about that. You know where I'll be at the usual time, Miss Halliburton. The choice is yours."

When she heard the click in her ear, Cass set her phone on top of Max's head and looked into his big brown eyes. "What do you think, boy?"

He sighed as only a dog can sigh.

"Yeah. I don't like ultimatums, either. I wasn't lying about having a whole other crew here by tomorrow, but I don't think she was necessarily lying about being ready to round all my guys up, either."

He didn't say a single word.

"You're right. Go get your leash." He jumped off and padded to her bedroom. She would go, not because the detective wanted her to, but because Max wanted her to.

They arrived at the beach at the same time and Cass let Max loose, laughing as he ran up and pounced on Bo, almost knocking her over.

"Whoa, there, big boy!" She looked up at Cass. "Have you got a saddle for this thing? I know a rodeo or two that could use a Clydesdale."

"Nah, he says it makes him look fat."

Bo knelt down and scruffed Max behind the ears, nuzzling his nose with hers as she made baby noises to him. "No, a big handsome boy like him could never look fat."

Bo stood up, dusting the sand off her pants. "Did you bring him to distract me?"

"No, he wanted to come for a walk, so I brought him along. Why, is he distracting you?"

Bo gazed in the air thoughtfully and then said, "I guess it depends on what you're trying to distract me from."

"How devilishly good-looking I am."

Bo looked surprised and Cass could see a slow blush creeping up her neck. "It would take a lot more than a big dog to do that."

"Then I guess it didn't work." The air between them had grown thick, and Cass could feel her stomach twisting at the look in Bo's eyes. "On the plus side," she said, changing the subject, "you're no longer concerned with information about my goings-on in Galveston."

She swore she could see Bo's balloon pop and swore silently at herself for killing the moment.

"What do you want, Miss Halliburton? Why are you here? I believe you're not trafficking, and you and I will figure that out together, but why are *you* here? Is it drugs? Is that it? Are you trying to cut the cartel out?"

Cass couldn't help but smile. "Would it be so bad if I were? I'm not saying I am, because frankly I have no idea what you're talking about and I've already told you we're not, but would it be so bad? We've already established that the cartel is dangerous and violent, and you know there's no way in hell you're going to completely rid the island of drugs because you're one of the biggest ports in the south and you're a direct line to the mainland. At least if I was in charge of it, you'd know where they were coming from, right?"

"No! More drugs means more people doing drugs which means more paperwork for me because there's more people to arrest and more people who die."

Cass grinned. "Detective, I already told you I'm not manufacturing. Why are you so set on drugs being the key?"

Bo grunted and crossed her arms. "I'm really just set on there being no drugs on my island at all."

"And you think that's possible?"

"I'd like to try."

Cass studied her for a moment and then smiled gently. "I'm not here to bring drugs on or off the island. I'm here because my father said I had to be."

Bo sighed. "You've already said you don't want to be his pawn anymore. Why don't you help me take him down, Cass? Let me try to protect you."

Cass shook her head. "I don't want your protection. I want to be free from any life that requires protection. I...I want to be a knight in shining armor, not a fucking princess stuck in a tower. I want to be the fucking dragon!"

Bo grinned and then laughed. "Dragons kill people, Miss Halliburton. If it helps, though, I already think you're a lot more badass than any princess trapped in a tower. Honestly, I really think if you and I had met in another time or place we could have been good friends."

Cass stepped up to her and laid a gentle hand on her chest as she looked up at her. "Who says we can't? I'm pretty sure there's no law that says we're not allowed to be friends."

Bo's breathing kicked up a notch and Cass watched her eyes darken. "I'm pretty sure there is." When she spoke, her voice was low and rough.

Cass took a chance and pressed closer, her chest against Bo's as she tilted her head. "What if no one knew? What if we didn't tell anyone? Could we be friends then?" Her lips were close enough to feel Bo's hot breath and she slowly closed the distance between them. The first kiss was soft, questioning. She leaned back and laughed at the look of mixed trepidation and terror on Bo's face. She waited, searching Bo's face for an answer. When it didn't look like she was going to make up her mind, Cass leaned in slowly, giving Bo the chance to say no before pressing her lips to Bo's once more, this time lingering, pressing in closer.

It took Bo a second to respond, but then she did. Oh, then she did. She opened her mouth, inviting Cass's tongue in, as her rough, calloused hands gently cupped her face and held her close, her thumbs lightly grazing Cass's cheeks.

Cass moaned as Bo kissed her hungrily, nipping at her bottom lip as their tongues pressed against each other. Her lips, the lips Cass had been fantasizing about for months, tasted like cherry Chapstick and fireball whiskey and Cass knew without a doubt that if she were on death row, this is what she would request for a last meal.

Bo's hips rocked into Cass's, but when she would have opened for her, Bo pulled back, her chest heaving as she fought to control her breathing, her forehead pressed against Cass's. "I'm sorry. We can't do this, Cass."

"I know."

"I mean I'm on a case and you, you're—"

"Bo." She leaned back and focused on her. "I know. Believe me, I wish I didn't know, but I know." She sighed softly and closed her eyes before focusing again on Bo. "I don't want my name mentioned unless it's absolutely necessary. Trust me when I tell you my father would know. Can you promise me that?" Bo nodded. "All right. I've got my second looking into what's going on with the girls coming in. I have a meeting with him in about an hour and then I'm going to sleep," she added when Bo opened her mouth. "I trust him. I don't think he likes the idea of trafficking any more than I do." She stood on her toes and gently kissed Bo's cheek. "I look forward to seeing you again, Detective. Maybe one day things will be different." As she called for Max and walked away, all she could think about was the smoldering fire in Bo's eyes.

Chapter Fifteen

B o waited until noon to call Nikki, knowing she wouldn't be up until at least then because Nikki's Place had hosted an up-and-coming local band the night before and Nikki wouldn't have gotten home until the wee hours of the morning. When Nikki picked up the phone, however, she was anything but groggy. In fact, she launched immediately into a diatribe so energetically Bo had trouble following at first.

"Did you know that the Texas Parks and Wildlife Rehabilitation Center classified birds as raptors? I told you, Bo. I told you I didn't like the black birds at Tortugas, and I told you I didn't trust them. Why? Because fucking raptors, that's why. They remember. They remember and they don't like being small, and damn it, they're holding it against us."

Bo tried not to crack up laughing. "Is this the same line of thinking that told you that Salem was a bitch because she remembers cats being worshipped in Egypt?"

"Okay, first off, Salem is people. She is a complete bitch and my ex-boyfriend has the scars to prove it. Second, *you're* the one who said she was worshipped in a past life so don't go putting that on me." Bo finally started laughing. "I'm going to feed you to the raptor birds, Bo."

"You're just jealous because they like me."

"I'm going to feed you to them and then you're not allowed to haunt my funeral. You'd bring them with you, because that's just the kind of asshole you are."

Bo really was trying not to laugh. Really, she was. "Does this mean we can't go to Tortugas?"

"Oh, no, we're going. I'm going to look them right in their beady little eyes and let them know I'm not fucking around."

"All of them?"

"At least one of them."

Bo grabbed a T-shirt from her closet. "Think of it this way. If we go to Tortugas and you *don't* look them in their beady little eyes—which, rude, by the way—you can try to make peace with our feathery friends, and when they eventually return to their full glory, they *won't* eat you. Or at the very least, they'll eat you last."

"Peace? There will be no peace! You pick up an injured seagull in the middle of the highway, throw a shirt over his head and call him 'Little Bird' and take him to the water. He gives you a tiny love bite and makes it on his merry way. I, on the other hand, pick up an injured bird in a much less chaotic place, call him a respectable 'Joe' and that little motherfucker goes bat shit crazy and pees all over my car! I didn't even know birds could pee, Bo."

"Well, I'm sure it's a biological thing. They do eat and drink. Besides, maybe it was a girl and she got offended at the name Joe."

Nik harrumphed. "I'm going to ignore your bird sympathizer tendencies and pretend you're still my best friend. I'll meet you at Tortugas. I love you, honey."

Bo chuckled to herself and said, "I love you, too."

She had just tossed her phone on the bed when it screamed again. She finished pulling her shirt on over her head and then grabbed it, answering without looking at the read out.

"Detective Alexander."

"Hey, Detective, this is Officer Dillon. Listen, I've got a woman in here that's asking for you and I figured I should give you a call. It, uh…it seems pretty urgent."

Bo shook her head, even though she knew the officer on the other end of the phone couldn't see her. "No. I'm not the one on call right now. All due respect, Officer, just hand her over to one of the other detectives in the station."

"Well, that's the thing, I tried that, and she refuses to speak to anyone else."

"Then she can wait until I come in tomorrow to speak to me."

The officer gave a bone-weary sigh and said softly, "I don't think she can wait until tomorrow. She came in here wearing those big sunglasses, you know the ones women wear. It's not bright in here but she refuses to take them off. Has a baseball cap on. She's acting real jumpy, too, and keeps looking at the door. I think someone may have hurt her."

Bo let out a long, exasperated breath. "What's her name?"

"Sarah Cassidy, she said."

Something in the name tickled the back of Bo's neck, but to her knowledge she had never heard it before. "All right. Put her in one of the interrogation rooms by herself. Don't bother with the cameras or anything, just keep her in there. If anyone suspicious comes through the doors, stop them. If anyone asks for her specifically, put them in another room until I can question them. I'll be there in a bit."

"Yes, ma'am."

Once he hung up, she called Nikki back but got her voice mail. "Hey, honey, I've got to reschedule lunch. Let's go to Jimmy's tonight, instead. I have a work thing that just came up. Give me a call back when you get this." She decided on keeping the surf shop T-shirt she had put on earlier and grabbed a button-up from her closet to put on over it.

When she got to the station, she sought out the officer who had phoned her, and he led her to the room the mystery woman was in.

"Do you want me to stand witness?"

She shook her head. "No, I'll call one of you in if she agrees to an official interview. Other than that, just give me the room."

He rendered a jaunty salute and then promptly walked away. When she entered the interrogation room, she was quick to take in the woman sitting in the corner. Her eyes were hidden by the bugeye sunglasses the officer had mentioned before, and her long brown hair was covered with an Astros baseball cap. That brown hair seemed to be a wig, though. At least, it was if the sprig of blond hair poking out from the woman's forehead was to give any indication. She could feel the woman watching her, and she was instantly on guard.

"Miss Cassidy. I'm Detective Bobbi Alexander. I was told you asked to speak to me. How can I help you?"

A slow, predatory smile spread across the woman's face, and Bo fought the urge to back up. When the woman spoke, however, her voice was playful and melodic. "Miss Cassidy? That's a new one. I like it. I think I prefer Miss Halliburton, though."

Bo glanced up to the camera to make sure the red light was indeed off. "Miss Halliburton."

A sound like a purr came from across the room as the now familiar smile—the real smile—replaced the one given to her earlier. She took off her sunglasses, glanced at the two-way mirror, and then walked over to Bo, pressing fully against her body before whispering, "I like that much better."

"You're insane, Cass." The husky timbre of her voice belied any admonishment her words might have otherwise held, and Cass gave her a knowing look.

She bit her lip and gently kissed Bo's cheek. "I decided I couldn't wait for you to call me. I have some information for you from my meeting last night. I didn't know any other way to get in touch with you other than through the department because you blocked your number when you called me, and showing up uninvited at your house again seemed like a bad idea."

Bo once again glanced up at the camera. "That's not on. Do you want me to turn it on?"

Cass shook her head. "No. I wasn't lying when I said that there couldn't be any evidence of me helping you. I don't really want to be here any longer than I have to be, but I needed to tell you what I know."

Bo frowned. "Okay, what's going on?"

"Someone in my organization is trying to upend the chain of command. I can't figure out for sure who it is, but my second went to my father with some 'rumors' he heard and now I know for sure my father doesn't know anything about the trafficking. I couldn't do it myself because if he *did* know, then he specifically cut me out because I'm a woman. That said, I don't know who it is. Is there any information you can give me on him that will help me figure out who he is?"

Bo shook her head. "The young woman I spoke to said they all used fake names. Is there anyone you know of that might be capable of a double cross?"

Something flashed in Cass's eyes. "I definitely do."

"Shit. Who?"

"That answer will most assuredly get me killed. Just know that whoever it is dealing with the Demons isn't doing it with our permission, so it's likely to make him even more dangerous than usual. He won't want to be caught by either of us."

Bo nodded and stepped a little closer. "I'll do what I can. I know you risked a lot by coming here so...thank you, Cass."

Cass smiled softly. "There's no need to thank me. I did it because it's the right thing to do. Look, I know you said we couldn't but..." She pressed even closer, not even bothering to hide the gasp as her hard, braless nipples brushed against the rough fabric of Bo's shirt. "Are we alone? I'm not going to lie, I think I'm kind of liking this adrenaline rush."

Bo felt a momentary jolt of panic but chose to ignore it and focused instead on the pleasant burning in her belly as she wrapped her arms around Cass. Squeezing her tightly, she gently ran her lips down Cass's neck. "Sarah Cassidy?"

Cass closed her eyes and tilted her head back, giving Bo better access to her. "Remember that information I told you Sav dug up? I changed my legal name before high school. I was born Sarah Cassidy, my mom's maiden name. She changed my last name to Halliburton when I was a kid."

Bo nodded and grunted as she nipped Cass's soft, sweet neck, drawing a small whimper from the her.

"You didn't answer my question. Are we alone?"

"I locked the door to the viewing room. We're as alone as we can—"

Cass cut her off with a hard, bruising kiss, thrusting her tongue deep into Bo's mouth.

There was no hesitance on Bo's part as she quickly backed Cass up and forced her to sit on the table she had been at when Bo came in. She took control, forcing Cass's head back as she placed hot, frantic kisses down the line of her neck. Cass immediately opened her legs and let Bo fit between them, moaning when Bo lifted her leg and pressed into her center.

"Oh. Fuck, Bo, yes."

Bo growled and kissed her again, biting down on her plump lower lip as she began rocking into Cass in earnest. Cass threw her head back, gasping for breath. She bit down and then sucked on Bo's ear.

Bo groaned as Cass's hot breath and the smell of her perfume and vanilla enveloped her, clouding all her senses. "I want to fuck you, Cass."

Cass moaned deep in her throat and begged, "Yes, please. Please fuck me, Bo."

Bo reached down for her zipper but was startled out of her stupor by the shrill ringing of her phone. She snarled and jumped back, yanking her phone out of her pocket to look at the readout. She sent Nikki to voice mail.

"Fuck! Is this your plan?" she growled. "To get me so fucked in the head I can't think straight and get me fired?"

Cass's chest heaved as she responded, just as loudly, "Are you serious? I don't have a fucking plan anymore, Bo. I risked getting killed just by coming here! If you seriously think you're the only one affected by this, you're out of your damn mind."

Bo opened her mouth to yell back but looked into Cass's eyes and shut it tight. She closed her eyes and stumbled blindly over to the wall to rest her head on it. "One of the other officers will see you out. Go out the door you came in and anyone out there will show you where the front door is."

"Bo—"

"Look where we are, Cass! I'm a cop! You're a drug lord! What part of that do you not get? My job is to arrest you not f—"*fall in love with you* "—fraternize with you."

The slight widening of Cass's eyes said she understood exactly what Bo hadn't said.

"Just go, Cass. I need a minute to get my shit together before they see me. Please."

Cass waited for another moment before quickly walking out, leaving Bo alone to her thoughts. When she heard the door click shut, Bo pulled out her phone and called Nikki back. "I don't need to reschedule, but meet me at Jimmy's. I'm still not feeling margaritas."

Twenty minutes later, she watched Nikki approach her on the right side of the small dive bar situated in the middle of the water on a pier. Nikki sat, and when the waitress came almost immediately, they both ordered a stingray with a burger and fries. Once she left, Nik turned to her. "What's on your mind, Bo?"

"What makes you think I have something on my mind?"

Nikki scoffed. "Because I've known you for fucking ever that's why." The waitress came and set their drinks in front of them and Nikki took a long pull through the straw of hers before continuing. "Don't even try to lie because if you do, I'll feed you to the raptors."

Bo took that opportunity to grab a fry that had been left on the bar to entice one of the said raptor birds over to them.

"Bo, don't do that! They're going to eat me!"

"I thought you said they were going to eat me?"

"Well, now I'm thinking of eating you so what are you going to do with that, huh?"

Bo simply raised an eyebrow and Nikki rolled her eyes, not having caught the double entendre of what she had said. "Fuck you."

"Pretty sure that's what you just said," Bo quipped.

"Bo, I swear to Go—" A raptor bird flew toward her and cut her off. She didn't say another word, and Bo grinned at the glare she gave to her.

"You were saying?"

Nikki sighed in a deeply exaggerated manner before saying, "You've got something on your mind. Seriously, Bo, what is it?"

Bo contemplated silently for a moment, voicing her extreme gratitude when the waitress set their food in front of them and thereby allowed Bo to stuff her mouth full, thereby disabling her speaking ability. Nikki just stared daggers at her.

"Speak, bitch."

Bo frowned deeply. "Fuck you, asshole." She took another few mouthfuls of burger before washing it down with her first drink of the now melting stingray. Finally, she looked up and asked, "How did you know you were in love with Brit?"

Nikki showed her surprise by choking on the drink in her mouth. Bo let her stop coughing before she apologized softly.

"No, no, it's fine. I just wasn't expecting…that."

"What were you expecting?"

"That you were pregnant with fucking Attwater's babies. I don't know. Not that."

"Can you please just answer the question?"

Something in her voice must have broken through to Nikki because she sobered quickly. "It was just something I felt, hon. We met and I thought she was fun, and so I wanted to hang out with her more one on one. Eventually, I just…knew. I knew that I loved her. It was like she had taken over this part of me, and it wasn't quite right if I wasn't with her. And when I saw her, my whole chest just…fucking felt like it was going to explode or something."

"Oh, that's lovely. Exploding chest, got it."

"Bo, what's going on? Why are you asking me this?"

Bo didn't respond for a long while, but finally, she said, "I think…there might be someone. But it's complicated."

"How so?"

Bo shook her head. "It's just complicated. And I've never really had any attachments to anyone but you, so I don't really know how to proceed."

"How do you not know how to proceed? It seems pretty natural to me, honey."

"Well, like I said, it's complicated. I don't know if what I'm feeling is real or if it's just a result of the fact that she's completely infuriating in all the right ways but utterly unavailable to me."

"She's married?"

"No. Well, at least I'm pretty sure she's not. She's…involved."

"So, she's got someone else?"

Bo frowned. "Multiple someones, really. And she's involved with the case I'm working on. I just…I've had to spend a lot of time with her lately because of the case and I'm thinking that maybe the close proximity mixed with high strung emotions may have turned into something else."

"So, she's a witness."

"Something like that."

Nikki rolled her eyes. "Goddamn it, Bo, will you just tell me what's going on?"

"I'm pretty sure I've got the serious hots for Cass Halliburton. I'm not falling for her, obviously, but..." Bo thought back to their encounter at the station. "She's got me so fucking wound up I'm not thinking straight. I can't get out of my head with this one."

Nikki munched on a fry and looked at her for a moment. "Okay. Why?"

She looked up in surprise. "Just okay?"

Nikki shrugged. "I could freak out very easily, but I'm choosing not to right now. Why do you think this?"

Bo shook her head and chewed on the inside of her cheek. "At first, we just screamed at each other any time we were together in the same room. I mean shit, she hit me in the fucking nose the first time we were face to face." She took a few minutes to think everything over, and Nikki silently let her.

"She started flirting with me after a while. I knew at first that she was just trying to get a rise out of me, but then...I don't know. Something changed. She changed. *I* changed. Suddenly she wasn't just trying to screw with me."

"Why do you think something is different?"

"I...could feel it. When she kissed me."

Nikki choked on her drink again. "Goddamn it, could you wait for the earth-shattering revelations until I've at least swallowed?"

"My bad." Bo grinned and tossed a fry into her mouth.

"So. She kissed you. How was that?"

"Earth-shattering revelation pretty much sums it up. Hot as hell would work, if not."

Now Nikki was chewing the inside of her cheek. "Bo, how long has it been since you've gotten laid? Like really laid. Like all night in a bed multiple orgasms laid, not just a hookup in a bar or anything."

Bo thought about it and then replied honestly. "The last time you and me and Brit got together. So, a couple of months or so."

"Holy hell, Bo, that's your problem right there. You need to get laid."

"I'm definitely not going to deny that."

"Look, I have a friend at work who has a cousin who's been asking around for a date. She seems to be exactly your type."

Blonde and chaotic? "What type is that?"

"Hot and DTF. Not looking for any strings, just wants to have a good time with someone who knows what they're doing."

Bo grinned at the *down to fuck* acronym. "So naturally, you decided to pimp me out."

"Well, I've got to make money off of you somehow and your computer skills are completely useless."

"Not my fault Mama couldn't afford MIT."

"The corner it is, then. What do you say? I can give her your number and y'all can set something up."

Bo nodded slowly. "All right."

"I know you're not keen on this. I'm not sure why, but I can tell, so I'm going to ask you something. Is Cass Halliburton worth losing your badge over? Because that's what's going to happen if you have an affair with her." When the widening of her eyes was Bo's only answer, Nikki said, "That's what I thought. Just go out with this woman, Bo. See what happens, okay? If, after you've had a good roll in the hay, you're still jonesing for this chick, then… maybe you have sex with her."

Bo just nodded. She'd do whatever she needed to in order to get Cass from under her skin.

Chapter Sixteen

Billy had chosen an outside seat for their impromptu meeting, but as he shifted to face her, his face scrunched up into a grimace that displayed his obvious discomfort. Cass glanced up at the sky to ensure no bird bombs were on their way.

"You look constipated, Billy. Is the food here really that bad?"

When she called him to meet, she'd given him the opportunity to name the place, and he mentioned his cravings for Tortugas nachos, a place she hadn't tried yet. "No, this chair just doesn't fit my ass, apparently. Or it fits a little too well, if you wanted to look at it that way."

She smiled slightly as she raised an eyebrow in question.

"The chair went up my ass, ma'am."

She burst out in laughter as she took a seat in front of him. "Well, I could only assume that would definitely be uncomfortable for a big man like you, Billy."

"Yes, it's certainly a change from Dave." He laughed, but Cass was lost. He realized what he had said and clarified. "Dave is my husband."

She couldn't have been more surprised if he had told her the pope just took a trip to the moon. "You're...gay?"

He grinned. "Yes, ma'am. Married to a big burly bear for about thirteen years now."

"I...never would have guessed, Billy." Cass was momentarily speechless, and Billy seemed to be trying not to laugh.

"Well, why would you? It's not like it's something I advertise or throw around like some of these other men do—bragging about this lay and that. I'm simply a man married to another man."

"That's a very astute way of putting it. Most of those men you speak of are so closed-minded they would think you couldn't be gay simply because you're a biker."

He laughed loudly and shook his head. "Yes, well, so would most of society, I'm afraid. But as I stated, I'm simply a man who loves his husband. Nothing more, nothing less."

"And the chair is not a good substitute." She chuckled.

"No, I would have to say not. Too hard."

She laughed again and had to admit to herself that it felt good to be unreserved for once. She quickly sobered when she realized just how lonely and stressed out she had been lately.

"So, hard chairs be damned, how can I help you, Cass?"

Most of the people in their crew wouldn't dare call her by anything other than "boss," but there was just something about Billy that made her prefer her name when he spoke. She felt the unease seeping into her consciousness as she thought over what she needed to tell him. The smile dropped from her face.

When she didn't immediately answer his question, he supplied helpfully, "The fajita nachos are really good. You should order some when the waitress decides to get off her ass and come take our order."

She stared at him, but he simply smiled. She was after all, his boss, and he was obviously content to let her speak when she was ready. She chewed her bottom lip for a moment and then finally said quietly, "I need to know…" She grimaced and shook her head.

"It's okay, whatever it is, Cass."

She glanced up at him and saw a look she hadn't seen since her mother had died. She didn't know if it was love or understanding or something else entirely, but it broke down the reservations she had been harboring. "I need to know, if our business maybe…goes south a little, and my father decides to put his foot in it…I need to know whose side you're on."

He took a moment and seemed to be considering exactly what she was saying. "You're asking me whether I'm going to back you or your father if things come to a head between the two of you. Am I reading that right?"

She met his eyes and nodded once.

"You're aware that, should I be so inclined to back your father faithfully, I could report this conversation to him as soon as you ride away with no fear of the repercussions?"

Cass took a very deep breath and then nodded once more, her eyes never leaving his. "I am very much aware of that, Billy. And in all honesty, I wouldn't fault you for it if you did. I know what kind of things you had to do to make it to my second, and I'm under no illusion who you were doing them for. I just...I maybe get the feeling that..." She sighed deeply and ran her hands through her hair, shaking her head. "I don't know what feeling I got, but I have to ask you that question, Billy, because frankly you seem like a really good guy and you're a great second and you're an excellent Voleur, even though you seem like an extremely nice man when you're not having to do some crazy shit."

Cass hated the vulnerable feeling engulfing her in that moment. She hated feeling trapped and unable to move, unsure who she could trust. "Someone in this club was ballsy enough to go behind everyone's backs to make a deal with the Demons. I think we both know that given the opportunity, Daniel will want in on it. Sure, he's going to severely reprimand the member that made the deal, but in the end, all he'll care about is money." She met his gaze. "I can't let that happen. And for me, that pretty much means mounting a shadow war against someone in my own club, if not my father himself. By any means possible. Even—"

"Let me make one thing clear, Cass."

She stopped just before she started another ramble and looked at him expectantly.

"I didn't join the Voleurs because I wanted to be a criminal. I joined the Voleurs because my best friend, Sheila Cassidy, decided when she was old enough to make her own decisions that bad boys in leather jackets were much more attractive than good men in designer suits."

He was doing that whole pope on the moon thing again.

"I joined the Voleurs to make sure your mom stayed safe and..." He swallowed and his eyes looked glassy. "When she was gone, I stayed to make sure her legacy was safe."

"How well did you know my mom?"

He nodded. "I knew your mom very well. I tell you this to say, unequivocally, I am on your side, Cass. I am here for you and only you. Everyone else be damned."

"Why didn't you say anything before? How have you been friends with my mom all these years and I never knew who you were? Why tell me now?" She felt her anger rising with the anxiety and she growled before yelling, "To get me to let my guard down?"

He shook his head. "No. As you well know, Daniel didn't come into your life until after you were born. He was already an up-and-comer when your mother met him and he didn't like the idea of having another man hanging around, so your mom asked me to keep my distance. I did because I would have done anything for her, and I stayed with the Voleurs so I could stay close to her. Before she got with Daniel we pretty much flew under the radar as low-level members. Once she died, I only did enough to make sure I kept you in my sights. As for why I stayed away, well, it seemed like a good idea. Keep low, keep watch, by being part of the shadows, you know? If I got too close I might not see things, but from a distance I could keep a good eye on everything around you. When Marcus was killed and I became your second, I realized just how much I'd missed of your life by keeping away, but I didn't want to make it a thing—I mean would you have believed me anyway?"

She stared at him for a long moment and then dropped her shoulders as she let her breath out. "No. I wouldn't."

"Exactly. So instead, I made sure that everything you needed was taken care of, and I made sure you knew I was dependable. You got the idea I was trustworthy on your own. Before that anything I said would have been cannon fodder. Now—"

"Can I take your order? I'm so sorry it took us so long to get to you. We're super short staffed."

Cass had never before felt so inclined to murder someone. She opened her mouth to tell the woman as much, but before she could get a word out Billy interrupted what was likely going to be a delightful speech by saying, "Two plates of fajita nachos, meat and cheese only, one chicken and one beef. You put lettuce or jalapenos on my plate I will die because I'm allergic. That's all, thank you." He turned to face Cass. And the waitress, thankfully, took the hint and walked off.

"You were saying?" she asked quietly.

"I think Pigsty is the one going behind our backs with the Demons."

"Shit, Billy, don't pull any punches, please."

He smiled but it didn't reach his eyes. "Cass, if I'm right this just got a whole hell of a lot more dangerous. Sty wouldn't do something like this without long-term planning, it's just the way he and his family operate. I don't have any solid evidence yet, but if it's true it makes sense."

"Goddamn it, this is a fucking shit storm. What makes you think it's him?"

Billy shrugged. "More of a feeling than anything. I was asking around to some of the guys I trust not to run their mouths, seeing if they heard anything about ways to make extra cash. A couple of them mentioned that Sty has been whispering about one-upping you, since he seems to think you usurped him from the throne. It doesn't mean much, but with everything you've told me from the detective…" He didn't finish his sentence and she didn't need him to. Sty was a fifth generation Voleur. He was supposed to be vice presidente, and in fact the job had been promised to him until she came along and made waves as the first woman to wear the bandit on her back. She wasn't kidding herself that her chance was given to her for any other reason than her last name, but in the end she had rightfully earned her position just the same. After all, if you couldn't deal with El Presidente himself, who better to garner a deal with than the VP, right? And she knew better than anyone the best way to get a man to agree to a deal on the Voleurs' terms. At the end of the day she just made better business decisions than Sty.

"What does he hope to earn by working with the Demons? Going into business with them on the money laundering is one thing, and most of us weren't sure about that to begin with because we have no control over them. But trafficking will get us nailed to the wall. It's way too visible, and it makes me sick."

"Yeah. You, maybe. But not your father. And if Sty can get in good with the Demons and get a lucrative business set up without you interfering, that would probably make him look a hell of a lot better in Daniel's eyes than someone that, to him, purposely deviated from a potential cash pot just because of her feelings."

"What I have for Detective Alexander is not…feelings. It's simply my body refusing to see reason until I see her naked."

Billy's eyes were as wide as the plates on their table. "I meant your feelings about trafficking, but if you're seriously considering sleeping with Detective Alexander then you need to be even more careful. And you need to get that shit out of your system quick."

"I'm fucking trying. She just…I don't know. She's opened my eyes. She's making me think about what a life outside the club might look like."

Billy shook his head. "You need to be careful. If Sty really is the one going behind your back, then having an affair with the detective will get you killed."

Cass shrugged. "I'll just tell them I'm sleeping with her to get information on the case. It's not like my father hasn't already suggested it. Hell, so did Sty. It will just look like I'm doing what they wanted me to."

"And if they don't buy it?"

"Then I guess I'll cross that bridge if I ever come to it."

CHAPTER SEVENTEEN

The date Nikki had set her up on had been disastrous and Bo hadn't been able to leave the restaurant quickly enough. The woman was vain, vapid, and altogether uninteresting. She'd only agreed to go on it to get her mind off Cass, but she'd ended up playing the comparison game instead. It hadn't taken long before she'd begged off, saying she wasn't feeling well, and left the woman sitting dumbstruck at the table.

Bo closed her eyes and dialed a number she knew full well she shouldn't be calling, but she couldn't help the smile that broke out at the sleepy hello that answered her phone call.

"What are you wearing, Miss Halliburton?"

The soft, deep moan that filled her ear seemed to baptize her with fire and burn out every inhibition she'd held thus far about the woman on the other end of the phone. The seductive, knowing laugh that followed finished the job and set Bo ablaze completely. "Why do you ask, Detective?"

Bo tried to school her voice to sound professional, but knew she was unsuccessful when she said, "I'm afraid it's pertinent to my investigation."

There was another moan, this one followed by a soft, almost inaudible gasp. "I'm wearing silk panties. And absolutely nothing else." A soft whimper. "I think they may have to come off soon, though. They seem to be…wet."

Bo wished she had at least taken a to-go water from the restaurant. "I think I'm going to need to see that. For investigative purposes. Are you awake enough to meet me?"

A throaty growl sent chills down her spine. "I have a better idea. You know that blue house right up from our meeting spot?"

Bo barely managed a yes.

"Meet me, there, Detective. I'll be waiting."

Bo ended the call and turned toward the beach, trying to quell the knowledge that this was a bad idea in every possible way. She gripped the steering wheel and hit the accelerator.

Cass opened the door, and she could feel Bo's eyes on her back as she walked into the house, not bothering to turn on the lights. She was nervous—that much she could admit—and she was silently thankful when Max pushed past her to say hello to her. He distracted Bo long enough for Cass to turn on some soft music and settle herself.

She knew that by inviting Bo into her house she was crossing a line that there was no coming back from. They weren't there for her job, and they certainly weren't there for Bo's. They were there for each other. She could tell Billy something else all day long, but she couldn't lie to herself while she listened to Bo walking around her house.

She watched Max amble down the hall to her bedroom and turned to meet Bo's eyes.

"You should know, no one but me has stepped foot in this house since I bought it. I have an apartment somewhere else on the island listed as my official address."

"No one but you, Cass?"

Cass shook her head slowly. "I've done everything I could to keep this house private. I don't even think my father knows about it. No one but me. And now you."

"Why now?"

Neither of them moved closer to the other, and Cass shook her head. "I don't know. Why did you call me?"

Bo look uncharacteristically shy. "I went on a date."

Cass simply raised her eyebrows. The statement *shouldn't* have made her jealous.

"I went on a date to prove to myself that going completely crazy and risking my badge over you was just a byproduct of not getting laid."

There was that ugly green monster again. Cass held out her hand, and when Bo took it, she led them both to the couch. "And it didn't go as planned?"

Bo shook her head and placed soft kisses on every one of Cass's knuckles before gently kissing up her arm. "No."

"Because she was a terrible date?" Cass wanted it to be more than that. She needed to know.

"Because she wasn't you, Cass. It didn't matter what she did, I kept thinking of you. I thought about the conversations we've had. I thought about everything I know about you and you know about me and I just couldn't lie to myself."

Cass slid closer to Bo on the couch, gently running her free hand over Bo's shoulders, down her chest. Her stomach clenched at the sharp inhale she heard when she reached the silver buckle at Bo's navel. "And what was your verdict, Detective? Is what you're feeling for me real or just a byproduct?"

"I don't know what the fuck it is. But I know I want you."

When the warm, dark scent of Bo's cologne drifted to her, Cass moaned quietly and gently kissed the hard-beating pulse under Bo's jaw. At the slight stiffening she felt, she slowly ran her tongue over the same spot and was rewarded with a deep, strangled groan. "Can I touch you? Please? Just touch."

Bo stared deep into her eyes before nodding.

Cass straddled Bo's hips, letting Bo's breathing settle before she moved again. She could feel her every movement being watched as she ran her hands lightly down Bo's stomach to pull her shirt out of her pants, then she moved them back up to painstakingly undo each button, one by one, letting it fall to the side to expose the stark white shirt underneath. She slowly moved her hands up Bo's shoulders and down her arms to slide the shirt off completely, her fingertips gliding over Bo's goose bumps.

She ran her hand through Bo's thick, wild hair and pulled just hard enough to force Bo's head back before she bent down and placed a featherlight kiss on her throat. She could feel Bo's body trembling underneath her and sat back up, watching Bo grimace slightly as Cass settled against her center.

"Bo, if you need me to stop..."

Bo's only response was to take Cass's hand in hers and pull it between them, sliding it under her own shirt. Cass moaned and pushed her hand up Bo's chiseled stomach, forcing the shirt up and over her head. When she shifted to take it off, her hips moved and they both moaned as they pressed against each other.

Bo's eyes were deep, black pools of desire as Cass traced her fingertips over the tattoos she had yet to see in full. A dragon here, a shark there, a wolf going up her side. There was no rhyme or reason to the tattoos covering Bo's arms and chest, but just the same, they were incredibly sexy.

"You are so beautiful," Cass whispered. She didn't know where the words came from, but she meant them. There was no other way to describe the masterpiece beneath her.

She inhaled sharply and her eyes fluttered closed as she felt the rough, calloused pads of Bo's thumbs rubbing against the vee in her hips that was exposed when Bo's strong hands wrapped gently around her. She couldn't help the moan that escaped as Bo increased the pressure of her thumbs just slightly.

"Bo...you're making me so wet, baby."

Her body moved on its own, her hips beginning a gentle rocking motion as Bo tightened her grip. When she heard Bo's low, sexy growl, she bit her lip hard before finally reaching down to yank off her own shirt, giving Bo full access. She heard an appreciative groan as she felt Bo's hips start rocking against hers.

Bo slid her hands up Cass's sides before pulling her down and claiming her mouth with an intense, possessive kiss that left Cass gasping for breath as she wrapped long arms around Cass's body. Cass moaned into the kiss and felt sure hands reaching around to undo the clasp on her bra. She sat up only long enough to let it slide off before crashing back down into Bo's body to return the kiss with equal fervor. She felt Bo's teeth scraping her lips as their tongues danced.

Bo grabbed her ass and Cass threw her head back, groaning Bo's name as she arched against Bo's hard, warm body. She was so very close to coming completely unraveled, but when she looked into Bo's eyes, she saw the flicker of hesitation and put her hands against Bo's chest.

"Bo, wait. Are you sure?" It was the hardest thing she'd done so far, saying those words, asking that question, but she had to be sure. As a woman in her position, it wasn't in her nature to ask questions or make sure anyone else was okay. It had always been only her. There was just something about Bo that wouldn't let her be careless.

Bo's sigh was her answer. "I am. I just...I don't know. There's a part of me that's holding back. I know you want to, though, and I'm completely okay with that, Cass. If you're okay with letting me get there in my own time."

Cass bit her lip hard enough to taste blood and let her head fall to her chest as she tried to catch her breath. "You're saying you don't mind letting me come, but you're not sure you can right now?"

Bo's expression was so intense, so focused on her, it made her ache even more.

"Then...I think...we need to wait." Cass laughed shakily and ran her hands through her hair before taking a deep breath and leaning down to kiss her gently on already swollen lips. "As much as it pains me to say this, when I make love to you for the first time, I want it to be for both of us. I don't want it to be one-sided, even a little bit."

Bo swallowed hard before she nodded, her eyes never leaving Cass's. "So, what do we do now? Where do we go from here?" When she spoke, her voice was several octaves deeper than normal.

Cass exhaled sharply and said softly, "From here, if it's okay with you, you're going to follow me into my bedroom and we're going to hold each other while we sleep. And for just a few hours, we're going to pretend we're just normal people free to be with the person we want to be with."

❖

"Detective Alexander." Bo blinked against the grit in her eyes. She'd barely slept, as was the case lately. Her sex drive was on high and she couldn't bring herself to let go with Cass until this investigation was over. Instead, she spent her nights poring over the case documents, looking for the bit of info she'd missed that would shut everything down. She was so fucking close; she just needed that one last piece.

"Hey, this is FBI Special Agent Jamie O'Callahan. Do you have a moment to talk?"

"Of course, I'm just sitting at my desk. How can I help you, Agent O'Callahan?"

"You're currently running an investigation into the Galveston Island Voleurs. Is that correct?"

"All due respect, Agent O'Callahan, what's it to you?" Bo knew she was being ruder than common courtesy would dictate, but like most other cops, she was territorial about her cases and the thought that an FBI agent was going to try to take over irked her. Not that she had any conclusive shit to work with.

A soft laugh pierced her thoughts. "Calm down, Detective, I'm not calling to usurp you. My sister Callie works for GPD, and she's the one that told me to call you."

Callie was an acquaintance of Bo's on the force and the mention of her name settled Bo's nerves slightly. She also vaguely remembered a Jamie, Callie's twin, working a few years at GPD as well. "You're not the traitor that left to go to the Feebies, are you?" A hearty laugh gave her all the answer she needed. "Yes, I am investigating the Galveston Island Chapter. How can I help you, traitor?"

"Actually," Jamie chuckled, "I think it's how I can help you. A couple weeks back a random Coast Guard inspection found a printing plate hidden in a container from a Halliburton International shipping crate. You remember that?"

"Yeah, you guys picked up the guy that signed off on the crate though, right? My investigation has been stalled without that motherfucker."

"We're looking into some other stuff around that too, but that's not why I'm calling. A week ago, the state troopers picked up a member of the Demons heading somewhere from the island. I don't remember what he was picked up for, but he ended up being transferred to Huntsville State to serve out a federal warrant. Now, the boys at county didn't catch it, but guess what the corrections officers found in his belongings when they did inventory?"

"I'm going to take a wild guess it wasn't a pink dildo and a note that said, 'Sorry, Mama, I'm gay'?"

Jamie laughed. "No, but that would have been fucking hilarious. They found a rolled-up wad of ten-dollar bills. Every single one of them was counterfeit. They wouldn't have even noticed except, miracle of miracles, one of the guards used to work at a bank and knew what she was looking at. That got me thinking about that printing plate the Coasties found coming from your island and before you ask, Callie told me. I don't suppose your Port Police have given you any more cooperation than they gave me when I called?"

"Nope. Our liaison for Port is getting completely stonewalled."

"I figured. Look, normally this would go directly to the Secret Service, but I was venting to my sister and she pretty much begged me to let you guys have the collar. Since it was between you and the other guys, I decided a traitor's loyalty only goes so far."

Bo scratched her head, feeling more and more pieces of that nagging puzzle start lining up. "I appreciate that, but what exactly, specifically, are you asking me to look for?"

"I think either the Voleurs or the Demons are running a printing press right there on our pretty little island. I can't tell you for sure because the first guy we nabbed was a Voleur. We've got one and one, which suggests they're teaming up. The rest is up to you."

"Holy shit, that's it. I've been so focused on everything else I'm looking into that I didn't even think of that. It all fucking fits."

"Yeah, it seemed pretty obvious to me. I was wondering what the hell took you guys so long to put it together."

Bo decided to take a shot in the dark, but she had a gut feeling she already knew the answer. "My answer depends on yours. I don't suppose you've heard any whispers of a massive drug manufacturing ring right here in the middle of our pretty little island, have you?"

"I think if we had, you wouldn't have been able to stop me from taking it down myself."

"Yeah, that's what I thought. Listen, I appreciate the call, O'Callahan, but my answer to your question is that I've got a massive problem that needs to be fixed right now. Tell your sister I owe her dinner." She hung up without waiting for a reply and waved at Guthie to follow her into a conference room. She didn't want this conversation overheard.

"We have a problem, Gerald. And I'm very concerned about it." She waited for him to say something, but he seemed content to listen at this point. "I just got a call from an FBI agent who got wind of a Demon coming from our island with a wad of counterfeit bills in his pocket. Sound familiar?"

"Yeah, wasn't that fella down at Port picked up for a counterfeit plate?"

"Exactly. And he was a Voleur. So, tell me this, Gerald. What's a Demon doing with a massive wad of fake cash coming from the Voleurs? And if the Voleurs are really running a printing press, then why the hell aren't our undercover boys telling us that? Because the fact of the matter is there is no drug manufacturing ring. I've been through East End enough to know that. Not to mention we would have had a massive influx of drugs from the narco guys on the street. So, I ask again, why aren't our boys telling us the truth?"

"Maybe…" He looked uncomfortable, and Bo couldn't blame him. It was one thing to have false information coming from a gang member. It was an entirely different thing to have it coming from a fellow cop. "Maybe we're getting the same thing the narcs are. Maybe it's one specific person who's trying to throw us off by telling the department to look for the drugs."

She only nodded. She hated to agree with him, but it was better than the alternative of a whole slew of dirty cops. Her money was on whichever officer told Topher he had sex with Cass. She now knew that was untrue, and as hard as it was for her to admit it, it wasn't entirely uncommon for an undercover officer to go rogue.

"So where do we go from here?"

"For now, just go through the motions. We have a trinity of things to deal with—a dirty cop trying to throw us off the trail of a printing press, Classic Auto and Heartbreakers, and prostitutes. We need to figure out where the money starts and where it ends so we can wrap this all up." She lowered her voice. "I'm willing to bet whoever is lying to us about the drugs and the printing press is the one going behind the Voleurs to bring in the girls with the Demons. Unfortunately, we can't afford to bring anyone else in on what we suspect until we have more solid information. Whenever Topher gets back from his vacation, I'll pull in him and Sergeant Gill, but until then this remains entirely need to know. We don't know who we can trust to keep information at this point."

"I have a few new people I might be able to squeeze for information." He gave her a mock salute. "Detective Guthrie, on the job."

She grinned. "That's good. I may just have someone I can squeeze without raising too many red flags, too. Until I can talk to Topher and the sarge, it's no one but you and me. Got it?"

He looked like he was going to say something, but instead he just nodded. When he left, Bo called her source.

Cass watched as Bo approached her from the access point parking lot. Bo's eyes darted back and forth, scanning every shadow she could find for some sign of anything that didn't belong. Cass laughed quietly to herself. Always a cop, never a civilian. It didn't matter how many times they had met at this exact spot Bo never seemed to relax until she was absolutely sure they were alone.

Cass used the opportunity to study her outfit of choice. Today she was a beach bum like the rest of the B.O.I. natives with her cargo shorts and slightly baggy button-up white shirt. Her Reef flip-flops completed the image, and Cass smiled at the heat she felt between her legs at just how hot "off duty Bo" was. Too bad they continued to play for opposite teams.

"Your eyes give away your intentions too easily, Miss Halliburton," Bo called out. "Were I an honorable woman, I would wonder if my virtue were safe."

Cass grinned and ran her hands down Bo's arms, stepping forward into a hug when Bo squeezed her hands. "Were you an honorable woman, Detective Alexander, I would tell you that your virtue is without doubt in danger."

Bo smiled, but she looked serious. "Thank you for coming."

She leaned up and kissed Bo's neck gently before inhaling deeply. "God, you always smell so damn good." She knew instinctively that Bo's distinct smell would never get old for her.

Bo sighed softly and held Cass back to look at her. "I really do need to talk to you, Cass."

Cass bit her lip and looked into Bo's dark, stormy eyes. "How about we go for a swim instead?"

Bo shook her head. "Not this time. You're in danger, Cass. We both might be."

Cass frowned. "I wasn't really planning on talking shop when I came out here."

"I'm close, Cass. I have most of the pieces and I know enough now to know that whoever is going behind your back is probably doing the same thing to us."

She could feel Bo searching her eyes for the truth, but she wouldn't give it up. So the detective had finally figured out she had a dirty cop. The question was… "Can you tell me who it is? Because without that your information is useless."

Bo's face showed her remorse. "No, I can't. Interdepartmental cooperation is a pipe dream and they're not going to give me the names of their undercovers. Don't act like you don't know they exist, either."

Cass only smiled.

"I can only think of one reason for someone to go behind everyone's back on this big of a scale, and that's to take you down. As much as I really want to start kicking down every door I can, there's a really big part of me that is worried you might get hurt in the crossfire. This is the part where you need to be completely honest with me."

Cass took a moment to formulate her response. She could feel it in her soul that this was the moment where the path to her final destination forked irrevocably. "What do you want from me?"

"I want you to tell me who in my department is dirty and let me go after them. Then I want you to lay out exactly what your part in the original operation on the island is and who all the key players are on that. I want to take down every single motherfucker trying to sully my island and I want you to help me." She paused for what seemed like an eternity. "I want you to let me protect you. I want *you*."

"Detective, you have no idea who *me* is. You have no idea what I've done in my life to get to where I am. There are men who have murdered people in cold blood who are afraid of me." She reached up to hold Bo's face, forcing her to keep her gaze. "You don't get to look away right now. What happens at the end of all this? What happens when the novelty wears off? Yeah, I'm fucking sick of this life, but that doesn't mean I didn't enjoy it once. And I was damn good at what I did. Still am."

Bo reached up and held Cass's hands. "Then you tell me everything. I'll wage a goddamn war if I have to."

Cass laughed softly and closed her eyes, dropping her hand as she turned her head up in mock prayer. "You make it sound so easy, don't you? Just turn against everything I've ever stood for in my entire life. Risk everything just so you can get the bad guy?"

"No. Risk everything so that I can do the same."

Cass stared into the green eyes holding her own captive. "So you can do the same?"

Bo nodded and took a step forward until her chest pressed gently against Cass's. "Yes. Risk it all on me. Because I'm going to risk it all on you. Trust me to keep you safe like I'm trusting that you're not using me."

So that was it, then. At her core, Bo didn't trust that if she let go and slept with Cass that Cass wouldn't turn around and get her fired, or worse. It was a quid pro quo of the best and worst sort, wasn't it? She stood on her toes and ran her hands through Bo's hair before kissing her slowly, thoroughly. She moaned when she felt Bo's arms wrap around her, holding her tight. In that moment, she really did feel safe. Bo's hands wandered, running the length of Cass's back before gripping her ass and pulling her hips tight. Bo growled hungrily as Cass rocked into her.

Cass broke the kiss, gasping for breath. "You taste so fucking good."

"Please, Cass. I'm not just asking because I want to sleep with you. I'm asking because I want to have the choice. And that means taking care of all this bullshit so you can be free to do whatever you want."

"Assuming my father lets me walk away?"

Bo didn't answer, but *God*, the hunger in her eyes was almost enough to make Cass say yes right then and there. Almost.

"You're asking me to risk my life so you can risk your job."

"We both know I'll be in the direct line of fire for all of this too, Cass. Especially going after a rogue cop. Don't belittle this by pretending otherwise."

Cass sighed. "Let me think about it. Give my second a couple more days to come up with something concrete. One way or the other you'll have your answer." She turned to walk away but stopped when Bo called her name.

"Just one thing before you leave. If none of this was going on—no Voleurs, no cops, no nothing—what would you do?"

Cass turned back to Bo and pulled her hard against her body. She yanked her head down and kissed her hard enough to bruise, not stopping until she felt Bo move against her again. "If none of this was happening, I would have had you in bed a long time ago."

CHAPTER EIGHTEEN

Bo was glaring at the wall when Gerald walked in. She spared him a glance before motioning to the seat in front of her. "I just got a phone call that Dusky Nelson was taken off life support."

Gerald slumped into the seat in front of her. "Fuck."

"Yeah. And that sucks because I think I may have figured out where most of our pieces fit and I was really hoping he would wake up to confirm it for me, seeing as how my source isn't sure she wants to go on record."

Gerald seemed lost in thought as he murmured, "What do you think is going on?"

"We know the Voleurs are printing counterfeit bills on bleached singles. We haven't gotten any calls for fakes because to the untrained eye they seem real. The corrections officer in Huntsville knew they were fake because she used to be a banker. I couldn't figure out what was nagging me, but it was the acetone. It's a common chemical used in bleaching bills for counterfeiting. They give the Demons the counterfeits at Heartbreakers and then the Demons give them real cash at Classic Auto under the premise of buying a car. So they're essentially buying the counterfeit money from the Voleurs, but the real cash goes through a legit business so there's no hand to hand exchange and it gets funneled directly into their bank accounts. No massive flag raising deposits necessary. All the pieces make it that much harder to get a handle on it, which is why it took us so long. It all fucking fits. Except the prostitutes. Are they part of the Voleurs' work? Or part of the Demons' work? Who made that call, and how does it fit with the counterfeiting operation? Or is it totally separate? But it can't be totally separate, because they're having the girls make the handoffs of the fakes."

"Maybe it's exactly what you said. Obviously, this isn't just a single one-room deal so they use the prostitutes in the clubs to hand off the money to the Demons. The lower ranking members don't have to come into contact with a rival gang and risk a fight, and to anyone looking on the outside it just looks like the Demons are enjoying a good time, courtesy of a new business partner."

"Shit, that actually kind of makes sense."

"And our problem is that we can't get a warrant because we have no real proof, and we don't know where they're printing."

Bo shook her head. "That's far from our only problem. It's not even our biggest problem."

Gerald sighed. "Why haven't we heard a word about any of it from Topher and his narco guys?"

"Exactly."

"So, what do we do?"

"We go fucking talk to narco ourselves and get this shit figured out once and for all."

He followed her as she stormed out of their unit office and into the narcotics squad room. She strode in without knocking and was treated to a glare from the lieutenant that had taken over for Topher on his vacation. "Detectives Alexander, Guthrie. How can I help you both?" His tone made it clear that his implied politeness was in no way authentic.

Bo leaned on his desk. "You can tell us why the fuck you guys are dicking us around, making us chase a false lead on narcotics manufacturing while the Voleurs are starting up a fucking printing press and sex trafficking ring right under our goddamned noses."

By feeding the other officer pertinent information right off the bat, she could watch for telltale signs of subterfuge, but she didn't think either of them expected the loud guffaws that they were given.

"Are you fucking kidding me, Zander? You really think if we thought there was a drug fucking manufacturing ring, we'd bother telling you guys? That's literally our fucking job, and we'd have dealt with it. We've been suspicious for fucking ever that the Voleurs are trying to print, which is your fucking department, not ours. It's been a running fucking joke in my unit for months. Topher's had a great laugh telling us how every time he brings you guys even more evidence, you just keep turning it down and saying, 'it's not enough, it's not enough.'" He made the last statement in a way that directly reflected what he thought of their intelligence level. "Once I heard through the grapevine that counterfeits were being found, I was seriously about to go to your captain and report you guys because Topher was refusing to do it and as far as I'm concerned you guys dropped the ball hard."

Bo couldn't help it when her jaw dropped. "Topher told you what now?"

The other officer rolled his eyes but repeated himself, just as rudely.

Bo composed herself. "Would you mind if I called Sergeant Gill and you repeated exactly what you just told me?"

The lieutenant growled this time. "Why?"

Bo simply smiled. "I'd just answer the question if I were you."

Something in her eyes must have put him on guard, because he stiffened and gave a curt nod.

When Bo put the phone on speaker, the first thing the group heard was, "Bo, I swear to God this had better be good," followed by the muffled rumblings of what was obviously her husband.

"Sorry to interrupt your nookie time, but I figured you'd want to hear this. Lieutenant Parris?"

He repeated his story for the third time, leaving out the inflected tone this go-round. When he was finished, the other end of the line was silent for a full minute before a soft, "Fuck me. Holy fucking shit. Topher Dusek, huh?"

Suddenly, Parris slammed his hand down. "Someone better fucking tell me what's going on right now."

"Go ahead, Bo," Sergeant Gill said.

"For the entire length of our investigation, Topher Dusek, the liaison between your narcotics unit and our unit, has been feeding us information that there was a drug manufacturing ring in the middle of the island that his undercover boys weren't ranked up enough to get hard evidence of. He's been pressing us to squeeze our sources and telling us *he's* the one who needed more information. Not us. The only reason we even thought to track the printing press was because of an accidental find from a friend in the Coast Guard looking for something else entirely. To be clear, Topher never mentioned the press, and he let us think it was drugs you guys were after, but you couldn't make a bust yet. We needed the undercover officers we *thought* he was getting his information from, so we continued to allow him in on our investigation, even when it became apparent something was off. We thought we were working on a drug trafficking ring until we started putting a few more pieces together."

"First thing's first," Sergeant Gill spoke up. "We need to get this whole operation taken down as soon as possible. Lieutenant Parris, you're still in charge of the SWAT unit, right?"

Parris grunted in agreement.

"How long would it take you to get approval for a SWAT raid on wherever they're printing and washing these bills? Obviously, we won't use the narco squad because the 'manufacturing ring' was nothing but a wild goose chase made to keep us off track."

He shrugged. "Depends on how long it takes Detective Alexander to squeeze her source. I need to know the exact location and exactly what we're going in for. Once we get that, I'll put out the call. You guys are the ones that really know what we're dealing with, so I'll need you to get the proper warrants. It shouldn't take more than two days."

"All right, can you handle that for me on your end?" Not known for listening to superiors in other units, she didn't wait for him to respond before she continued. "Now, before I hang up, we need to address the elephant. Topher Dusek has an outstanding record with this department and has more than ten years of exemplary performance. LT, unless you have a problem with this, I'd like for no one but the four of us to find out he had anything to do with this until we can get him face to face and give him the chance to explain himself. When he gets back from his vacation, I'll pull our lieutenant in and have him there for the questioning process. Is that understood by everyone? Everyone okay with that?"

There was a chorus of "yes, ma'am" before she continued, "Bo, you call up your source and then the judge and work on getting the warrants. Call Judge Nelson directly, Bo. We know we can trust him. As of right now, no one except those absolutely necessary is to know about any of this. We're pretty sure it's going to be in the medical district since that's where most of their buildings are, so we need a couple of patrol units to monitor the area so that we'll know if they catch wind of this and scurry. They don't need to know anything other than bare essentials, though. If they got to Topher, they could have gotten to anyone, and we don't need this blowing up in our faces. Bo, take care of that and let me know when you have everything ready to move. Until then, it's business as usual. Understood?"

Another round of agreement proceeded the click of her hanging up.

Bo waited until late that night to call Paige back. "I need to talk to you about something very important and I need to know it's not going to go anywhere until I can get a handle on it."

"That depends on what you're about to tell me, Bo."

"I have reason to believe that Topher may also be double-crossing the Voleurs and making a deal with the Demons. I think our suspicions about human trafficking were right and he's trying to start smuggling women."

"Jesus fucking Christ, Bo, you've waited until just now to fucking tell me this?"

"I still have no proof other than one single prostitute's word. My source is pretty fucking sure, though. The problem is if I'm going to convince them to go on the record, I have to be damn sure they're not going to get killed, because they will if any of this gets out before we at least get Topher."

"Bo, I can't keep a lid on this! If we have proof of human trafficking we are obligated to report it. This is way above my pay grade."

"My source is getting proof together from the inside. Either we keep them safe or this shit doesn't get stopped because I promise you this isn't something we're going to be able to take down if we have to defend ourselves from three different sides."

Paige sighed. "What are the three sides? I want to be crystal clear on this."

"The Voleurs, the Demons, and Topher. If we can wait to move on this until we can get solid proof to take Topher down, my source can give us what we need to take down everyone else, too and we can stop this before it gets out of hand. But we have to wait."

Paige waited so long to respond that Bo thought she hung up. "Fine. Get the information about the printing press. Tell us where to go. I'll work on getting WITSEC for your source so we can call the feds in and cut this shit out now. I'm done trying to deal with this much shit by ourselves."

She hung up and Bo felt the emotions in her depths warring with each other. The familiar elation at closing a case, the adrenaline of an impending bust. But underneath it all was sheer terror. She knew in the end it was entirely possible Cass wouldn't walk away from any of this. She hated to admit that she was beginning to question the decisions she had made.

❖

Cass's hands shook as she reached behind her back to pull up the zipper on the form fitting royal blue dress that hugged every curve of her body. After some debating with herself, she had called Bo and asked her out on a date. She wanted to dress up for her. She wanted to hold her, to dance slow with her. She wanted to be pressed against Bo with no one interrupting them, and honestly, that feeling scared the ever-loving shit out of her. She had weighed her options over and over and over again before finally breaking down and making the call. The fact of the matter was, one way or another, this life would probably end up with her dead, and if she could at least have one moment of doing what the fuck she wanted, she was going to take it. Even if that meant putting a target on her back for being a rat. She was fucking done with the subterfuge that came with back alley dealings. She wanted out, and Bo had given her a window into another life. Maybe, just maybe, she could turn her world around.

The legendary Kourtney Van Wales, now performing without her stage name simply as Vancie Vega, was in town and would be doing her award-winning Cher and Dolly Parton impersonations at the F Bar to help raise money for their upcoming pride celebrations. It was an event where she would be completely anonymous and could be herself with Bo without having to worry about who was watching. And she could be open and honest without having to worry about who was listening.

Cass sighed and looked at herself as she thought back to every moment that had led her to this spot, in front of her full-length mirror, eyeliner in hand.

She thought about every hand that had ever touched her body for the good of the club, every time she had waited anxiously at the doctor when someone refused to practice safe sex and she didn't have the choice to say no to them. She thought about Bo's sister and the look on Bo's face when she talked about the drugs that had ended her young life, and the conviction in Bo's voice when she spoke of her own personal war on those drugs. She thought about her mother. If her mother had never been a Proud Voleur Old Lady, would she still be alive? Would Cass's sister? The dam hadn't broken, but the cracks were getting bigger. This life just wasn't worth what it took away anymore. Her anticipation rose as she watched Bo make her way through the crowd. Vancie's performances could draw a crowd in Houston like no one else. Bo leaned down and kissed her gently on the cheek. "You look beautiful tonight."

"Do I not look beautiful every other night?"

Bo grinned as she sat down, lifting her arm to allow Cass to settle into her side. "Breathtaking."

Cass smiled and leaned into Bo's warm body, inhaling the scent of her. "You always smell so good when we're together."

Bo looked somewhat shy as she shifted to look down at Cass. "I noticed that night in Pearl that you seemed to really like this cologne so I've kind of made it a point to wear it whenever I know I'm going to be around you. I usually have quite a few that I go through on a weekly basis, but you never reacted to any of the others so..."

She trailed off, and Cass was momentarily speechless. She shook her head slightly and murmured, "They broke the mold when they made you, Bo Alexander."

Bo simply smiled and held her tight as they watched Vancie belting out a Frank Sinatra song between her impressions. Cass could feel herself tensing as the show went on, unable to let go completely of the turmoil of the past few weeks, but Bo rubbed her arm and leaned down to whisper in her ear, "Let's just enjoy this for right now. Don't make it about anything else except this amazing performance, okay? Relax."

Cass felt her shoulders loosen as Bo continued her soft ministrations. When the show was over, the DJ came out and started up the music, encouraging all the guests to get out of their seats and dance with their partners. Cass took Bo's hand and led her to the dance floor. When Bo held open her arms, Cass stepped into them, marveling at how naturally they seemed to fit together. Bo's left hand was wrapped perfectly around her right, Bo's arm around her waist.

Bo leaned down to nuzzle Cass's neck, and Cass pressed into her as Bo whispered in her ear, "It's so nice to be dancing with you willingly this time."

Cass threw her head back and laughed as Bo spun her to the music. "Don't lie to me, Detective. If you didn't enjoy it even a little bit, you wouldn't have kept coming back for more."

Bo grinned from ear to ear and twirled Cass again. "I'm a red-blooded American lesbian, Miss Halliburton. There's very few of us who wouldn't enjoy having your hand between our legs in some capacity."

Cass smiled and leaned in to kiss Bo as she whispered huskily against her lips, "Yes, but you're the only one whose legs I actually want my hands between."

Bo seemed to hesitate for a moment before saying calmly, "That can't happen if we're on different sides of the law. It'll get me fired and you killed if I don't have a reason to offer you some sort of official protection."

Cass held Bo's gaze for a long time before nodding. "Okay. But I need you to understand something. I'm not doing this solely to sleep with you. I'm doing this because I want a chance at freedom."

Bo, surprisingly, grinned. "Miss Halliburton, I wouldn't fool myself for a second thinking one woman would be enough to get you to turn on your people. Even a woman as devilishly charming as me."

Cass laughed and allowed Bo to twirl her in time to the music before stepping in closer. "I won't give a written statement and I won't do a recording. I will tell you what I know right now, and I will agree to stand as a witness should this come to a trial, provided my name stays out of anything until then. Can we agree to that?"

Bo dipped her and a girlish squeal came out before Cass could stop it. Bo's eyes were stormy as she nodded. "I understand. I'll have to tell the judge my source for the warrants, though, since we haven't found anything concrete."

The music stopped and Cass looked around, noticing the DJ was going on a break. "Let's walk outside." She led the way through the door and sat on a bench connected to the brick exterior. "None of the judges are in our pockets so that's fine, but my name can't be on any documents."

"We can make that work."

Cass took a deep breath and took a final look into Bo's eyes, still expecting to see some sign of ulterior motive. All she saw was strength and understanding and she nodded. "I'm sure you've figured out by now you've got a dirty cop in your ranks."

"Yes. I just don't know how he managed to hide all this from the department."

"Because his family has been in the Voleurs' pocket for generations. Once you get that kind of pedigree, no one really looks too hard at you, and they got good at hiding their secrets. He never went into meetings until he worked his way to becoming an undercover officer. Before that he used emails and phone calls to get his orders from the club leaders. Once he became an undercover, anyone who saw him go in just assumed he was gathering intel. When he 'earned' his patch, it was assumed it was for the greater good and still no one looked too close. The club already knew who he was, so there was never a fuss about him going into the PD. With me so far?"

Bo nodded, her focus intense and unwavering.

"GPD's interdepartmental communication is nonexistent and he used that to his advantage to play you guys. Narco isn't interested in counterfeits, and you guys aren't interested in drug busts. As long as he could give enough false info to keep both sides satisfied, no one got too suspicious."

Bo sighed deeply and rubbed her face with her hands. "So, is he the one moving behind your back within the organization?"

Cass nodded. "I'm pretty sure. We call him Pigsty. It's starting to seem like he's gathering a following to vote me out of my seat. He'd be using the connection to the Demons to do that."

"So where do they come in? The Demons, I mean." Bo laid out her thoughts, reiterating what she and Gerald had discussed, and Cass listened, correcting her where she was wrong, which was only once.

"Yes. The Demons deliver money to Classic Auto under the guise of buying a car. Around the same time, another group would collect the counterfeits from Heartbreakers. Tiffany was never a part of anything. I used her to make a statement because I didn't want anyone talking to you at that point. That really was just a coincidence. They weren't being used as go-betweens at all. For me, at least. I think you might be right, though, that Pigsty is using her to his own ends. It makes sense that he'd be rounding up the pimps to make sure they didn't interfere with his new business and he'd want to make sure our girls would show the new girls the ropes. If he was already dabbling in trafficking, then he most likely wouldn't have a problem forcing someone to comply if they didn't want to work with him."

"Which would be why Tiffany was warning me away. She knows he's a cop."

"That would be my guess, yes. And behind all of this is my father. I will testify that he's the one who orchestrated the entire counterfeiting deal with the Demons, among other things. I'll tell you exactly which building to look at and I'll give you all the information I have on Sty and his trafficking deals. When they come for me, because they will, I'll need to know you have my back."

Bo chose that moment to kiss Cass gently. "I have a lot more than your back. I'm going to keep you safe, Cass."

"I shouldn't believe you, but I do."

A buzzing sound split the silence of the night and Bo cussed. "That's my work phone." She pulled it out of her pocket and glanced at the readout. "That's going to be a SWAT call." At Cass's look of confusion, she added, "Not for you, don't worry. I'm on the rotation this week and it's an emergency. Listen, I have to go, but I'll call you as soon as I can, okay? Write everything down for me that you can. With regards to the trafficking, I need every name you can think of. Once I have all that I'm going to forward it to my partner and he's going to get everything ready for the warrants because once we start this, I'm not going to leave your side until I know you're safe." She looked like she was going to say something else but instead leaned down and kissed Cass again before walking away.

CHAPTER NINETEEN

Cass and Chubby waited nervously on Bo's couch, Cass having decided not to wait for a phone call, and it was all she could do not to stand up and pace. She had tried that already, and Chubby quickly told her to stop. She hated the void of information she suddenly found herself in. All she knew was that Bo was in an extremely dangerous and volatile situation, and there was nothing Cass could do to help her.

When the doorknob wiggled, Cass and Chubby stood, but when Bo walked in and Cass saw all the blood, she almost fell back down. Bo seemed to realize this, because she held up her hand. "It's not mine." The relief, however sweet, was short-lived in the face of just what horrors Bo had to have faced in order to be covered in so much of someone else's blood.

Cass swallowed hard and took a step closer. Ignoring the blood, she ran her hands lightly over Bo's chest, feeling the bumps and ridges of the bulletproof vest under her shirt. This one item, more than any other, served as a stark reminder that the people Cass employed would gladly shoot her without even a second thought. She gently cupped Bo's cheek, and when Bo leaned into the touch, Cass took the time to wipe off a small spot of blood before kissing the spot she had cleaned. She bit Bo's lip before she kissed down Bo's neck. She didn't stop until she felt a little of the tension in Bo's body release. She gently bit down, feeling Bo tense again, and she whispered softly in her ear, "Let me have this, Bo. Please."

She took a step back to look in Bo's eyes and saw the desire Cass wanted, but there was also the fear and trepidation she had fought so hard against. Tonight, though, Cass refused to let her go. She took Bo's hair in her hands and forced her mouth down, kissing her hard. She was surprised when Bo kissed her back.

Cass kissed with everything she had, hoping she could somehow erase the distance between their worlds. When she heard the soft moan against her lips, she pulled back, and was glad to see only stark, raw, white hot desire mirrored back at her.

With shaky hands, she reached between them to lift Bo's shirt over her head, exposing the black vest underneath. She paused just for a moment before grabbing hold of the strap and yanking it free. The sound of the Velcro coming undone was like a shot ringing out in the silent apartment. Cass tried so hard to keep going, but her own anxiety was getting the best of her. Bo gently took the strap from her hand and completed the process before lifting the vest off her shoulders and over her head.

"I've got to take a shower. Can you wait for that?" Her voice was rough with need and her eyes were almost black they were so dark. All Cass could do was nod her acquiescence and watch Bo back up slowly before turning to go into her bedroom to shower. She returned a short time later dressed in dark sweatpants and a white shirt that was plastered to her by the water still dripping down her body.

"You didn't think to use a towel?"

"Seemed like a moot point."

"But the shirt wasn't?"

"Figured you might like something to play with."

Cass smiled and walked over, feeling like she was in a trance as she leaned her hands against Bo's chest and gently licked the water running down her neck. Bo groaned quietly and wrapped her arms around Cass, her eyes closing. Cass heard herself whimper as she bit down on the thick muscles and lightly ran her hands up Bo's etched stomach, lifting the wet shirt up and over Bo's head. She moaned as she felt Bo's strong hand on the back of her neck.

Slowly, she kissed across Bo's chest, her own clit throbbing as she felt Bo's erect nipples rubbing against her. She took one between her fingers, squeezing slightly as she took the other one in her mouth. She was rewarded with a low, strangled moan and her name being whispered like a benediction as Bo tangled her hands in Cass's hair, holding her there. She felt Bo's hips begin to rock into her own as Cass pulled more of her breast into her mouth, licking and nipping at it while she twisted and pulled at the other nipple until Bo was moaning uncontrollably.

Cass dropped to her knees, tasting every inch of the skin covering Bo's stomach as she ran her hands up Bo's back before gently dipping her tongue in Bo's navel and biting at the soft skin surrounding it. She yanked Bo's pants down, laughing and moaning when she realized Bo hadn't put on any underwear. She slowly kissed lower, biting at the sensitive skin just below Bo's waist.

Bo groaned as if in pain and tried to push Cass's head down. "Oh, God, put your mouth on me, Cass. Please, baby." Cass couldn't have said no to that even if she wanted to. Seeing Bo so completely out of control and begging robbed Cass of the ability to do anything but obey.

She frantically took Bo's clit in her mouth, moaning as she felt the throbbing against her tongue. She began sucking in earnest, flicking her tongue against the sensitive tip as she did. She felt the sharp pain of her hair being pulled as Bo rocked her hips harder, groaning Cass's name over and over. "Don't stop, baby. Don't stop. Please. Make me come in your mouth."

Cass moaned loudly against Bo as her own clit threatened to explode, and then Bo pulled her hair again as she cried out, her taste flooding Cass's mouth and all her senses. As she came, Bo slid to the floor and into Cass's embrace. Seeing her big, strong cop made weak and vulnerable made Cass feel more powerful than holding a gun to someone's head ever had.

She pushed Bo to the floor and straddled her hips as she kissed her thoroughly and with abandon, claiming what was hers in that moment. She moaned as Bo grabbed her hips and they began to move in an age-old dance. Bo took control of the kiss, thrusting her tongue into Cass's mouth as she thrust her hips against her. Cass moaned deeply and threw her head back before ripping her shirt off and pulling Bo's hands to her throbbing breasts. She groaned as Bo squeezed. She made Bo stop just long enough to get completely naked before settling back down, yanking Bo's head up to her breasts to replace her hands. "Mouth. Now, baby, suck on my nipples."

Bo feasted hungrily and Cass gladly let her take over as she gave in to the pleasure of Bo's hands all over her body, Bo's ravenous mouth devouring her, Bo's hips pressing incessantly against hers, hitting her clit over and over, forcing her higher and higher until she screamed out Bo's name and coated her stomach completely.

As she rested in Bo's arms, Cass felt Bo roll out from under her before lifting her effortlessly and carrying her to the bed, where she promptly fell asleep wrapped in Bo's arms.

The shrill ring of a cell phone broke Cass out of her sex filled dream. Bo had woken her up on the verge of orgasm and they had spent hours exploring each other. The more she thought about it, the more she wanted to ignore her phone. She could still feel Bo's strong hips between her legs, hear her grunts of pleasure and her deep groans as she came again and again. Bo had started with her mouth, her skillful tongue working Cass over until she wasn't sure she could go any more, and then she had pushed her fingers inside until Cass lost count of her orgasms. As wild as Bo might have been out of the bed, she was exponentially more so in it. The phone went to voice mail as Bo rolled over and pulled Cass against her, gently kissing down Cass's neck. Cass moaned softly and wrapped her arms around Bo's shoulders.

Bo stopped kissing her to look deeply into her eyes. "I have a question."

"Yes?"

"Would you mind terribly if I put on my strap-on?"

Cass grinned and pulled Bo back down for another deep kiss before she whispered against her ear, "Only if you promise to fuck me just like this." She felt Bo's hips jerk and smiled as she hopped off the bed to run to the closet, coming back out with a velvet bag. The strap-on was a little bit larger than Cass was expecting, and Bo seemed to notice her trepidation.

"I promise I won't hurt you." Once she had the boxers-cum-harness properly in place, she slowly walked over to the bed, and

Cass couldn't help but run her hand along the shaft of the cock. Bo's low groan said she didn't mind one bit.

"Condom?"

Bo nodded and pointed to the nightstand beside Cass. She reached in and pulled out the foil square, ripping it open and pulling out the condom before looking up into Bo's eyes as she slowly rolled the rubber down the long length of her. Cass lay back on the bed, pulling Bo on top of her. She gasped when the tip of the strap-on slid easily inside her. "Oh...oh, that's so nice."

Bo grunted and held herself up with an elbow on either side of Cass's head, her hands gently running through Cass's hair. Cass rocked her hips, slowly taking more of Bo inside her, watching as Bo's eyes slid shut as she let Cass set the pace. Her entire body was trembling with the effort of holding back. She was so fucking sexy.

Cass leaned up and sucked her earlobe into her mouth, positioning herself to take even more of the strap-on. She whimpered and Bo's hips jerked again. Cass took a deep breath and then whispered in her ear, "You have to go slow for me, baby, it's been a very long time. Can you do that? I want you to take me like this."

Bo groaned and Cass smiled as she slowly took Bo in, inch by inch. She moaned as she was filled completely, and she wrapped her legs around Bo's calves. "Fuck me, baby. Just like this."

Bo cried out and began slowly rocking her hips, pulling almost all the way out of Cass before shoving back into her again. Cass dug her nails into Bo's ass, urging her on as she rocked her body in sync with Bo's. She whimpered her name as Bo's thrusting brought her higher. "Harder, baby. Oh, come on, I know you want to fuck me harder. It's okay."

"Oh, my God." Bo growled as she lifted herself up, using Cass's shoulder as leverage to thrust harder into her. Cass moaned loudly and was on the verge of screaming. She had never screamed before, but with Bo it seemed like she couldn't stop.

"That's it, baby, fuck me just like that. Does that feel good? Does it make you hard when I tell you to fuck me?"

Bo grunted and nodded as her jaw clenched and Cass could feel her stomach tightening as she fucked her faster. Cass clawed at Bo's back, feeling the skin breaking under her nails as her own orgasm rapidly approached. "Don't stop, baby, come with me!"

Bo threw her head back and arched as Cass screamed Bo's name. She felt like she was in space. She pulled Bo down flush against her and kissed her before her phone rang again. She groaned and shook her head, and Bo smiled gently.

When she spoke, her voice was rough with the aftermath of their lovemaking. "Answer your phone, sweetheart. I need to go clean up and I don't want you to get in trouble." She got up and Cass waited until the bathroom door was closed before answering her phone on the fifth ring.

"Halliburton."

"Cassidy." Her father's voice was eerily calm, and Cass was instantly on guard.

"Yes, sir?"

"I've called you twice already. Have you decided my calls are no longer important, Cassidy?"

"I, uh..." Her sex clouded brain struggled to come up with a good answer, so she settled for a half truth. "I was asleep, I'm sorry. I must have missed the first call. I thought the second was an alarm and I fell back asleep."

"Hm. I'll assume that's true for now. Just the same, I'm in town and I have something I need you to look at. I'll be in your office in thirty minutes, Cassidy. I expect you to be there." His tone made it clear that refusing was not an option.

"Yes, sir. I'll be right there."

He hung up and she shuddered at the sense of foreboding that suffused her.

When Bo walked out of the bathroom, she couldn't contain her smile. When she saw Cass standing beside the bed in her jeans, her face a study in anxiety, she frowned.

"Cass, what's wrong?"

Cass tried for a smile but failed and just shook her head. "I just hate talking to my father. He's an asshat and always has been."

"Do you have to leave right this second?"

Cass bit her lip and then shook her head.

Bo smiled gently and lay on the bed, then held her arms open. "Come here, baby."

Cass curled up against her side before rubbing her hand lightly up and down Bo's stomach, which was left exposed by the sheet at her waist. "Have you always been this muscular?"

Bo smiled and ran her hand through Cass's wavy hair. "That's an odd question, but no, I haven't been. Believe it or not, if I didn't work out every single day, I'd be roughly the shape of an elephant. And not a cute one, either."

Cass smiled at that and leaned up to kiss Bo gently. "I happen to think elephants are adorable."

Bo rubbed her nose against Cass's as she shook her head. "Not as humans, they aren't. When I first started the academy, I was actually in pretty rough shape. I wasn't fat by any means, but I definitely couldn't chase a suspect if I had to. I used to joke that if a suspect ever ran from me, I'd just shoot him because making me run was an obvious attempt on my life."

Cass laughed and Bo relished the sound. She grinned and leaned down to kiss Cass gently. "You have such a beautiful laugh."

Cass returned the kiss just as softly but shook her head. "You wouldn't think that if you hated me."

"But I don't hate you, so I do."

Cass just rolled her eyes and started playing with Bo's hair. "So, what happened then?"

Bo thought for a moment as she gently rubbed Cass's back and smiled when she felt Cass relax into her. "Once I graduated, I got hired on at GPD and barely made it through the in-house academy alive. I think at some point I actually had an asthma attack. That's when I realized that if I seriously wanted to do this job and make it home every night, I was going to have to get my ass in shape. I started working out once a week, then twice, and now if I'm not at the gym I'm running on the beach."

Cass smiled slyly and moved her hand just under the sheet. "So that's where that stamina comes from."

Bo grinned and rolled over on top of her. "Absolutely." As she settled her weight between Cass's legs, Cass's expression changed, and Bo frowned slightly. "What?"

Cass reached up and gently touched Bo's cheek. "You are without doubt the most amazing person I've ever had the pleasure of meeting."

Bo cocked her head. "Is there a *but* to that statement?"

Cass laughed and shook her head. "Not to that statement, no. But would you mind terribly if I asked you to tell me more about when you were younger? What was it like before you were the famous Detective Bo Alexander?"

Bo rolled off and shook her head as Cass once again began playing with her hair. "I don't mind at all. What do you want to know?"

"Tell me about your very first arrest." Cass curled up and spooned against Bo's side, laying her head on Bo's chest. Bo wrapped her arms around her, and for a moment, they both just lay there. Cass whispered, "You have such a strong heartbeat."

Bo placed a finger under Cass's chin and gently tilted her head up to kiss her, and then murmured against her lips, "During my field training with my training officer, or after, when it was just me?"

Cass ran the tip of her finger down Bo's ear and said, "After."

Bo captured her hand and kissed it before returning it to her ear. "It was actually one of your people, but I can't for the life of me remember his name."

Cass smiled and traced Bo's lips with a fingertip. "What was the charge?"

Bo closed her eyes and took Cass's finger in her mouth, sucking gently. She was rewarded with a soft moan. "I originally stopped him for speeding and was honestly planning on letting him go with a warning because it was only maybe ten miles over, but then he started getting belligerent so I invoked RICO on him and told him I was going to search his bike. Found a couple ounces of cocaine and put him away." Bo gasped as she felt warm lips on her neck. "Cass..."

She felt Cass's mouth at her ear and her warm breath as she whispered, "Shh." She felt the tip of Cass's tongue licking along the edge of her ear and moaned softly. "Just let me touch you, Bo. But keep your eyes closed for me."

Bo whimpered quietly as she felt Cass's hands barely graze her nipples before she felt nails dragging down her stomach.

Cass gently kissed Bo's chest as she straddled her hips. "Tell me about your academy."

Bo moaned as she felt Cass begin a gentle rocking motion against her center. "I can't concentrate when you touch me like that." Her stomach clenched as Cass braced her hands just above the sheet covering the soft curls between her legs.

"Keep talking to me, Bo. I want to hear your voice change. I want to hear how your breathing gets faster when you get turned on." She pushed her ass against Bo's clit, eliciting a deep groan.

"I promise you I'm already turned on."

Cass stopped her ministrations and moved off the bed. "Open your eyes, Bo."

Bo obliged and looked up at Cass with hooded eyes. "They're wide-open, baby."

Cass held Bo's gaze as she slowly ran her hands from the top of her own neck, down her chest and over her breasts and stomach, before stopping at the button of her jeans. "Tell me about your academy, baby."

Bo swallowed and Cass watched her eyes grow impossibly dark. "I was twenty-one when I started. My first day was my birthday."

Cass popped the button and slowly slid her zipper down, her hips undulating as she moved her hands back up her body. "When is your birthday?"

"July. Twenty-seventh."

Bo's voice was breathless, and Cass smiled slightly before undoing the buttons on her shirt one by one. As each button fell to the side, she felt as if her shirt were baring more than just her body, and was surprised to find that in that moment, she *wanted* to be completely exposed. "Were you the youngest in your class?" She slid her hands up her bare stomach, squeezing her breasts before slipping her shirt off and letting it fall to the floor with the last brick of every wall she had ever put up around her heart.

Bo groaned and shook her head. "There was a guy who turned twenty-one halfway through. Valdez."

Cass tilted her head back and closed her eyes as she rubbed her erect nipples through her bra. "Who was your favorite instructor?"

Bo's response was strained, hurried, and when Cass looked down at her, Bo's chest was heaving. Cass had never in her life been looked at with such reverence, such awe, and no one had ever made her feel as genuinely beautiful as Bo did in that moment. She struggled to form a coherent thought and she could feel her breath catching as she took a moment to breathe deeply before she resumed her effort wholeheartedly. The world outside these walls would have to wait. She wasn't giving this moment up for anything.

"Favorite class?" She reached down, sliding her hand into her pants as she slid the other hand under her bra to squeeze her nipple. She couldn't help the small moan that came out.

"Oh, God, uh…ground fighting. They paired me with a bitch who hated me, and we kicked each other's ass."

Bo's voice was deep and husky, and Cass slowly walked closer to her before pulling Bo's head to her stomach, moaning as she felt Bo's hungry mouth on her. "Oh…"

Bo reached up and slowly pulled down her jeans and Cass gasped as she felt Bo's tongue slide lower. "Take off my bra, baby." Bo did as she was told and Cass guided Bo's head to her breast, moaning her name as Bo took her nipple into her mouth. "Yes…God your mouth is so hot, baby…you make me so wet…"

Bo groaned around her nipple and Cass pulled Bo's hand between her legs. "See?" She made a high-pitched sound as Bo gently moved her panties aside and slid her fingers in. "Oh, baby, yes. Make love to me just like this…"

Bo groaned even louder, and Cass reached down to rub Bo's clit as Bo moved her fingers slowly, steadily in and out. She rocked her hips, riding Bo's fingers as she circled Bo's clit. "Don't stop…don't stop…" she whispered as she felt her muscles clenching around

Bo's fingers. She tried to make it last as long as she could, tried to memorize every sound Bo made, every thrust of her fingers that took Cass higher and higher until she just couldn't hold on anymore.

"Can you come with me baby? Oh, Bo please let me feel you when you come, I'm begging you." Bo shifted to take Cass's fingers inside her and they both cried out as their orgasms peaked together. "That's it! That's it! Yes!"

Bo bit down on Cass's nipple and Cass screamed as she came again, her mind soaring somewhere into the stratosphere where she let herself believe for just a single second that they could stay this way forever. When she came back down, she fell in an ungraceful heap on top of her. Neither spoke for a very long time, both content to live in the moment. It was Cass who broke the silence.

"You make me feel things no one else ever has before, Bo." She tried to keep her voice even, but she failed miserably.

She felt Bo's lips at her neck and turned to capture them with her own, trying to push every ounce of feeling she had into that one kiss.

Bo yanked her head back and gasped for breath as she replied, "I would definitely say the feeling is mutual."

A silence heavy with unspoken words and promises settled on them before Cass looked up and bit her lip. "I've never done that before."

Bo's eyebrows shot up. "You've—you've never…that was your first—"

Cass held up her hand to stop her. "No, you walnut. If you'll recall, I've had sex more times than I care to say out loud." She paused and bit her lip again, cursing the fact that her eyes started to water. "That was the first time I've ever made love to someone."

Bo closed her eyes and pulled Cass tight. "Oh, honey, don't cry."

Cass shook her head and slid out of Bo's arms. "I needed to make love to you. I needed to feel you everywhere."

Bo held her face and pulled her into a deep kiss, and Cass thought back to the moment she had very first tasted Bo's kiss. She had been right—it was a final death row meal fit for a queen.

"Cass, I—"

"And now I have to go."

Bo frowned and Cass steeled herself as she stood up to begin dressing once again.

"What do you mean you have to go?"

Cass took a deep breath. "My father called. I have to go."

Bo nodded slowly and Cass couldn't help but look over her naked body, leaning casually against the headboard. Bo gave a knowing smile and held her head a little higher. "Can you come back after?"

Cass met her eyes and nodded, resisting the urge to run to her and touch every inch she could. Deep down, she knew there wouldn't be an after. This was the one and only, and she'd take it with her to the grave.

Bo held her gaze as she slowly ran her fingers down the ridges of her own stomach, her hips arching slightly. "I love the way you look at me."

Cass's mouth was dry, and she knew she needed to leave, but she couldn't help herself. She walked over, stopping just before her body met Bo's. "I love looking at you."

Bo's voice was husky, her eyes hooded as she leaned in and gently kissed Cass before whispering, "Hurry back, Miss Halliburton."

❖

Cass hadn't been gone five minutes when Bo's personal phone rang. She grabbed it, frowning at the readout. "Guthrie. Why aren't you calling me on my work phone?"

"Because your work phone has either been off or dead for the last, oh, eight hours or so."

She picked up her phone, grimacing when it wouldn't turn on. "Yep. Dead as a doornail. My bad. How long have you been trying to get hold of me?"

"However long your phone has been dead for." He laughed. "It wasn't particularly important until now so I waited as long as I

could to call your personal cell. Figured you could use the sleep."
His tone implied he knew she was not, in fact, sleeping.

"Yeah, I appreciate that. What's going on?"

"We got the approval for the SWAT raid. I think Sergeant Gill
was actually trying to call you, too."

"Shit, she's going to be pissed."

"Probably, but I'm sure if you show up on time with donuts it'll
make it up."

"What time is on time?"

She heard the sound of papers rustling. "Raid is going to be at
2000 hours tomorrow night. Brass wants us at the station at 1700 to
go over the plan and make sure that everything goes according to
that plan."

"I'm assuming we have people watching the Demons, too? The
ones I emailed about, from Halliburton's intel?"

"Yeah, it's all covered. We're going to hit a few hotels quietly
without a fuss, but the warehouse they've got the press in...well,
that's a different story."

"So, basically, it's time to take these motherfuckers down GPD
style?"

He laughed loudly. "Fuck yeah. Guns ablaze."

"Hey, speaking of ablaze...I don't suppose Dusek has checked
in yet, has he? He's supposed to get back from vacation tomorrow
morning, so you'd think he'd check to see what's been going on,
right?"

"Do I even want to know how you went from ablaze to Topher?"

"Well, for some reason my mind went to 'ass on fire' and that
made me think, 'liar liar.' So, Topher."

"I'm just going to pretend that makes sense, but no, no one has
heard from him yet. At least none of our people. I did hear someone
mention that he was supposed to have been back already and his
lieutenant hasn't been able to get hold of him."

"Fuck. He's fucking in the wind, isn't he?"

She heard his beard scratching the phone as he shook his head.
"I can't be sure one way or the other. Seems to me like he picked a
hell of a time for a no call, no show, though."

"What about the raid? Is that compromised?" The only thing that would keep Cass safe for sure was bringing Daniel Halliburton down for good, and the raid was the first step.

"Not to my knowledge."

"All right, man, you said 1700?"

"Yep. Raid is at 2000 hours."

"Roger that. Now if you don't mind, I'd like to get some sleep."

"Okay. Charge your phone, honey."

"Suck my dick, baby."

"Don't get anyone pregnant."

She hung up on his loud guffaws and rolled over to put her phone on the charger. She was hit with a tinge of sadness when she realized Cass still probably wouldn't be back for a while, yet. That thought was followed quickly by the realization that if Topher did know about their raid then Cass was very likely in serious danger. She was filled with dread as she thought about what the meeting with Cass's father was going to entail. "Fuck. Okay, Bo, think." She could only hope that Daniel wasn't going to have Cass executed on the spot, because that would cause far too much mess right now. That meant she had a small window of opportunity to get Cass the hell out of Dodge. All she could do was wait for the phone to ring, because if she called Cass in the middle of the meeting, mess or not, Daniel might not be so merciful.

Daniel Halliburton's massive wooden desk was imposing enough, but the man who sat behind it was infinitely more so. His blond hair and bright blue eyes belied his true personality, and right now those cold, killer eyes were focused on her. In that moment, Cass couldn't help but feel Daniel was every bit as evil as his Nazi ancestors. The only thing on his desk was a single manila envelope, and it stood out like a landmine in the middle of the ocean, sending chills down Cass's back.

She didn't have to ask; she just opened the envelope and took out the pictures inside. Most of them probably could have been explained away, but there were definitely a few that couldn't. Her stepping out of Bo's truck, obviously distressed, soaking wet from the rain. That was taken a few blocks from their warehouse, and anyone who knew that could tell. Her on the beach she had thought so safe, looking up at Bo. It was only the back of Bo's head, but she didn't have to be visible to be recognizable. She looked like the cop she would always be, and Cass went cold inside. That picture had been taken just the other night, after she had agreed to think about turning rat on the club. She looked, plain and simple, like she was falling and enjoying it. They'd been watching her, and she hadn't had a fucking clue.

"You told me to distract her. I don't see the problem, since it was your idea in the first place." She tried for nonchalance, but he wasn't fooled.

"If you had done your fucking job, we wouldn't be having this conversation, Cassidy!" He slammed his hand down on the desk as he leaned over and hollered in her face. "I told you to distract her! Not take her to the fucking prom!"

"And she was distracted, Daniel!" *Fuck, fuck, fuck.* She kept her expression hard but inside she was shaking.

"So can you guarantee my business is safe? Can you tell me with absolute surety that she has no idea what we're doing on the island? What about where she's at in her investigation?"

Cass blinked, caught off guard, and that was enough of an admittance of guilt for him.

"Exactly. You don't even know. So, tell me, Cassidy. What's the point of you sleeping with the enemy if you can't even get good intelligence out of it?"

"Oh, I don't know, maybe to get off so I'm not as cranky as you?" She slammed her hand on the desk, mimicking his actions as she stood up. He didn't need to know anything anymore. "If you want to know about the fucking investigation, why don't you ask Topher fucking Dusek? He's the fucking pig, right? And since you obviously know everything, I'm sure you know about the side deal he's made with the Demons? No? You're the one that fucked up and didn't have him killed when you had the chance. I've stonewalled Detective Alexander every chance I've gotten."

When Daniel narrowed his eyes, she knew she should have kept her mouth shut.

"You're right, Cassidy," he replied, his voice suddenly calm. "I did fuck up not having him killed when I had the chance. Especially since he's now disappeared. It's not a mistake I intend to make again." He grabbed a cigar and clipped the end of it before lighting it. "You see, Cassidy, it's been my experience that women in love tend to make mistakes. Especially," he took a long drag and blew it in her face, "when they fall in love with cops. Just like your stupid whore of a mother. Her actions got my daughter killed."

"You...my mother?"

"Your mother, my dear adopted daughter, seemed to have the same proclivities for loose lips as you do." He glanced down at her crotch before meeting her eyes again. "In more ways than one. I'm a man who learns from my mistakes. I'm just glad Topher caught you early enough in this to spare any unnecessary deaths. His father was a little late in the pickup to avoid messes."

Cass could see all the little things that never made sense in her mother's final years suddenly fall into place. She remembered every hand that had defiled her body since her mother passed and knew with absolute certainty that she'd been made to pay for a mistake that wasn't her own. She could feel her heart being ripped out again, just like it had when she'd come home from a romantic comedy with her first girlfriend to learn she was suddenly an only child. She could feel the breath being sucked from her lungs. "You killed my mother." She could only be glad her voice didn't shake.

"And now I'm giving you a choice. You or Detective Alexander. You choose who lives and who dies. You have until midnight tomorrow to make your choice, Cassidy. Otherwise I will use my connections to do more than just keep the pretty detective away from my business." He took another drag of his cigar, and she stood and walked out of his office. When the door was closed behind her, she looked to make sure she was alone before letting the tears fall, cascading in an unstoppable flow into a puddle on the floor and taking with them any chance of happiness she had. When she felt she could talk, she picked up her phone and called Billy.

When she ended the phone call with him, tears streaming down her face, she called Bo.

"Hey. I figured you'd be back in person. Is everything okay?"

Cass took a deep breath, trying to steady herself against the onslaught of emotion. "I have to leave, Bo. Someone told my father about us and now he's on the war path. I have to run."

Cass could hear the sharp intake of breath from the other side of the phone "Cass. What are you saying? I told you I can protect you. You just have to give me the chance. I promise, baby, he won't hurt you."

She stifled the sobs that wracked her body and drew a shaky breath before continuing. "It's not that easy, Bo. He's threatened you, too, if you continue this investigation. You can't stand up against the entire club, and that's what I'm up against right now. If I leave, I can convince him to spare you because there will be nothing else to investigate that will bring him down, since the human trafficking doesn't involve him."

"Cass, no. Come on, you told me you trusted me. I thought…I thought you meant it. I can protect myself, and nothing is stopping me from going to that raid. I'll bring it down and I'll be safe. Let me do the same for you."

Cass could feel every shard of the thousand pieces her heart shattered into. "Bo, I needed you to serve a purpose. Daniel beat you to it and now that purpose is null and void. I'm sorry, Bo, but I have to go, and you need to call off your investigation once the warehouse raid is over. At least do that, and maybe he'll leave you alone." *Please don't fight me, baby.*

"There has to be another way! Cass I…I…."

Cass laughed harshly, hoping it would be enough to sever the ties that bound her to the island. "I can't stay for something there aren't even words for. We played, we lost. Good-bye, Bo."

CHAPTER TWENTY

B o leaned back in her chair and looked around at her brothers and sisters in blue. Gerald was lying to a woman about her son's whereabouts. He had been shot in a gang war. Paige was talking about cheating on her husband, who loved her with all his heart. Two officers in the room she knew were addicted to pills.

Liars. Every single fucking one of them.

And she was supposed to trust them with her life while Cass Halliburton, the most infuriatingly honest woman she'd ever met, went on the run because Bo wasn't fast enough to protect her. Because she had agreed to help a department of fucking liars and it bit her in the ass. There was no North on her moral compass anymore. When Gerald tapped her on the shoulder, she jumped and smiled at him sheepishly. "Sorry. I've got a lot on my mind." All she could think about were Cass's last words to her. On a phone call no less. She tried to take a deep breath to steady herself, but it didn't work very well.

He clapped a hand on her shoulder, and she was suddenly very aware of just how much smaller than him she was. Any other time, she would have felt unstoppable before a raid like this one. This time was different in so many ways. "Do you want to talk about it? I'd really hate for you to go into this raid without a clear head. Not to mention," he added very seriously, "my wife would kill you if you let me get dead."

She laughed and shook her head. "It's nothing serious, just some girl trouble. I do have a question, though. Have you heard anything about Halliburton being at the warehouse tonight? I asked one of my sources and they think she turned tail and ran."

"Why, you going to stalk her now?"

He laughed, but Bo couldn't bring herself to laugh along with him. If Cass really had left, she hoped the information would have made it to him. It was all Bo could do to keep her breathing even while he composed himself over what he obviously thought was a hilarious joke.

"I wasn't planning on it, but I'm thinking it could do me some good."

He grinned. "I didn't hear where she was going, only that she took off out of town sometime last night. I guess this proves Topher really was dirty, huh? Rat bastard warned her, and she took off like a bitch with her tail between her legs."

"I thought no one had seen Topher?"

He shrugged nonchalantly. "Obviously, he found out."

Or Daniel Halliburton forced her to go on the run. "If Topher knows about the raid then won't that compromise our safety? We'll be going into a trap."

"I don't know, Bo, that's above my pay grade. Are you okay? It kind of sounds like you don't want to do this."

Her jaw clenched and she had to force herself to relax. She could tell he noticed but was glad he chose not to mention it. "Guess I just wanted the pleasure of shooting her myself," she laughed as she spoke, hoping to cover her momentary lapse in control. She motioned for him to turn around so she could strap up the back of his plate carrier, and he did the same to her. They both grinned when the SWAT commander called for them to move out.

Sitting beside him in the van, Bo started to get nervous. What would happen to Cass? She knew in her gut it wasn't a warning from Topher that had her leaving. Something had gone horribly wrong to the point that she no longer trusted Bo with her life, and it was all Bo could think about. She looked at Gerald, and he seemed to understand she was anxious. He clapped her on her shoulder. "Don't look so scared, Zander. You've done this before. Besides, if we end up in a gunfight, at least it won't last that long, right?"

She went along with his misinterpretation of her feelings and asked, "What do you mean?"

"Well." He grinned. "You know the numbers better than I do. Statistically speaking, gun fights only last about five seconds."

The briefing from the SWAT commander was quick and clear, and the tension in the room was intense. There was silence in the van as they moved into place and spread out around the warehouse, and Bo was right behind the first line of SWAT that surged into the warehouse just after 2000.

The crack of the door preceded the first crack of gunfire. Adrenaline surged through her body as she fired off her first round, dropping someone to her left holding an automatic rifle. Everything slowed as she saw the sparks from stray bullets flying up all around her. She raised her rifle again at someone stepping out of a door and gasped as her eyes met Cass's. Icy cold fear raced through her body because in that moment, she knew.

Cass glided toward her, her eyes already the lightless, dull color of someone who had long given up, and in that instant, Bo understood. She had no intention of walking out of the warehouse. Cass would have freedom, even if it cost her everything.

Bo ran, heedless of the firefight around her, trading shots only with the people preventing her from getting to Cass, but it felt like she was running through water. Each step seemed to take a massive amount of effort, and she didn't feel any closer to her than she was when she started. But damn it, she ran.

A bullet grazed her ear and she cried out as another bullet ripped through Cass's middle, a bright red circle appearing on her stomach. The second two shots sprayed Bo's face with her blood as Cass fell.

She caught her, gripping her tight and immediately searching for something to put pressure on the wounds turning Cass's shirt crimson. "Cass! Come on, baby, hang on!"

Cass coughed and blood sprayed from her mouth. "Hey, Detective?"

"Yeah, baby?"

"You were totally fucking worth it."

Her eyes slid closed and Bo shouted at her to open them. She heard the sirens but refused to look up until a strong hand gripped her shoulder. She was ready to turn around and punch whoever it was, until she saw the strong confidence and sympathy in Brit's gaze. "I've got it. Take care of your team."

Bo looked around and noticed that everyone on her team was purposely not looking at her, but none of them seemed hurt. Gerald tilted his head for her to come over.

"Our report is going to say you stopped to administer lifesaving first aid because she was a key witness in the case. We all have your back, Bo, but we've got to go. Let the EMTs take care of your girl."

His words blasted through the haze in her mind as she realized that he knew. Somehow, they all knew, and no one said anything. No one thought to tell them they weren't being careful enough and now Cass was bleeding out on the floor.

"Let's go write this fucking report." She turned to Brit. "You tell me the second you drop her off and who signs the transfer paperwork."

They made it to the door, and she saw a lumberjack looking man being walked out in handcuffs. "Who is that?"

"He said he's her biological father, in case she needs blood."

She stared at his back, confused. Did Cass know? She shook her head. There'd be time for more questions later. Back at the precinct, she was barely cognizant of writing her report. The words flowed easily across the screen surrounded by the familiar smells of rocket fuel coffee and tile cleaner, but she couldn't have told anyone what she was actually writing. She couldn't make it to the hospital fast enough. When she finally reached the ER, she rushed in, glancing at the nametag of the woman at the desk. "Cassidy Halliburton. She was brought in with—"

"Multiple GSWs, critical condition. Eryn Scott. I'm the charge nurse."

"How is she? I'm the officer in charge of the case."

Eryn's expression said she didn't believe the obvious lie, but instead of responding, she glanced over Bo's shoulder. Bo turned around and noticed for the first time the two men in sharp black suits with American flag pins on their lapels, who were waiting outside one of the doors. What were the feds doing there? Were they guarding Cass? She didn't remember seeing them at the raid. She turned back to the nurse, her mind going a hundred miles an hour.

Eryn cleared her throat. "Miss Halliburton was brought in in critical condition. I'm sorry, but we couldn't save her. She died before she made it to the operating room."

Bo felt the floor drop out from under her as she fell to her knees. Something was there, in Eryn's gaze, something off, but she couldn't place it. All she could hear were the words…Cass was gone. She saw her walking through the warehouse, unarmed, looking at Bo as the first bullet hit. Bile rose in her throat and tears slid down her face. "What…what happened? What do I do now?"

One of the men walked over and Bo felt herself being lifted up by surprisingly gentle hands. "You finish the case, Officer. Find these bastards and bring them down."

Bo felt the hard grip of conviction around her heart. "Oh, make no mistake. I will."

About the Author

JD grew up in the deep East Texas woods and on the coast of Galveston Island. When she's not working somewhere that requires a holster and a gun, she enjoys spending quality time with her massive pack of dogs (aka writing buddies) and going for stereotypical long moonlit walks on the Galveston beach. She highly recommends anyone who makes their way to the island try a frozen stingray from Jimmy's on the Pier.

Follow her on Twitter: Little Behemoth

Books Available from Bold Strokes Books

A Far Better Thing by JD Wilburn. When needs of her family and wants of her heart clash, Cass Halliburton is faced with the ultimate sacrifice. (978-1-63555-834-0)

Body Language by Renee Roman. When Mika offers to provide Jen erotic tutoring, will sex drive them into a deeper relationship or tear them apart? (978-1-63555-800-5)

Carrie and Hope by Joy Argento. For Carrie and Hope loss brings them together but secrets and fear may tear them apart. (978-1-63555-827-2)

Death's Prelude by David S. Pederson. In this prequel to the Detective Heath Barrington Mystery series, Heath discovers that first love changes you forever and drives you to become the person you're destined to be. (978-1-63555-786-2)

Ice Queen by Gun Brooke. School counselor Aislin Kennedy wants to help standoffish CEO Susanna Durr and her troubled teenage daughter become closer—even if it means risking her own heart in the process. (978-1-63555-721-3)

Masquerade by Anne Shade. In 1925 Harlem, New York, a notorious gangster sets her sights on seducing Celine, and new lovers Dinah and Celine are forced to risk their hearts, and lives, for love. (978-1-63555-831-9)

Royal Family by Jenny Frame. Loss has defined both Clay's and Katya's lives, but guarding their hearts may prove to be the biggest heartbreak of all. (978-1-63555-745-9)

Share the Moon by Toni Logan. Three best friends, an inherited vineyard and a resident ghost come together for fun, romance and a touch of magic. (978-1-63555-844-9)

Spirit of the Law by Carsen Taite. Attorney Owen Lassiter will do almost anything to put a murderer behind bars, but can she get past her reluctance to rely on unconventional help from the alluring Summer Byrne and keep from falling in love in the process? (978-1-63555-766-4)

The Devil Incarnate by Ali Vali. Cain Casey has so much to live for, but enemies who lurk in the shadows threaten to unravel it all. (978-1-63555-534-9)

His Brother's Viscount by Stephanie Lake. Hector Somerville wants to rekindle his illicit love affair with Viscount Wentworth, but he must overcome one problem: Wentworth still loves Hector's brother. (978-1-63555-805-0)

Journey to Cash by Ashley Bartlett. Cash Braddock thought everything was great, but it looks like her history is about to become her right now. Which is a real bummer. (978-1-63555-464-9)

Liberty Bay by Karis Walsh. Wren Lindley's life is mired in tradition and untouched by trends until social media star Gina Strickland introduces an irresistible electricity into her off-the-grid world. (978-1-63555-816-6)

Scent by Kris Bryant. Nico Marshall has been burned by women in the past wanting her for her money. This time, she's determined to win Sophia Sweet over with her charm. (978-1-63555-780-0)

Shadows of Steel by Suzie Clarke. As their worlds collide and their choices come back to haunt them, Rachel and Claire must figure out how to stay together and most of all, stay alive. (978-1-63555-810-4)

The Clinch by Nicole Disney. Eden Bauer overcame a difficult past to become a world champion mixed martial artist, but now rising star and dreamy bad girl Brooklyn Shaw is a threat both to Eden's title and her heart. (978-1-63555-820-3)

The Last First Kiss by Julie Cannon. Kelly Newsome is so ready for a tropical island vacation, but she never expects to meet the woman who could give her her last first kiss. (978-1-63555-768-8)

The Mandolin Lunch by Missouri Vaun. Despite their immediate attraction, everything about Garet Allen says short-term, and Tess Hill refuses to consider anything less than forever. (978-1-63555-566-0)

Thor: Daughter of Asgard by Genevieve McCluer. When Hannah Olsen finds out she's the reincarnation of Thor, she's thrown into a world of magic and intrigue, unexpected attraction, and a mystery she's got to unravel. (978-1-63555-814-2)

Veterinary Technician by Nancy Wheelton. When a stable of horses is threatened Val and Ronnie must work together against the odds to save them, and maybe even themselves along the way. (978-1-63555-839-5)

16 Steps to Forever by Georgia Beers. Can Brooke Sullivan and Macy Carr find themselves by finding each other? (978-1-63555-762-6)

All I Want for Christmas by Georgia Beers, Maggie Cummings, Fiona Riley. The Christmas season sparks passion and love in these stories by award winning authors Georgia Beers, Maggie Cummings, and Fiona Riley. (978-1-63555-764-0)

From the Woods by Charlotte Greene. When Fiona goes backpacking in a protected wilderness, the last thing she expects is to be fighting for her life. (978-1-63555-793-0)

Heart of the Storm by Nicole Stiling. For Juliet Mitchell and Sienna Bennett a forbidden attraction definitely isn't worth upending the life they've worked so hard for. Is it? (978-1-63555-789-3)

If You Dare by Sandy Lowe. For Lauren West and Emma Prescott, following their passions is easy. Following their hearts, though? That's almost impossible. (978-1-63555-654-4)

Love Changes Everything by Jaime Maddox. For Samantha Brooks and Kirby Fielding, no matter how careful their plans, love will change everything. (978-1-63555-835-7)

Not This Time by MA Binfield. Flung back into each other's lives, can former bandmates Sophia and Madison have a second chance at romance? (978-1-63555-798-5)

The Dubious Gift of Dragon Blood by J. Marshall Freeman. One day Crispin is a lonely high school student—the next he is fighting a war in a land ruled by dragons, his otherworldly boyfriend at his side. (978-1-63555-725-1)

The Found Jar by Jaycie Morrison. Fear keeps Emily Harris trapped in her emotionally vacant life; can she find the courage to let Beck Reynolds guide her toward love? (978-1-63555-825-8)

Aurora by Emma L McGeown. After a traumatic accident, Elena Ricci is stricken with amnesia leaving her with no recollection of the last eight years, including her wife and son. (978-1-63555-824-1)

Avenging Avery by Sheri Lewis Wohl. Revenge against a vengeful vampire unites Isa Meyer and Jeni Denton, but it's love that heals them. (978-1-63555-622-3)

Bulletproof by Maggie Cummings. For Dylan Prescott and Briana Logan, the complicated NYC criminal justice system doesn't leave room for love, but where the heart is concerned, no one is bulletproof. (978-1-63555-771-8)

Her Lady to Love by Jane Walsh. A shy wallflower joins forces with the most popular woman in Regency London on a quest to catch a husband, only to discover a wild passion for each other that far eclipses their interest for the Marriage Mart. (978-1-63555-809-8)

No Regrets by Joy Argento. For Jodi and Beth, the possibility of losing their future will force them to decide what is really important. (978-1-63555-751-0)

The Holiday Treatment by Elle Spencer. Who doesn't want a gay Christmas movie? Holly Hudson asks herself that question and discovers that happy endings aren't only for the movies. (978-1-63555-660-5)

Too Good to be True by Leigh Hays. Can the promise of love survive the realities of life for Madison and Jen, or is it too good to be true? (978-1-63555-715-2)

Treacherous Seas by Radclyffe. When the choice comes down to the lives of her officers against the promise she made to her wife, Reese Conlon puts everything she cares about on the line. (978-1-63555-778-7)

Two to Tangle by Melissa Brayden. Ryan Jacks has been a player all her life, but the new chef at Tangle Valley Vineyard changes everything. If only she wasn't off the menu. (978-1-63555-747-3)

When Sparks Fly by Annie McDonald. Will the devastating incident that first brought Dr. Daniella Waveny and hockey coach Luca McCaffrey together on frozen ice now force them apart, or will their secrets and fears thaw enough for them to create sparks? (978-1-63555-782-4)

Best Practice by Carsen Taite. When attorney Grace Maldonado agrees to mentor her best friend's little sister, she's prepared to confront Perry's rebellious nature, but she isn't prepared to fall in love. Legal Affairs: one law firm, three best friends, three chances to fall in love. (978-1-63555-361-1)

Home by Kris Bryant. Natalie and Sarah discover that anything is possible when love takes the long way home. (978-1-63555-853-1)

Keeper by Sydney Quinne. With a new charge under her reluctant wing—feisty, highly intelligent math wizard Isabelle Templeton—Keeper Andy Bouchard has to prevent a murder or die trying. (978-1-63555-852-4)

One More Chance by Ali Vali. Harry Basantes planned a future with Desi Thompson until the day Desi disappeared without a word, only to walk back into her life sixteen years later. (978-1-63555-536-3)

Renegade's War by Gun Brooke. Freedom fighter Aurelia DeCallum regrets saving the woman called Blue. She fears it will jeopardize her mission, and secretly, Blue might end up breaking Aurelia's heart. (978-1-63555-484-7)

The Other Women by Erin Zak. What happens in Vegas should stay in Vegas, but what do you do when the love you find in Vegas changes your life forever? (978-1-63555-741-1)

The Sea Within by Missouri Vaun. Time is running out for Dr. Elle Graham to convince Captain Jackson Drake that the only thing that can save future Earth resides in the past, and rescue her broken heart in the process. (978-1-63555-568-4)

To Sleep With Reindeer by Justine Saracen. In Norway under Nazi occupation, Maarit, an Indigenous woman; and Kirsten, a Norwegian resister, join forces to stop the development of an atomic weapon. (978-1-63555-735-0)

Twice Shy by Aurora Rey. Having an ex with benefits isn't all it's cracked up to be. Will Amanda Russo learn that lesson in time to take a chance on love with Quinn Sullivan? (978-1-63555-737-4)

Z-Town by Eden Darry. Forced to work together to stay alive, Meg and Lane must find the centuries-old treasure before the zombies find them first. (978-1-63555-743-5)